TWICE
IN
A
LIFETIME

TWICE IN A LIFETIME

A Novel

MELISSA BARON

alcove
press

Copyright © 2022 by Melissa Baron

All rights reserved.

Published in the United States by Alcove Press, an imprint of The Quick Brown Fox & Company LLC.

Alcove Press and its logo are trademarks of The Quick Brown Fox & Company LLC.

Library of Congress Catalog-in-Publication data available upon request.

ISBN (trade paperback): 978-1-63910-136-8
ISBN (ebook): 978-1-63910-137-5

Cover design by David Drummond

Printed in the United States.

www.alcovepress.com

Alcove Press
34 West 27th St., 10th Floor
New York, NY 10001

First Edition: December 2022

10 9 8 7 6 5 4 3 2 1

To Art, for loving me in every timeline.

This book contains depictions of death, depression, anxiety, and suicidal thoughts. These depictions may be difficult to read, and if you'd like to proceed and need support after, there are resources at the back of the book.

CHAPTER ONE

The text came through at 8:33 PM.

Isla saw the notification pop up on her laptop and promptly ignored it. She didn't recognize the number, and she was already on the phone anyway. And also busy logging back in to her work desktop, under extreme duress, to request time off.

"Did you do it?"

"Yes, m'lady," Isla said. She had no idea why Willow had woken up this morning determined to lock down Isla's plans for a birthday three months away, but a promise was a promise. "I will come back for my birthday. I just put in the time-off request."

"Excellent. I'm making dinner reservations and I need to do it now, because I'll forget and then it'll be too late to grab a table."

"This sounds like a fancy date, Will."

"For your thirtieth birthday? It has to be."

Isla smiled, letting her closest friend's warmth chase away the cool edges of gloom. "Are you still visiting me on Friday? I don't have any fancy dinners planned, I'm afraid."

"None required, and yes. I can't wait to have some time off work. I've gotta tell you about this one customer I had on Monday . . ."

And Willow was off. Isla listened dutifully as she logged out of her virtual desktop. Will had a great way of telling stories and even made Isla laugh a few times. Homesickness for Will drenched her in a sudden downpour. It had never been her intention to leave Chicago, not up until six months ago. She loved the city even when it suffocated her, when it couldn't be quiet. She loved the lake and the sun-dappled streets and the festivals she attended (when she could cope) and the restaurants and the myriad of cultures. She even loved it in winter, when Chicago became cruel and cold and bitter as a jilted lover.

But that was before the breakdown, when the sound and fury of her emotions and her surroundings had gotten the better of her. Isla's ability to cope left suddenly and without warning, and she had no idea how to put herself back together again.

So she'd fled. She wanted no neighbors, no street parking battles. She wanted green space and a city just within arm's reach. It took her away from her friends, but it would be better. *She* would be better. She could work mostly from home and still have a life. She'd still participate in society. She would not hermit. She would talk to real live people, on the weekends.

She was talked out now, though. It took Isla another fifteen minutes to gracefully end the call, leaving her in the soothing silence of her new cottage. Her back was sore from finally putting together the bed frame, but at least she wasn't sleeping on a mattress on the floor anymore. She'd finally unpacked all the books and put them on the bookshelves, which was hilarious, considering she hadn't read one of them in . . . she couldn't remember how long.

Her phone lit up with the missed-text notification. *Look at me*, the device seemed to plead. *I am the connection to the world you can never sever, and I want your attention right now.*

No thank you. Isla talked to people all day, in person and over email. The text could wait.

She rose to walk through her little cottage. The walls were a dreamy, quiet blue—a lake on a windy day, the breeze ruffling the water's feathers. Pewter wood flooring like the wide planks of a ship. A bathroom like the shower area of a community pool, white and blue and periwinkle mosaic tiles. She could almost smell the chlorine. The kitchen was a ship's galley. The blue-and-white-striped wallpaper was peeled and stained in the left corner above the stove and along the scuffed wood countertops.

Most of the things she'd filled her new place with came from resale and antique shops, but she liked it that way, this patchwork theme cobbled together like puzzle pieces from mismatched sets. Antique lamps, hanging plant pots, bookshelves made out of wine crates, trunks from the 1930s, plates and cups and bowls from six different kitchenware sets. It looked like the inside of her mind, and Isla liked that too.

She ignored the dirty dishes in the sink and set water to boil for pasta. Then stared at the dish pile with an increasing amount of guilt. They'd sat for over two days.

"Do the dishes," she said out loud to herself. The sound of her own voice startled her. "Pick up your clothes."

The trick was not letting herself think about it too much. No guilt. Just action. She put on music, turned on the hot water, and cleaned until it was time to put the pasta in. After, she made herself pick up the last weeks' worth of leggings and sweaters and put them in the hamper, continued to ignore the piles of forwarded mail by the front door, and put away the shoes cluttering the front door. Everything in its place.

She felt lighter when she sat down on the couch with her bowl of pasta. The phone came with her, and she finally unlocked the screen and read the text.

It hasn't been the same without you, Buttercup.

Her lips curved at *buttercup*. The number wasn't saved in her contacts. For a brief moment, she envied the person the message was intended for. *I'm sorry*, she typed. *I'm afraid you have the wrong number.*

A new text appeared right away. *I'm afraid I have the correct number.*

That was a little cheeky. *No*, she wrote back, *I'm afraid you don't.* But then she second-guessed herself. Was it someone she knew and they were just teasing her, or had they gotten a new number and not added her as a contact yet? She asked, *Who is this?*

After a long pause, the messenger replied. *I'm sorry. I didn't realize this number had already been reassigned.*

Reassigned? This number had been hers for years. Just to be sure, she texted the person her phone number with a question mark. They confirmed that was the one.

I don't understand, she wrote. *This has been my number for ten years. Are you sure this is it?*

The response was immediate. *I know this number by heart. Who is this?*

"Why do *I* have to prove myself?" Isla grumbled. *My name is Isla.*

There was a long, long pause, and she found herself waiting for their response impatiently.

Then: *You are not Isla.*

"I beg your pardon," she countered out loud. Her fingers flew over the phone's keyboard. *Excuse me, but I have been Isla for the past 29 years. And who are you?*

Her entire body stilled as the next message came in.

Is your full name Isla Elizabeth Abbott? Born in Grand Rapids, Michigan to Caroline and Arnold Abbott? Employed as a graphic designer?

Fear spread through her like a biting frost. Who the hell was this person? How did they know her? Were they stalking her? Was this some kind of sick joke?

Isla wanted to block the number to be done with it but found herself typing, *How do you know me? Did you look me up online?*

Can you confirm? the messenger asked. *Please. Please just confirm your identity. I can't explain why but I need to know if you're Isla Abbott.*

Nope. Isla shut down the thread and ignored it, shaking with the adrenaline rush of such a bizarre, unexpected exchange. She didn't know who they were or what they wanted, and it was suspicious as all hell that they wouldn't identify themselves, but she would not entertain their delusion.

And yet she couldn't bring herself to block the number.

* * *

Isla woke up with a stomachache on one of the two days she had to drive to St. Louis for work. After she took her medication and packed her bag, she noticed one more text from the messenger: *Please. I mean you no ill will; far from it. Please tell me if you're Isla.*

No, she typed.

Nothing for the rest of the morning. She picked at bland food throughout the day to help settle her stomach. A new project found its way into her lap first thing in the morning—something she had never done before.

"If you have any questions, just reach out to me," the project manager said. "Do you think you can have it done by five?"

Isla inwardly blanched. "Yes, probably. It'll be tight, though."

"Do your best, and we'll have the client review it tonight."

Do your best. Isla stared at the project instructions in the email blankly, the listed requests not translating well to her brain.

Fatigue and haggard stress, those old uninvited guests, wanted to tiptoe into the room, and she tried to jam the door shut with every lock and barrier she could think of. This job's workload was nothing like her last. No one had asked her to work over the weekend yet, or help finish a project at ten, eleven, midnight for an early delivery. It was too soon to worry that she'd walked into more of the same. So this was nothing.

Except it's not nothing, and you can't do this, she suddenly thought. You don't even know how. You're new and they've overestimated your ability.

Isla swallowed back the inbred panic that rushed up as she tried to detangle what she needed to do, then started to work. Every line fretted over, the composition critiqued down to the last layer. Which never met the high bar of her own standards. She could ask her design manager's opinion, but no, no. Lay it out as best as you can and then ask, he can't do anything with this until he sees a more complete design.

The client was seeing it tonight. *Tonight.*

They would hate it, and she'd be told to do it over again. Best-case scenario. Worst-case, they'd realize it was a mistake to hire her, let her go, and then she would have moved to another state only to be jobless within a month.

It slowed her down, and before Isla knew it, it was after three, and the project wasn't finished. Panicked, she worked faster, putting on headphones to drown out the noise of the rest of the office. It helped her ignore the insidious whispering in her ear. *This design is sloppy. They'll wonder why they hired you in the first place.*

Isla made it under the wire at 4:55. Muscles burning between her shoulder blades, neck stiff, stomach in knots. She stood and stretched her legs after submitting the document, catching the attention of her manager.

"Take a load off. You've earned it," he said, before turning back to his computer.

"I might just go home, if that's okay." Her hands shook, and she didn't want anyone to know she was on the verge of hyperventilating from the pressure and sudden relief.

"You have my blessing. Nice work; it looks great."

Isla smiled wanly and grabbed her things. As she headed out, two of her coworkers stopped her. She nearly cried.

"Hey, Isla. We're grabbing drinks and a bite to eat after this. Want to join us?"

Her first reaction was an inward cringe and a mental snapshot of her bank account. Could she afford dinner and drinks? But then she recalibrated, because yes, she could now. It had taken her three years to scrape up the money to buy her small cottage, because living alone in Chicago was tough, even on her decent salary, and the leftover money after paying for Mom's funeral only went so far. It was a sacrifice she had willingly made, because finding a stranger for a roommate had been so panic-inducing that she didn't even try. Now that she owned right outside the city, she had actual disposable income to use.

Her second reaction was confusion. Why were they asking her? They barely knew her. Maybe they're being nice, she guessed. Their gazes were open and friendly. But no. No. She didn't feel well, and she was wound up like a coiled spring.

But if she didn't, they'd probably never ask again. And she was so painfully new to Missouri.

"Where?" she asked carefully. "I'm sorry, I don't know St. Louis very well yet."

"It's a gastropub five minutes away."

Hadn't she promised herself to try more? Do things with people, even if it scared her? She did like these girls. Janelle was a developer, and Eleanor worked in events, and they were friendly and great to work with. Unless they didn't want to hurt her feelings and had extended the invite just to be polite. Maybe they hoped she'd turn it down.

Stop it. "I'd love to, thank you. But I can't stay terribly late."

Eleanor beamed, turning her round apple cheeks rosy. "Excellent! Let's head out in ten."

When they arrived downtown, a scant two miles from their Midtown office, Isla cast an eye around at the buildings and compared them to Chicago's wide downtown streets and stunning architecture. She couldn't help a gasp of surprise, however, when they passed a gorgeous street art mural on the side of a building—she knew that artist's work. He created under the moniker Woo. No one knew who he was. He'd done a piece in Uptown last year, and everyone had gotten in a frenzy over it. This mural looked like someone had tossed the contents of a dozen different paint cans onto the wall, the colors dripping down to the alley in candy-coated trails.

One drink with dinner ended up being two, because she didn't get a nice buzz going until the second, and that made the noise and the close quarters of the bar seating more bearable. Eleanor excelled at including more than one person when she spoke, making eye contact and asking personable questions; it was why she was so good at her job. Isla listened wistfully when she talked about the travel she did for events:

Madrid and Amsterdam and Vancouver and all over the country. Janelle seemed to know a little bit about every topic, and Isla held her breath every time she spoke. She was a talented coder, and her whole aesthetic was so effortlessly cool and stylish—like the peach-toned blazer contrasting beautifully with her dark-brown skin—that Isla harbored a bit of a crush. She didn't want to sound foolish or out of her depth in front of these competent, put-together women, so she kept silent for most of dinner.

"So tell us," Janelle started, looking over at Isla. "What took you from Chicago to here? How was your work up there?"

"Intense," Isla said. Understatement of the year. She'd nabbed a job at an ad agency right out of college, and she'd learned a hell of a lot and grown as a graphic designer, but at a cost she couldn't pay anymore without accruing enough mental debt to put her student loans to shame. Late nights, weekends, and insane deadlines had been doable before Mom got sick. After, when she was working out of a hospital room and stepping out to find empty waiting rooms for conference calls, Isla felt her mind slowly crumble under the pressure. The nervous breakdown was just as much from work as from her mother's sickness.

It had taken Willow all but moving in for her to keep functioning like a normal person, and Isla had realized she needed to make a change.

She'd much rather talk about the work than what it had done to her and why she'd left, and she latched onto that like a lifeline. "I enjoyed it, and I had great coworkers, but the work-life balance was nonexistent. I just wanted a change of pace for a while. Do either of you go to Chicago often?"

Eleanor confessed that she hadn't been in years, but Janelle had some family in Bronzeville and visited a few times a year. Isla thought she had safely turned the tide of conversation away from herself, but Eleanor later circled back around with, "So what is it you do when you're not at work?"

The question froze Isla's brain.

What did she do?

. . . she couldn't think of anything interesting. All the hours of her life not spent at work were unpunched time clocks. Whole blank sheets of paper. "I . . ." She cleared her throat and, to give her mouth something to do, took another drink. "I draw," she blurted out. "I paint, and . . . occasionally do commissions, but most of my work stays at my place, so . . . I also read." Jesus Christ, she had to be the least interesting person ever.

"That's awesome!" Eleanor said. "Can we see? I mean, do you have pictures?"

Yes, I do, and no, you can't see them. Isla was instantly irritated with herself. What good is your art if no one sees it? It's already online. She's not going to trash your paintings. You need to get over this fear of showing them to people.

"I have an Instagram account. I can give you my username."

Having all this attention on her and then watching Eleanor and Janelle scroll through the photos was worse than handing over a design to her boss. Before she knew it, her back was ramrod straight, her hands clasped tightly together in her lap. It didn't matter that they said nothing but positive things (although Janelle noticing the use of broken color in a sunrise made her feel good—she wasn't dishing out compliments just to be nice, she was *paying attention*); having them look at her work made her feel exposed. She was relieved when they finally tired of looking and put their phones down.

It was getting late, and neither woman showed signs of wanting to leave. Isla wanted to leave. Her reserves for being social had depleted. All she had to do was say a variation of "It's getting late, and I don't live in the city, so I have a drive ahead of me," but it would reach the tip of her tongue and get caught there like a sweater snagged on a hook.

"Ladies, I've gotta go," Janelle finally said, flagging down the bartender to close the tab. "We're getting client feedback on that app first thing, and I need to head into the office early."

Isla's shoulders sagged with relief. "This has been great. Thank you for inviting me."

"Anytime! We should do this on the regular."

Isla both loved and hated that idea.

Home was a quiet, blessed relief, with one exception: another text from her incessant messenger. *I'm sorry. I don't mean to scare you. I don't think you know me yet, but you're someone I care very much about. If you're the Isla Abbott I know.*

Maybe it was the drinks. Or self-pity for being so bad at socializing, for how unbelievably hard it was for her to do something so simple. A twinge of sympathy reverberated through her like a plucked violin string. She sighed. She didn't want to do this, because she hated sending pictures of herself to anyone, but if he looked her up online, he'd see a few anyway. And it would settle this bizarre disagreement. Isla found a semi-decent picture she didn't hate, from a coworker's wedding a few months back. Her old company employed a lot of great photographers and one of them had gotten a good shot of her in the hotel lobby, so she'd kept it.

Isla sent it. *That's me at a wedding. Is this the Isla you're looking for?*

She forced herself to pocket her phone and headed for the bathroom. On the way, she bypassed the small second bedroom where a nested collection of canvases she had painted lived, the oils in their case on the floor.

She hadn't opened them in months.

But tonight, the tubes of color inside the case drew her into the second bedroom/storage room. So did the canvases. Nothing too expensive: wooden frames from a discounted craft store, the pastels a gift from Willow's parents on her twenty-fifth birthday. Isla lifted one of the slim canvases from the pile, a wild, green-black forest path at twilight. Deep shadows obscured the edges of the frame, and the painting's camera lens aimed down a poorly lit path. Thick, moss-covered tree trunks stood guard on either side, their arms overgrown with boughs of black and dark-green leaves. It looked vaguely sinister, the impressionist technique giving it a depth that let the path stretch on endlessly. Although she didn't know where the path led, it never made her feel like there was real danger. It would look, she thought, much different in the daylight.

After setting it down, she went back to the living room. Four more of her pieces were on the walls, more at home with the house's blue hues. The shores of an opaque, dark, yet calm sea; a wet, thickly packed brown sand strip, overgrown with beach grass. Gray-and blue-woods, fresh white snow piled at the bottom of the painting, with an owl in the center, perched on a snow-covered branch. His ear tufts pointed straight back in a curious manner, his eyes worried. He was her favorite. His name was Digby.

She could do another.

The drop cloth was right in the hall closet with her easel. Isla rose to get them, then paused at the closet door, looking down at the folded-up easel and cloth.

Was there a point, if it would just join the other hidden canvases in the bedroom?

She didn't know why she painted. Yes, she enjoyed it, but she wasn't particularly good at it. On her bad days, it felt like a waste of time, tangible evidence that Isla fancied herself an artist but wasn't actually one. On her good days, it was a source of comfort and creativity and made her feel alive and expressive and, dare she think it, beautiful for having created something that once solely resided in her imagination.

Isla shut the bedroom door.

Her mystery texter had responded by the time she checked again.

Yes, they said. *Yes, you are the Isla I'm looking for.*

Great, she replied. *Now who are you?*

The response appeared within seconds.

Your husband.

CONNECTION

CHAPTER TWO

Isla laughed out loud. Oh, that was a good one. *I'm afraid I don't have one of those*, she typed back. *You legitimately have the wrong number.*

The typing bubble appeared, then disappeared. He had to respond, because she could not go to bed until he did. Isla felt more awake and alert than she had in longer than she cared to remember.

And then a picture came through.

It was the dress she'd worn at the wedding, in the picture she'd sent him.

Same three-quarter-length sleeves. Same collared neckline. Same tiny burst of color in the left shoulder; peacock feathers embroidered into the sleeve, stitched wisps of yellow and green and purple. It was lying on a bedspread, like it was just waiting for her to wear it again.

It was in her closet in the next room.

She made a distressed squeaking noise as her hand went to her mouth. He followed the picture with, *The Isla, born on June 26th, who owns this dress and who is in the picture you sent me, is my wife.*

Isla had a large imagination, with many rooms and castles in the sky and dungeons in the basement, and even that one struggled to process what he alluded to. Was she supposed to believe that this stranger claiming to be her husband was an actual husband she didn't have? And that he was, what . . . communicating to her from some future point in her life? As in, actual facts from the future?

Horseshit.

Anger bloomed like nightshade. This was a joke. No, she could not explain how he had, on hand, a hard-to-duplicate dress that she'd gotten from a boutique in Lincoln Park, but she could not accept that some random guy texting her out of nowhere was her *husband*.

Time travel was not a thing.

A husband was an even less likely thing.

Isla was not an attractive woman. Men rarely noticed her, much less wanted to date her. Therefore, he was a liar. A mean, cruel liar.

Don't ever contact me again, she told him. God, had she turned on the heat? Her body was a lava flow of rage, her anxiety spiking like an erupting volcano. *This is not funny, this is not a joke. I don't have a husband, and I am not your wife. Please go confuse some other poor woman.*

His response was immediate. *Isla, wait. Please. You just moved to Missouri, is that right?*

She didn't respond.

Your mother passed away sixteen months ago.

Isla fired back, *Anyone with a shred of research skills could pair my name with that obituary.*

He continued unabated. Text after text. *She was sick for six months. You worked ten-hour days and took care of her on the weekends and took her to her appointments, and it was exhausting and heartbreaking. But you also said it was the most time you'd spent together since you were little, and you didn't regret that part of it.*

Your favorite memories of you and your mom were the long car rides she used to take you on. You always wanted to drive across the country using the same route she did when she was younger and drove to the Californian coast. She used to tell you that she wasn't a brave person, but you thought that had been so brave of her. Doing something like that by herself.

Grief cupped its hand around her heart.

Your artwork is brilliant and you hate sharing it because it feels like sharing a piece of your soul. You like to repurpose old things. You love cherries. You don't like sushi, and that's a character flaw we overlook, but it was almost a dealbreaker.

Isla laughed despite herself.

When you were eight, you almost drowned in a friend's swimming pool and you've been scared of deep water ever since. You collect fonts like people collect stamps. Your favorite is something called Bambi.

Bembo, she corrected automatically, unconsciously smiling over his flub. She held the phone with trembling fingers. She could barely type. *Who are you? Who are you really?*

My name is Ewan.

She couldn't help herself. *McGregor?*

Isla could almost hear the sigh imbued into the words on the screen. *I've endured enough Obi-Wan Kenobi jokes in my life to almost believe it myself, but I am not a Scottish actor.*

Last name? she asked.

The typing bubble was slower to appear this time, and lasted longer. *I don't think I should tell you that. I don't fully understand how we're able to communicate or what's going on either, but it feels irresponsible of me to give you information that would have you looking me up prematurely.*

It was Isla's turn to sigh, literally instead of presumably. *This is not how we build trust, Ewan.*

I know. I'm sorry.

I don't know how I'm supposed to believe this. My God, what an understatement. *I don't know you. I've never met you. You won't even tell me your last name. I don't believe in time travel or time loops.*

I don't get it either, he admitted. *But I'm not crazy. And I really, desperately don't want to lose touch with you. I can't explain myself, but just . . . please keep talking to me, okay? You have no idea how important you are to me. How vital this connection is.*

No one had ever said words like that to her.

If it helps, he added, *I can give you a little more than my first name.*

An Itemized List of Ewan:

1. *Favorite color: purple*
2. *I love hiking. I went to college in Colorado and I've summited eight 14ers.*
3. *I hate social media. Correction: I hate how all-consuming these tiny computers are, and people develop way too many neck and back issues and poor posture habits because of them and tablets and computers and everything that cranks your head down and puts upwards of 50 pounds of pressure on your neck. (but let me tell you how I really feel).*
4. *I had a pet rabbit for about five minutes as a kid.*
5. *I've traveled to Thailand, Vietnam, Japan, a few European countries, and South Korea multiple times (once with you. My grandparents live there. I'm second generation).*

What's a 14er? she asked.
Mountain peaks above 14,000 feet.

Damn. Clearly the man was in shape. And she was jealous that he was so well traveled. Isla scanned over each line of precious information, and the third made her straighten her slouched posture and rub a hand over the back of her vaguely sore neck. *50 pounds of pressure, really?*

Really. Your head weighs about 10 pounds in neutral, right? For every inch you tilt forward and look down, the weight your neck and spine carries increases by 10 pounds. That's a lot of stress and pressure on your joints and your spine. You're doing it right now, aren't you?

Isla straightened her posture again, then tilted her head left to right and felt the tight pull of stiff muscles. *No.*

Every time you tell a lie, a kitten gets punched in the face.

She would not find that funny. *I'll bet you're doing it, too.*

I'll have you know I'm texting at eye level.

Isla snorted. *Okay, pal. Are you a chiropractor?*

No.

She sighed. She wasn't ruling out a doctor of some sort. Or maybe just someone really, really passionate about spinal care. *What was your pet rabbit's name?*

Petrie.

Isla giggled despite herself. *Like from The Land Before Time?*

Exactly like from The Land Before Time.

She felt a thread of kinship reaching between her and this Ewan. Those movies had defined her childhood and that brief, shining moment when she had wanted to be a paleontologist. *Who's my favorite character from the series?* she challenged.

Ducky, of course.

His correct response jolted her right out of the comfort zone she'd tried to slip into. *This is just . . . I don't know what to do with this, Ewan. I can hardly believe it.*

Just keep talking to me, he begged. *You don't have to believe. I can barely believe it myself. Just humor me.*

Okay, she typed. *Okay, weirdo, I'll humor you.* And that's all she could do. Humor him until this strange interlude was over and it became a funny story she'd tell Will about later.

Thank you, Isla.

Even though they were just words on a small screen, Isla felt warmth from them. Like he meant it. Like it wasn't a hoax. She only then realized how late it had gotten, and didn't want to stop talking, but the whole ordeal had exhausted her . . . although in a weirdly good way, the way that painting for hours exhausted her.

I have to go to bed, she told him. *In case you don't hear from me.* She wasn't sure why she felt compelled to tell him that, but there had, in fact, been a sense of urgency in his pleas to stay in touch. No matter how bizarre the situation, she didn't want to cause another person undue stress. There was already so much suffering.

Sleep well, Isla, he said.

Holding the phone to her chest, Isla stayed where she was and stared blankly at the dark TV screen. Her heart pounded beneath the warm surface of the phone and her sweaty palms.

Sleep eluded her as she tried to ignore the phone, even turned her back to it and stared at the wall. It's a practical joke, she thought as she finally drifted off. You'll see in the morning. Things like this don't happen to people like you. Ewan is not real.

But it was nice to pretend, in the few hazy minutes before Isla fell asleep, that he could be.

*　*　*

The next morning sprinted up to her as soon as she closed her eyes, and daylight aggressively shone in her face before she was ready. Isla groaned as her alarm sang at her. She shut it off, rolled over, and dozed for another ten minutes.

It sang again. She thought about pitching it across the room.

Then thought of nothing but getting ready for work until she was digging into her closet for clothes that made her feel like a working adult.

She remembered when she pulled out a sweater and saw the navy-blue dress tucked behind it. Fully expecting that entire thread to be absent from her text messages, Isla swiped open her phone.

The unprogrammed number was still there. The last text: *Sleep well, Isla.*

"Oh my god, it wasn't a dream," she breathed. She sank onto the bed, work temporarily forgotten. She scrolled back through the conversation, shaking her head at the impossibility of it.

Just humor me.

Was *he* out of touch with reality? Or was *she*?

Isla's stomach dropped to her knees. Was this entire thing a product of her mind? Some grand delusion born from a mountain of stress and isolation and some pathetic, desperate need to connect with another person? But how could her brain fake an entire give-and-take conversation with a random number?

Why hadn't he reached out since then? If he *was* real, had he decided the game wasn't fun anymore? Had it been a joke all along? A joke from an external force . . . or some colossal misunderstanding on the part of her broken brain?

She wouldn't know unless she contacted him. Or . . . typed into the void. Whatever. Just text back, she told herself. Anything. Then get on with your day.

Isla set the phone down, paced in front of it, walked away to brush her teeth, then stared at her phone the whole time as if it were an EVP reader tuned into a future ghost, liable to shriek out an alarm when it picked up the right frequency.

She texted before she could keep overthinking it. *Why buttercup?* Then tucked the phone into her back pocket and went into the kitchen to brew coffee. She successfully ignored it for the first two hours of work, deliberately keeping it on silent while she worked on a design for an email campaign. Jamming on headphones to flood her ears with EDM music also helped.

Ewan's message came through at ten fifteen. *I don't really want to say why. It's my nickname for you. You seemed to like it.*

The last sentence intrigued her. *Seemed to, past tense?* she asked.

We're not together anymore.

Oh. Isla was bummed for this metaphorical future her and Ewan. *I'm sorry?*

Don't be, he replied quickly. *You don't owe anyone an apology.*

Interesting turn of phrase. Had he done something wrong? Was it an amicable separation or breakup? Imaginary Isla had a much more interesting life than Real Isla. International trips to South Korea, a husband, a dramatic and tragic ending to a grand love affair. A pining lover. Isla flushed at the very idea of having one of those. To say that Isla was inexperienced was a gross understatement. Even if she'd thought it was worth the effort, there hadn't been much time to date with an anxiety disorder, depression, and a dying mother taking up a large chunk of her life.

Two short-lived boyfriends was all the experience she could boast. Isla hadn't dated in high school because she'd been too busy falling apart, and guys ignored her anyway. Which was fine. Years of bullying in school about everything from her teeth (corrected with braces five years too late) to her freckles to her clothes to her gangly awkward preteen body were the perfect recipe for a wallflower to quietly want to die rather than endure another day of school.

Potential love interests had been the least of her worries then. And when it became time to even consider them, well . . . she was too painfully shy, anxious, and odd-looking (on a good day) to try very hard or even think about competing with all the more beautiful girls that were smart and funny and giving and everything she was not. So the idea of having a lover, much less a lover she'd end up marrying, was both intoxicating and ridiculous. She couldn't take it seriously. There was no one out there for Isla.

The indignation of someone suggesting otherwise, introducing this new variable that directly conflicted with her worldview and experience of it, filled Isla with anger anew. She was being catfished, she thought. That was it. He'd found her online somehow and maybe seen in her face that she was a vulnerable introvert with low self-esteem. Ah, yes: the perfect prey. Gullible and passive and willing to believe anything because she was so desperately lonely. He wouldn't be the first to have thought so.

Well, she had news for him. She'd made her peace with being single, and *liked* being single, and enjoyed the fact that she was able to pick up all of her shit and move to a different state just because she wanted to. She'd held down a job, done work she liked and was good at, *and* taken care of a sick mother, because that's what family did. She liked her new house and she was going to start painting again, maybe, when she got around to it. She didn't need this. She didn't *deserve* this.

No, she texted him. *You know what? I don't know what your game is or what you want out of this, but I can't be a part of it. You know how ridiculous this all sounds, don't you? I am married to no one. I know no one named Ewan. I don't know how you knew those things about my mother or any of the other stuff, but it doesn't matter. I wish you luck in . . . whatever it is you do.*

And another thing, she added when she could see the typing bubble appear and wanted to head him off. Did he have a job? Was he just sitting by his phone, waiting for her to reply? *I don't even know if you're real. Maybe you're a bot for a long-game pyramid scheme. Let me break it to you gently now—I don't want any of your Nutriboom and I'm not signing any contracts.*

That was it. That was *it*. Isla opened the caller information and scrolled down to the last choice on the page: *Block this Caller*. Her finger hovered over the option. And hovered there. And hovered there.

"Damn it," she sighed. And closed the page.

She'd give him a chance to counter. As if that would even matter, but it felt . . . nicer. And he could just wait for her to cool down before she'd pick up this bag-of-cats conversation again.

After all, she had a friend visiting tomorrow.

* * *

Isla hated being out in public alone, but she made an exception for coffee.

She got to St. Louis way too early and decided to settle in at a coffee shop near the office that her coworkers recommended. She liked it instantly for the strings of popsicle-shaped lights and bright stars hanging from the kitchen, the exposed brick walls, and the beautiful art prints. It helped that RISE made one hell of a latte.

It was also highly trafficked on Friday afternoons, so Isla kept her head down in her book. College students and remote workers appeared to make up most of the sit-down crowd, covering tables with textbooks and papers, laptops or tablets, earbuds in and focused. When her phone pinged a reminder to leave, she got back in line to order another latte to go, and spent the time enjoying whatever cologne the man in front of her wore. It made her think of mountain air on a cool spring morning.

She could still smell it when she pulled up to the train station. Gateway Station was a crowded gray building with a charming series of candy-colored glass panes that reminded her of the brightly colored tiles that kids built with. She distracted herself by staring at them while waiting for the Amtrak train to arrive. Even with her sunglasses on, she wanted to flinch every time a stranger glanced at her on their way past. Until it wasn't a stranger.

Willow embraced Isla first before retrieving her luggage. "Hey, shy girl," she said. "I made it."

CHAPTER THREE

"I am dubiously eyeing your choice of location."

"It's pretty," Isla protested.

"It's remote. It's where people go to turn into conspiracy theorists and hoard five years' worth of grain in their basements 'just in case.' It's where you ward off any visitors with a shotgun."

"It's less than an hour from St. Louis. And I don't own a shotgun."

Willow was not amused. Isla's oldest friend slid her sunglasses down her nose to properly take in the gently rolling green hills, wheat fields, tree groves, and sun-soaked Route 61. Took it all in, judged it, dismissed it with a push on the bridge of her sunglasses.

"I wanted this," Isla said, more firmly. "I needed it. Everything became too much."

"I know, babe," Willow said. "I just didn't think your first foray into homeownership would be out *here*." She kicked off her sneakers, pulled off her socks, and put her feet on the dashboard. Isla glanced at her friend, and that familiar pull of pride and envy tugged, like a rope attached to a bucket of old, unwanted feelings. Willow's heart-shaped face, sharp, intelligent dark eyes, and long black hair made her gorgeous in a way that sucked the air out of a room. Her low-key confidence commanded a room like a captain commanded a ship.

Sometimes, simply being around Willow made Isla braver. And sometimes Isla felt her own physical lack as acutely as a reflex hammer slamming into a kneecap. Which was why Ewan was full of shit.

Ugh. Isla made a face at herself in the rearview mirror, her heart now an open sore. Her thoughts were such unruly, unpleasant things, now more than ever. It would be nice, for once, to enjoy Willow's visit without picking herself apart like a scab. Will didn't own a car, and she'd come all this way on a train. No one else would have done that for her.

Isla's heart pounded pleasantly when she turned onto the dry, cracked country road. Trees with lush, thick leaves bowed over the asphalt on either side, occasionally parting their tresses to showcase a tiny farm with hilly land where horses roamed, tails flicking at flies. She'd never ridden a horse in her life. Brush grass swayed in the breeze and wildflowers grew near the gravel. The cottage's front faced a grassy field by the country road, and the back faced the edge of a small forest outcropping.

"Is that a shed?" Willow asked as Isla slowed to a stop in front of the small cottage.

"It's *my* shed," Isla shot back, still smiling. "I can even sit on the toilet without banging my knee against the radiator."

Willow laughed. "Christ, that was the tiniest bathroom I have ever seen!"

"It was cozy," Isla grinned. Her first apartment in Chicago had been, well . . . not exactly guest friendly. But this new place?

Tumbled brick exterior. White wraparound porch. A hip roof of brown shingles. A small back porch and room for a garden. Isla had never planted a garden except for the tomato vines she used to grow on the little balcony at her last apartment.

The pair walked across the creaky wooden porch, and Isla let them into the wide open living room that led into the kitchen; small by house standards but the biggest place she had ever lived in on her own. A tiny fireplace sat in one corner.

It was *her* shed.

"This is nice," Willow grudgingly admitted. She wandered each room, then followed Isla onto the back porch. "You need a little patio set back here, maybe a fire pit."

"I'll just roast marshmallows by myself," Isla said sarcastically.

"Well, damn, you wouldn't have to if you hadn't moved to another state!" Willow took the sting out of the comment by slinging an arm over Isla's tense shoulders, then sighed. Her voice was gentle when she asked, "Did you call your dad?"

Isla closed her eyes. "Not yet."

"Babe, you've got to tell him you moved, at the very least. Want to call him while I'm here?"

"No. Yes. No. Maybe. Can we eat first?"

* * *

They put off the call until the next day. Willow came with her to find a patio set, and then they went out to lunch in St. Charles, a smaller city along the Missouri River with cobblestone streets and antiquated storefronts. When the sun began to set, Isla placed the call and put it on speakerphone.

Her father surprised her by picking up on the third ring. "Hello, Isla."

"Hi, Dad." Isla squeezed the throw pillow in her lap.

"How's the new place?"

Whatever script Isla had haphazardly thrown together for this conversation flew out the window. "I . . . was actually calling to tell you that. I closed on the cottage two weeks ago." He'd known she was looking to get out of Chicago and saving to buy her first place, but she hadn't told him yet that she'd found one.

"Heard it through the grapevine."

"Wouldn't have killed you to reach out," Willow muttered. Isla shot her a wild-eyed glance, praying her father hadn't heard.

"Yeah, I . . . the, ah, the move went well. I started my new job too."

She braced herself for any of the shade she expected him to throw over her relocation in general. He had not approved of her wanting to leave, and he had been vocal about it. His only daughter, moving to another state. Leaving her good job, her good city life, to take a pay cut somewhere else. What a waste.

But he didn't, and she allowed herself to relax. It made her feel like she could talk about it. Ask him. He had done a surprisingly decent job of checking in on her last year, although they'd already fallen back into their regular rhythm. The least she could do was set aside her own discomfort and give him the same courtesy.

"How are you doing, Dad?" Isla asked.

There was a long pause, and then he cleared his throat. "I'm doing all right," he said slowly. "Keeping busy. Took some time off to go see your uncle Greg out in Idaho."

I meant Mom, she thought. Were they talking about Mom? Maybe it was still too painful. Yeah, they'd divorced, but they *were* married. She didn't know what that was like.

What kind of grooves wore into someone's mind after years and years of sharing a life with someone, even if you weren't happy? Maybe especially because you weren't happy.

Who are you?

Your husband.

Isla closed her eyes as that violin string plucked again, releasing one long, quivering note. "Really? When did you go?"

"Couple weeks back. Next time I'll bring you with. Your uncle hasn't seen you since you had braces," he continued. "I didn't think there'd be anything in Idaho to see worth shit, but it was nice out there."

"I'm glad you went." She was a little hurt that he hadn't told her—she had a soft spot for Uncle Greg—but that road went two ways, didn't it? She literally hadn't told him she'd bought the cottage until two weeks after she'd moved into it. They both sucked at reaching out to each other, and she knew that getting in touch with her had been like pulling teeth over the last year. She couldn't blame him for not letting her know every detail of his life when he wasn't even sure she would pick up the phone.

He's done the same to you for most of your life, she reminded herself.

Isla sighed. She was trying to put all that behind her. She only had one parent left.

"That wasn't terrible," Will said after the conversation was over.

"No," Isla agreed.

"And now you get your reward for doing the thing you kept putting off." Willow bounded off the couch and went over to her weekend bag. Isla snorted when she pulled out a bottle of wine.

"I could make sangrias with this, or we could enjoy it as is." With the discreet class of a future sommelier, Will presented the label to Isla. "I give you a Crianza Rioja. A perfect summer wine to enjoy on your new back patio. This Spanish red has been aged for two years, and it will pair well with the green olives I found in your cupboard. Why are you grinning?"

"You're so cute when you talk wine to me."

Will sighed, dropping her arms to her side along with the wine bottle. "I was going for knowledgeable and sophisticated."

"And you are those things too. But also cute."

Willow bowed with a flourish. "I'll pull out some wineglasses, and then you tell me what you taste, okay? I didn't tell you what to expect because I want to see what you pick up."

"I can't promise I'll taste anything but vague hints of fruit and something I can't label, so I'll just call it *toasted*."

"Oh, Isla, you can do better than that. Show your new neighbors how cultured you are."

"That would be lying."

*   *   *

The day she finally reopened Ewan's message thread, Isla woke with a dull headache. She slouched over the wooden counter, head in her hands, as coffee brewed. There was a storm coming; she could feel it in her sinuses.

She worked at a snail's pace on a flyer and half a dozen posters for a conference and picked at a website redesign. They weren't hard, but Isla's brain couldn't differentiate among the deadlines and so made all of them high priority. The fluttering of Isla's pulse and the shakiness in her breath took a few hours to give way to longer, cleansing breaths and a quieter heart. When the workday was over, she was mentally worn out and disappointed with herself. This new job, this move—it was supposed to help, wasn't it? Everything about it had been carefully constructed not to feel overwhelming.

But it was anyway.

She soothed herself by cooking breakfast for dinner and then breaking into a package of cookies. Isla remembered Ewan when she was on her third cookie. She had enough mental bandwidth now to handle whatever curve ball had been held suspended in midair over the past few days, hiding behind the bright-red *4* attached to the message icon. Isla opened the thread.

Wait, he had texted.

1. *I am not a bot trying to get you to sign an 85-year contract for Nutriboom. Boom boom.*
2. *I've given you irrefutable evidence to the contrary. Is it impossible to suspend your disbelief, even just a little?*

Isla?

Damn it, he'd gotten the *Brooklyn Nine-Nine* reference. A bot wouldn't get that. Would it? Maybe this was a point in favor of the Ewan Is Legit theory. He had great taste in TV shows, at any rate.

Irrefutable, huh? she texted back. She would *not* be impressed that he used *irrefutable* in a text message. *You showed me a picture of a dress that maybe you got from someone else's Instagram or a review of it online, I don't know, and you told me a few things about myself that you could easily get from someone who knows me back in Chicago. You won't tell me your last name or anything else about yourself. If it's money you're after and you're looking to extort some funds, boy do I have news for you. I already signed a contract in blood to give all my money to UIC. You'll have to take it up with them.*

He got back to her right quick. *Thank you for texting me back. I was . . . worried.*

She waited, and he added: *You really still don't believe me. I knew about *Ducky.**

Of course I don't. There's an entire show devoted to people like you.

Do I need to tell you more about yourself? he asked.

No, it'll creep me out, she wrote, but that didn't stop him.

An Itemized List of Isla

1. *Favorite color: Prussian blue*
2. *Loves painting with oils (one of my favorites is the one you did of the backyard of a boutique shop in Michigan. Salmon pink walls, a garden, a pond, a blue patio set.)*
3. *Judges the font choice of every sign and home décor item she sees*
4. *Unabashedly loves playing with legos*
5. *Orders a vanilla latte in every city she visits. Her favorite is from a little town by the Puget Sound in Washington. (You haven't been yet, but you will.)*

That painting was sitting in the spare bedroom. She'd never shown it to anyone, and she'd never sold it. Just to be sure, Isla sprinted into the other room and thumbed through the canvases until she found the painting of the garden and the pink walls.

But of course *she* knew about her own paintings, didn't she? The word *delusion* flashed across her brain again in Franklin Gothic Heavy font, the kind used for period drama films about politics and espionage. Blocky letters with thick, sterile black lines, screaming against a stark white background. Your brain could be making this up as you go along, she thought. But even as the idea of suffering a mental break so bad that she'd created a whole other person to talk to made her want to curl into herself with a new kind of despair, she hesitated to make that self-diagnosis.

When she got back to her phone, he had sent a picture.

Their wedding picture.

There she was. In a beautiful, vintage-inspired bridal gown of delicate lace with sheer cap sleeves and a lace-embroidered upper back. The teardrop pearl necklace around her neck was her mother's; Caroline had worn it on her own wedding day. Isla's light-brown hair was in an admittedly beautiful crown braid updo, and she looked . . . she looked . . . like a *bride*. A pretty, glowing bride, her face upturned as she gazed into the eyes of the man next to her.

Isla tried to look away from this foreign version of herself, this happy stranger, to look at Ewan, to study every facet of him that the picture captured. This was her messenger.

Oh no. Oh no, he was gorgeous. Black hair that fell to his forehead and framed the kind of face that showed up in paintings hung in the Louvre or the Met. Square jaw, beautiful smile. Handsome, almost boyish features offset by a tall, lean body tucked into a tailored dark-gray tux. She couldn't handle the way he looked at the Isla in the picture. Like it was the greatest day of his life.

It couldn't be real. It *couldn't* be real.

Photoshopped, she texted desperately. No matter how badly she wanted it to be real, that was the only sane explanation she had left to keep her feet grounded in reality.

He sent another photo.

The painting of the boutique shop's backyard, hanging on a wall. Same salmon-pink walls, same blue patio set, same waxy green leaves and flowers that she'd hand painted. He appeared to have it in his possession.

Isla threw her phone away from her, and it thudded onto the carpet, facedown. She dropped her face in her hands and sat there, willing herself not to cry, and sucked in deep, shaky breaths.

People didn't go out of their way to create hoaxes this grandiose. At least, not to mess with someone of such little note. And the way he talked about her . . . there was familiarity there, and friendliness, and dare she say, affection. They had a *wedding photo*. He owned the original painting in her spare bedroom. She didn't know how it was possible . . . and she couldn't entirely rule out her faulty brain playing a role. But she had enough proof to suspend her disbelief in order to let whatever this was play out to its conclusion.

Whether that meant checking herself into a treatment facility or meeting this stranger in person. Because if he was her future, her present would eventually reach out to meet him.

If he existed.

CHAPTER FOUR

She found a flurry of texts waiting for her when she picked up the phone again after pacing around the house, willing herself to calm down.

I'm sorry, I know this is scaring you, he wrote. *I would be scared and skeptical if I were you, too.*

I don't know how this is happening either, but I think it's safe to say that we can establish a clear time difference between us, and that I'm more advanced in the timeline than you are. Your present is my past.

Can we establish that as a fact?

Isla?

I know you have a million questions and I don't have a lot of answers. Hand to god, that is our real wedding photo.

If you need me to shut up about this for a while, I can do that. Just please let me know you received these texts.

I got them, she typed. *And yes, we can establish that as a fact.*

Okay. Okay. I'm afraid to tell you too much about your (our) future because I've watched enough science fiction movies to know that changing things in the past affects the future. Isla,

I would protect this connection with my life. I don't want to do anything that would hurt you.

Oh, she did not like the way that was worded. *What's happened? Where is future me? Why are you saying this to me and not her?* It didn't feel like just a separation. If they'd gotten divorced and he had the ability to communicate with his wife again—and he still loved her—sure, maybe he'd want to try to fix things somehow. But he wasn't leading the conversation in that sort of direction. He was still being too vague.

It seemed so cruel, to have just learned that he existed and they would fall in love and get married, and in the same breath realize it would all end.

For imaginary her. But at this point, trying to mentally distance herself from this and blame it on bad brain wiring worked about as well as carrying loaded bags of groceries with her pinkies.

I have reasons that I can't disclose right now. It's hard to explain. I think being able to talk to you like this is the only chance I'll get to make things different. I don't know what that looks like yet, but we'll find out.

Understanding dawned, cold as a gray winter sunrise. *Did I die?* she asked him. *Am I dead, Ewan? Or sick?*

He didn't answer.

"Oh shit," she breathed. She was already seated, so she stood and paced, slowly, around her living room.

Death wasn't a stranger to her. Isla had been in the room when her mother died. She and her aunt and cousins had kept a vigil all night on that last night. Slept badly on the overnight cots the hospital provided, then given up entirely and stayed awake until the end. Death had arrived with little fanfare. One moment, her mother was there; within three breaths, she had left.

Confronted with the real possibility of a death that wouldn't occur in some distant future, when she was eighty and riddled with arthritis and afflicted with some form of cancer related to what took her mother, was unsettling. It scared her, but in the same way the thought of accidentally leaving the stove on when she left the house scared her. The inevitable would arrive early, and she was now having a discussion with someone trying to stop that; to "make things different."

But how?

Isla stared at the phone on her couch. The screen lit up. She swiped it open to see his response.

The answer is not that simple, he said. *I don't want you to worry about that, because it isn't quite what you're thinking. If there is something you need to know, I promise I will tell you.*

She was cold in the center of her chest, as if she'd swallowed an ice cube. *I believe you,* she told him, feeling as if someone else's fingers were typing her words, some impersonal party on her behalf. *I assume there's still time, since we haven't met yet. But if there's a place I should avoid or a car I shouldn't get into, please do me a solid and let me know.* And she should probably find a new primary care physician and schedule yearly physicals again. Although if it was an illness, traceable back to a certain point or a missed growth of some kind, she assumed he would just tell her. He acted as if it was more complicated than that.

Don't obsess over this, Isla thought, as if she ever listened to the rational voice in her head. The idea that you'll die one day is not a new one.

I would tell you, he repeated. *I need time. For now . . . keep talking to me. Please.*

I can do that, Ewan.

* * *

In-office days meant morning treats at RISE coffee shop beforehand, and it was there that she realized she couldn't contact Ewan after leaving the house. The message failed to send every time she tried. *Interesting*. So their connection through time existed only within the cottage. When she bought it, she hadn't seen any clauses about time loopholes, but there was a first for everything.

She found herself staring repeatedly throughout the day at the picture he'd sent her. When she had small breaks between assignments or meetings, she'd sneak a look at it and marvel at her excellent taste in wedding dresses and stare at Ewan to her heart's content like she hadn't done since the sixth grade at the poster of Bowie's Goblin King on her wall.

She could look him up. With enough time, she could probably find him, and it would settle the real or fake internal debate. She could do an image search with the picture too; facial recognition might pick him up.

That surprisingly didn't sit well. He hadn't outright asked her not to, but he didn't have to. He'd made it clear he didn't want her to know more than she needed to. And to be honest, taking a shortcut to find him prematurely felt like betraying him and cheating herself of a reveal that would be far more satisfying if she waited.

Be patient. See this through. Don't Google him.

She couldn't drive home fast enough. She wanted to talk to him, because it occurred to her that she knew almost nothing about him and she wouldn't unless he divulged it or she dragged it out of him. As soon as she was in the door, she texted him.

Hey. How was your day?

It felt odd to ask him such a banal question instead of the more probing ones she wanted to throw at him, but it was something she'd ask anyone she cared about; she didn't have to treat him any differently.

She watched the typing bubble appear, then stop. Then appear, and then stop, as if his first responses weren't satisfactory and he kept erasing them.

Hi Buttercup. It is . . . lovely to hear from you. I keep thinking this is a dream, and then you message me. My day was fine. How was yours?

She hated how madly her heart fluttered at the reappearance of the nickname. It was cute and sappy and intimate. *Same. What's your, ah, 9-5 look like? Office? Hospital? Do you travel for work?*

I help people, he said, helpfully. *You were one of them.*

Would you like to elaborate on that?

I respectfully decline.

Ugh. Since he refused to be forthcoming about concrete details, Isla changed tactics. *What did you have for breakfast this morning?*

A misugaru latte and a hardboiled egg.

What's a misugaru latte? Score one point for the Ewan Is Real theory; she had *no* idea what that was.

It's a Korean drink. My mom used to send me off to school with one. She always sweetened it with honey and milk. I add espresso.

Does Future Isla like them, too?

She does ☺

Isla almost forgot about her own dinner. When she came back after setting the oven to preheat for meat loaf, she was delighted to find that he had divulged more information, unprompted. *You got me into cooking at home more, although I'm not the best cook. We do Sunday breakfasts together.*

We have found the flaw, she texted. *Here I was thinking you're practically perfect.*

Oh, Isla, I am not perfect. Far from it.

Isla detected a sad air around his words and decided not to poke him with a stick about it. It was enough that she knew what kind of routines they had. Routines were so important. Routines kept her sane and calm.

How are you liking the area? Ewan asked her as she ate dinner on the couch.

I love it, she replied. *I've been meaning to drive up to Hannibal and do some Mark Twain tourism.*

You should, he said. *Play tourist. It's small, but it has a lot to offer.*

I don't have anyone to go with, she thought, her heart sinking. She wanted to, but she had such a hard time doing things alone. Whenever she went out alone, she felt too seen. Watched, judged. Most spaces found a way of crowding her out without anyone saying a word. She'd had so few friends even before she moved—she had no one to blame but herself for that.

As if he read her damn mind, Ewan continued with, *I know you're new in town, but it's perfectly natural to take a stroll where you live by yourself. People do it all the time.*

Those people aren't me, she replied. Could she tell him what it was really like? It wasn't as if he didn't already know. Even if she hadn't outright said it over the course of their relationship, maybe he'd picked up on it. But then again, her parents never quite did. At times, it had felt like she was a houseguest that they didn't know very well. *I have a hard time doing things alone*, she confessed.

I know, sweetheart.

Isla put her hand to her chest, right where it ached. She had no idea what his voice sounded like, but she could almost hear him say it. And it felt like balm on a wound. The urge to hear him speak came on as strong as a current. What did he sound like? Was it forceful and robust, or soft and low? Deep, or raspy?

Would you do it for me? he asked. *Tour Hannibal this weekend, and then report back to me. What you saw, how it made you feel.*

Isla smiled. *Do you want a paper, too?*

4–6 pages, double spaced. 3 sources minimum.

She laughed. Well, if she had a reason to go . . . it couldn't hurt. And she did want to act like a tourist in Hannibal, but she worried she'd get overstimulated and have a panic attack in public. And he knew that. Suddenly Isla did want to do it for him, because he asked her to, and because she felt like he'd be proud of her if she did.

Aye, aye, captain, she replied.

Isla tried to leave him be for the rest of the night and most of the next day, but it was annoyingly hard. She had never experienced this level of desire to talk to anyone. It was just because the situation was so strange. It wouldn't be like this if not for the inherent mystery of who he really was and how they would meet and why this was happening. She was less creeped out about everything now.

Plus, he was nice to talk to.

And funny and confident enough that he didn't seem to overthink his responses like Isla was prone to do. He only hesitated when he was afraid of giving away too much information.

How long had they, metaphorically, been together? She tried to get an age out of him, but he wouldn't tell her anything beyond *I'm in my thirties.* Isla found it remarkably easy to tease him and act, well, more confident than she really felt. Written communication always came easier to her than verbal; so did visual, for that matter. Words escaped her when she was confronted with real people. Words on a screen, however, she could deal with. She didn't have to worry about his body language or odd pauses or hesitations in person, whether he wasn't making eye contact or was looking down at his phone instead of her. Ewan's communication was exact and thorough because he cared enough for it to be, and that made a difference.

The weekend came, and Isla made good on her promise to go tour Hannibal, shooting him a text that she was off to explore, so he wouldn't hear from her all day. She was optimistic enough at the start, because the weather was beautiful. A lot of people were out and about on Main Street, so she blended in seamlessly. Mark Twain's boyhood home was her first stop.

Isla felt only a little bit weird about being by herself. There were a handful of other people taking the tour, and she made herself disappear among them, standing off to the side as she listened to the tour guide and looked around.

After poking through Mark Twain's home, she walked (and sweated) up the main street toward the statue of Huckleberry Finn and Tom Sawyer. Isla sat on one of the nearby benches and let the mild breeze cool her. Her phone pinged in her pocket; a text from Will.

You are so adorable I could eat you up. Thank you for the care package, babe. She ended the text with hearts.

Isla grinned, pleased. She decided to call Will back instead of texting it all out.

"I miss you," Will sighed as soon as she picked up. "I didn't know I needed a rice sock sloth in my life until I got one."

"You've worked hard on that sommelier certification, I thought it was time for you to get a congratulations surprise," Isla said.

"I'm almost in the clear; I can't wait to just work again. I never thought I'd say that."

They chatted while Isla enjoyed the breeze and the view of the Mississippi. When Will asked her what she was up to, she told her. "By yourself?" Willow sounded delighted. "Look at you! Take lots of pictures. Post them so I can see them."

"I will."

Isla had one more item on her list to check off that would give her the prettiest photos. She drove up to the Rockcliffe Mansion, parked . . . and stayed in the car. Staring up at the Georgian-style mansion-turned-bed-and-breakfast. She was intimidated at the thought of walking into a B&B with no reservation and just the explicit desire to look inside the house, but reminded herself that it had legit tours and functioned as a museum of sorts too.

No one will care if you go in. You're a tourist. They expect people like you to go inside. They give *tours*.

Isla's heart pounded anyway. All the negative thoughts she tried so desperately to keep at bay with work and painting and music and routines sneaked in, whispering at first, then growing louder when they realized they had her undivided attention.

You don't belong up there.

They'll know you're not from around here, and they'll wonder why you're there. You'll hang at the back of the group, alone, and they'll wonder why you're alone, and they'll judge you for it.

Don't even bother. Just drive away.

They don't want you there anyway.

Isla tried to refute it with common goddamn sense, but it was too late—the feelings were already planted and taking root in her chest. From there they would grow and spread, dispensing shame and fear and despair to whatever they touched.

It was such a simple task. It was so easy, so normal. And she couldn't do it. Because she was weak and a coward. Who on earth was incapable of walking into a building and doing a tour? Not normal people. Not people deserving of someone who talked to them and cared about them like Ewan seemed to. How could he, at some point in their future, look at her with anything but pity for how deeply flawed she was?

Oh god. It was really on a roll now. And Isla hadn't taken any medication today, since it had the tendency to make her tired. She dropped her head on the steering wheel and took slow, shaky breaths, fingers squeezing the wheel. Then, as the tightness in her chest increased and so did the urge to cry or curl into a ball, she turned the engine back on and went home.

Tail between her legs.

CHAPTER FIVE

Isla took her antianxiety medication before a real panic attack could set in. After drawing the curtains to block out direct sunlight, she curled up on top of her bedspread and didn't move for over an hour.

Why was she like this? Why was it always like this? She had been doing so well. So much better. Mom dying had acted like a reset button. She felt raw again, like the new fragile skin of a healing wound that would rip like tissue paper at the slightest provocation.

She fell asleep, waiting for the gnarled mess of disappointment, shame, and worthlessness to leave her. When she woke up again, the sun was setting, and the feelings were still there, albeit muted. Everything wrong or weird about how she acted or spoke or *was* had just waited for her to wake up to remind her that it still existed. That it would never leave.

And now she had to tell Ewan that she'd failed and copped out. That was the worst of it. She hated disappointing people or risking any sort of accusation or demand for a sensible reason to explain why she couldn't do the thing. She even hated canceling appointments and inconveniencing her doctors. Her ears were so attuned to the slightest hint of exasperation, annoyance, or hesitation that she did anything to avoid how that emotionally translated.

Her own mind exhausted her.

Eyes dry and heart heavy, Isla pulled herself out of bed, feeling ninety instead of twenty-nine. She had no will to cook and didn't want to leave the house to make the drive back into town for food or groceries (god no), so she ate a peanut-butter-and-jelly sandwich that her stomach violently rejected, besetting her with cramps that threatened to tear her insides in two. She hobbled into the kitchen for her stomach medication and waited out the worst of the cramps in the bathroom before curling up on the couch with a heating pad. The ocean-blue house was still, quiet, and growing dark in the waning light. It both soothed and suffocated her.

She ignored her phone until she felt both medications start to work, calming her mind and stomach and allowing her to endure the negative thought patterns without having a physical or emotional reaction to them. She was halfway through a documentary about the oldest cave paintings in the world before she looked at her phone.

Ewan. *How was your jaunt through Hannibal?*

. . . A bust, she typed. *I went through Mark Twain's boyhood home and then just . . . epically failed. I'll have to turn my paper in incomplete.*

Tell me what happened.

Isla hesitated. *I don't want to.*

This is a no-judgement zone, he wrote. *Isla, you can tell me anything. There's nothing to be ashamed of.*

Her eyes filled with tears. The hell with it. She might as well. Right now, he was just words on a screen. It hardly mattered. *I couldn't walk into the mansion. I couldn't do a simple, mundane thing because I listened to everything I don't like about myself and everything I tell myself about what I can and can't do, and if I had gone in, I would've fallen apart. So I went home. It sounds so silly and ridiculous. Children have meltdowns. I'm a grown woman and I have them.*

What do you tell yourself about what you can and can't do? he asked.

That I shouldn't take up space anywhere. Oh god, was she really typing this? Was she really telling him these private, damning thoughts?

Would you tell that to someone you cared about? Tell them that they're not allowed to take up space, or be seen in public places?

No, of course not.

Then why do you tell yourself that?

It made her pause. *I don't know. I've been telling myself that for so long that I just . . . accept it as a fact.*

Maybe it's a lie. And lies like that are designed to keep you feeling like you don't belong. Make you feel small. I did that to myself when I was younger, too. I was too Asian for my classmates and too American for the Koreans I knew. I internalized that for a long time before I decided that I was going to take up space anyway.

She pressed her fingers to her mouth and stared at his words for a long time before responding. *I can't imagine. I'm sorry you had to grow up with that conflict inside you.*

It is what it is, he said. *I'm sorry kids were so vicious to you when you were little. You never went into great detail, but you told me enough that I wished I could go back and kick 13-year-old ass. You didn't deserve it. And you don't deserve the way it's made you bully yourself.*

His word choice gave her a jolt. *That is not what I'm doing,* she argued.

Isn't it?

No one had ever phrased it like that to her, and that knife went in deep. He was not wrong. And it hurt to think that she was, what . . . that she had been continuing their work? The work of thoughtless, careless, casually cruel children? Did she have a mean preteen living inside her head, telling her awful things about herself to keep her on the ground, face in the dust? So she would always feel like that worthless thirteen-year-old who couldn't defend herself?

She finally returned to her phone to find another text. *Don't give them that much power. Fight it with kindness. Be the kid who stepped in to tell them they're wrong. From now on, I want you to stand up for yourself to yourself. As soon as that little shit pipes up that you're worthless and you shouldn't be there and you shouldn't say anything or take up space, tell her to stop talking about your friend like that. She's wrong. Be kind to Isla.*

Never before had Isla so desperately wanted to hear his voice. *Ewan, can I call you? Can we see if it works?*

There was a long silence, and then: *I don't know if it will.*

Just do it. Just do it. Do it do it do it do it. Isla tapped on his number and hit call before she could overthink it. Her heart pounded in her ears as the phone rang. And rang and rang, and went to a full mailbox.

I think that worked? she texted. *Do you see a missed call?*

I do, he typed. *But I can't pick up right now. It's not that I don't want to talk to you, sweetheart. It's that I don't think I'm mentally and emotionally ready for that yet, even though I want to so badly. I spent every week after you died sending you messages, pretending you were on the other end, getting them. And then you did, and I wanted to call you right away . . . but I couldn't do it. When I'm ready, we'll try this again, okay?*

Isla's heart wrenched for him. *I completely understand, honey. I really just wanted to tell you that your perspective makes sense, and to thank you for taking the time to tell me that. I don't know if I'll always be able to look at it this way, but I'll try.*

That's all you can do, he said.

Do you have a degree in psychology?

I have a degree in Isla Abbott, he said.

Isla flushed. There was . . . a lot to unpack in that statement.

But I didn't always listen like I should have, he added. *Some of this I've gathered in hindsight. You could say I didn't always pay attention in class, but I was really, really interested in the subject matter.*

You're getting into corny territory, she typed, smiling.

I could run with this metaphor for hours, he said cheekily. *Isla Musical Theory 101. The History of Impressionism: An Isla Dissertation Analysis 201. Good Design Versus Garbage Graphics 301, with an accompanying TED Talk.*

Isla giggled as he kept going. All of her friends had endured her rants about poor design in advertising and film. And she had no doubt Ewan would have suffered the same.

I've stayed up all night studying Isla, he added.

Her cheeks heated again. She tortured herself by pulling up their wedding photo to look at the happy future couple. Envisioned falling asleep and waking up next to him. The simple, vital pleasure of skin-to-skin contact. To simply touch another human being with the intent to bring pleasure would be a revelation.

And then the illusion shattered. She could count on one hand the number of people who had shown interest in her. What could someone as gorgeous as Ewan want with her? How could he be attracted to her? Most of the time, Isla felt so ugly that she couldn't stand it when photos of herself found their way to social media for the world to see. The very act of taking a picture felt ridiculous.

Why me? she asked him. *Let's face it, Ewan, I'm not pretty. At best, I'm inoffensive. So why?*

Attraction doesn't work that way, Buttercup. There are a hundred little things about you that I love and that are beautiful, and they include your youness and your body. How you give hugs. The way you find the best in people. How your hair is like silk under my fingers. The way you dress, your freckles; the curve of your neck. You have the softest skin I've ever touched. Your eyes are the exact gray of the mist that covers the valleys below the top of a trail I used to hike with my grandfather called Ulsanbawi. Every time I looked into them, I think of that sunrise and how those valleys took my breath away. I never told you that. I know you don't see yourself the way I see you. I wish you did. Because when you tell me that you think your eyes are too far apart, all I see are the mists in the valley.

Isla dropped her head into her free hand. The fear and longing and uncertainty and gratitude were so heavy in her belly that she didn't feel big enough to contain them.

You've made me cry more in the past week and a half than my own mother, she told him.

I'm sorry. But as long as you're hearing it and believing it, then I'm going to keep doing it. And any time you feel differently, I want you to tell me. The more you do it the less raw it'll feel. Tell me, tell Willow. People will understand. No one's harder on you than you are on yourself.

This is true, she admitted.

Do you promise to try?

I promise.

They talked well into the night. Isla treasured every tidbit he let slip about himself and their relationship until it started to feel more real and less like a promise that would never be kept. Isla marveled at the impossibility of their connection, at the how of it. It had to be something special about this cottage, or this particular patch of land. Isla went out into the backyard to sit on the patio in the warm summer night air and was still able to talk to him.

When the clock read one AM, Isla finally went to bed, hating that they had to sleep. Worried, in the back of her mind, that the tenuous connection would snap while she slept and he would disappear with the sun.

*   *   *

Gray swirled into emerald green in circular, dreamy brushstrokes. Swirl after swirl after swirl until it created the perfect shade of quiet green. Isla finished creating her palette, then stood over the blank canvas and began to work.

She had a few pictures as a reference to get the overall shape of it down and lightly sketched the design out on the canvas, but for the most part she let the soft, lovely feelings it gave her direct her hand. Music played in the background as she painted; the wind chimes danced on the back patio. Sunlight filtered in, unhampered by curtains.

It was a perfect Sunday for painting.

For a while, she didn't even think about Ewan; it was just her and the canvas. Isla remembered to eat only when her stomach was ravenous, and she ate fast in order to get back to the unfinished work. As the hours passed, the valley sprang to life, rising and falling in gentle swells like waves, carpeted by trees awash in the gold-and-pink light of sunrise. The jagged rocks of the mountain summit and the end of the trailhead framed the bottom of the painting, the serrated edges of bare rock rising up at the painting's edges like a doorway. The mists gathered in the center, hovering above the trees.

When it was finished, her back ached and her muscles burned between her shoulder blades, but a bone-deep satisfaction she rarely felt anymore filled her fiercely with its presence.

Pleased with herself, Isla snapped a photo and sent it to Ewan.

Sorry I've been quiet, she added underneath. *I was busy with this. Did I get it right?*

You nailed it, Buttercup. Please keep it for me, he wrote. *Don't sell that one.*

I don't sell my work, she replied. *Or rather, I haven't yet. I'll keep it for you.*

You should, he said. *Put your work out there. People always ask me who did the painting in my office, and I'm always proud to tell them it was you.*

There's a lot of competition out there, she replied.

And an audience for just about anything, he countered. *It's a shame for it to sit in hiding.*

She gnawed on her lower lip. She'd thought about it, certainly. But the will and energy and endurance it took to start an art career and get her pieces noticed had been beyond her for so long. It sounded exhausting on top of working full-time. She made those pieces just for her own enjoyment, because she had enough reasonable talent to not hate what she produced and the process was cathartic.

Isla had old classmates who sold their work on various online platforms, and some did reasonably well. It wouldn't be difficult to reach out to them to get some advice on getting started.

But later. Right now, she had to acclimate to the new job before she could worry about showcasing her work anywhere. She didn't even have a website yet beyond a simple graphic design portfolio.

I'll think about it, she told him. She didn't want to talk about it anymore; he was as talented at turning the conversation away from himself as she was. *What did you do with yourself today, Ewan?*

Cleaned, did laundry, took the dog for a walk.

We have a dog? she asked excitedly. *Picture, please?!*

He sent her a smiley face, then disappointed her with, *I think I'll leave that one as a surprise, but yes, we have a dog. She's a good travel companion. She's been on a few road trips with us.*

She loved that idea so much she wished she could hold it in her hands and squeeze it. Like the dog she didn't have yet. *Where do we road trip to?*

Out west. The national parks, the mountains.

I've never been, she typed, then rolled her eyes and added, *but you knew that. Do we hike together?*

A few times a year.

Where are your favorite trails?

Southern Utah and central Colorado. And my favorite road trip was the first one we went on. Watching you experience it for the first time was incredible. I've never met anyone who actually enjoyed driving through Kansas, but you loved it. Couldn't get enough. You find beauty in the oddest places. I love that about you.

Isla had to sit down again. What was he doing to her? She didn't quite have the words to describe the feeling in her chest. It was new, fragile, thin as gossamer wings but just as bright and incandescent. She believed this version of herself that he talked about. She recognized this version, saw fleeting glimpses of her on occasion. She *liked* this person. She did take joy in life's little pleasures, mostly because she felt things deeply, good and bad. He talked about this version of her with such affection, such . . . kindness. It didn't quite match the person she knew herself to be. But his interpretation wasn't incorrect. It was different.

And I can't wait to meet you to take that trip, she replied. *But I have one question. It's very important.*

What's that?

What are your road trip playlists?

. . . Promise you won't laugh?

Grinning, Isla curled up on the couch. *Scout's honor.*

You were never a girl scout.

You won't even know if I laugh at you. Tell me.

Gothic metal.

Delighted beyond her wildest dreams, Isla laughed so loud she startled a few birds out on her windowsill. *You're a metalhead!*

I am. Was. A little.

Please tell me you were a goth, please tell me you were a goth.

. . . I was a baby goth.

Oh, Ewan, this is the best news I've ever heard. I need to know everything. Did you paint your nails? Wear eyeliner? Leather pants? A DOG COLLAR?

. . . All of the above.

Isla squealed. *Ewan, if you're lying to me, it will be the greatest disappointment of my life.*

Why is this a thing for you?

Do you still go to shows? Do you have any of your goth wear?

I sometimes go to shows. Yes, some of it is hidden in a box in my closet. I was too embarrassed to ever tell you, and then you found out when you found the box while we were moving.

She was dying. Of all the things to be embarrassed about, this was the most endearing. He was adorable. *And what did I do when I found out my husband was a metalhead?*

You had the exact same reaction you're having now. I got offended, then you made me put it all on, kept teasing me, and then, ah . . . you took it off me.

I'll bet I did, she responded before she could second-guess herself. What was the harm in flirting with him? She was terrible at flirting in person, and it was so much easier this way.

W h y is this a thing for you? You never told me.

I love the goth aesthetic, she admitted. *I got along best with the goths at my school—even though I wasn't part of their group, they were always nice to me. I was never comfortable expressing myself like that through fashion. It's such a bold statement. I really admire it.*

Standing out does draw attention whether you like it or not. I did it on purpose, at first. A little rebellion on the home front and school front. If I couldn't fit in the way I wanted at school, then I really wouldn't fit in. My mother was horrified and my father thought it was hilarious and roasted me every chance he got. I couldn't dress like that at home, so I used to keep spare clothes in my locker and change when I got to school.

8-3 goth.

Yes. Then full time in college for a while before I toned it down, got a real job in a respectable field that almost-not-quite met my parents' standards.

I'm sure they're still proud of you. They'll love you no matter what.

Asian parent disappointment is on another level.

I'll take your word for it.

But they do love me. Even though they really hated the goth phase.

My parents wouldn't have appreciated that either. I, on the other hand, love your goth phase.

And for a moment, she didn't know whether she meant future Isla or herself.

CHAPTER SIX

Isla almost forgot that she was destined to die young.

She spoke with Ewan in the morning, on her lunch break, and after her workday ended. On Thursdays and Fridays, she went into the office and warmed herself with remembered conversations and the chance to talk to him again at night. He kept gently reminding her to not waste time and find a new therapist, so she started looking for one.

He wouldn't let her ignore the things she'd rather not deal with, particularly when it came to her anxiety and her lack of coping skills. He challenged her to go back to the mansion and tour it, but she wasn't ready to face that failure again. Instead, she tried to interact with more people at work, especially Janelle and Eleanor. When they asked her out for drinks again, she said yes, and it did not suck. It was actually fun. Twinges of self-consciousness still nipped at her heels, but the more interaction she had with them, the less it bothered her.

A solution to her problem with touring the mansion alone occurred to her when she was in the office, having a conversation with Eleanor over the graphic designs for an event campaign. Eleanor was dressed sharply, as usual, this time in a blue summer dress with her hair in a 1950s coiffed updo. It was glorious.

Isla just had to work up enough courage to face possible rejection. Even if Eleanor said no, she wouldn't be mean about it. It wouldn't hurt anything.

"So I'm still getting to know the area," Isla started in what she hoped was a conversational tone. "Do you go to Hannibal often?"

"I haven't been in years," Eleanor confessed. "I just don't think about it. I have family in Columbia, so I end up going there instead of ever heading north."

"I was thinking about playing tourist there." Isla paused, held her breath, and let it out. "If you ever wanted to check it out again, I wouldn't mind the company."

Eleanor's face lit up. "Oh yeah, that'd be fun! We could make a day of it. Let's see what Janelle's up to, she might like to come. When were you thinking? Did you know they have haunted ghost tours?"

The relief was so staggering that Isla felt light-headed. Before she knew it, she had actual plans to meet Eleanor and Janelle in Hannibal for lunch the following Saturday. She exchanged phone numbers with them, which was something Isla hadn't done with anyone in years.

On the drive home, she was genuinely happy—excited to talk to Ewan, planning what to cook herself for dinner— when a stray thought snuck in. There was no reason to get this excited over something so trivial. Normal people make friends. You haven't done anything special by inviting them out. They'll probably never do it again, because they're busy adults. Hell, they might even cancel on you.

Isn't your time on earth limited anyway?

"Whoa," Isla said out loud. God, why couldn't her brain be a productive member of society and help her make art instead of using all of its cells to turn just about any damn thing into an excuse to ruin *everything*? "Uncalled for."

She didn't know when it would happen; Ewan had never said. They could have been married for ten, fifteen years, if he was lying about his age. That was no excuse to not live her life. And even if Eleanor and Janelle canceled, which she couldn't possibly know in advance, it wouldn't be the end of the world. Isla thrived on canceled plans. It was a win-win.

Of course, it still rambled around in her mind like a tumbleweed when she got home. A date. A length of time. A countdown. She found a way to bring it up without directly addressing the thing he never wanted to talk about. *Ewan, did we have kids?* she asked bluntly.

No, he replied.

That was supposed to make her feel better, but it didn't. It just meant he was alone. In one way or another, she'd left him all alone.

Just like Mom.

That sucker punch knocked the wind out of her, and Isla couldn't breathe for want of air. Mom had left sixteen months and five days ago, the day after a blizzard hit the Chicago area and buried it under a foot of snow. A cold, miserable Tuesday had been her mother's last day. And here Isla was, just as alone in the world without her mom as Ewan was alone without his wife at some distant point in the future. Except he had the rare, inexplicable gift of being able to talk to her and maybe prevent whatever bad thing would befall Isla in the future.

No one had been able to save her mom like that. But Ewan cared enough to try to do it for her.

Isla's chest hurt so bad she thought it would cave under a pressure she didn't know how to release. She *hated* crying— hated it like nothing else in the world—so she sat with the pressure and tried to breathe through it, her throat clamped down like the jaws of an alligator around prey. All the while, her thoughts remained on a loop. Poor Ewan. That poor man. Her poor mother. Life was such a goddamn tragedy.

Once she could breathe without wanting to sob or kick something, she put the kettle on for tea and wrapped herself in the throw blanket that lay on top of the couch. The blanket that used to sit at the foot of her mother's bed.

When she was calmer, she messaged Ewan. *I'm so sorry for everything you're going through. I'm sorry for leaving you. It hit close to home today, thinking about my mom, then about you. I know you don't feel comfortable telling me much about your situation, and you don't have to, but I just want you to know that I think about you every day when we're not talking, and I worry about you, too. I hope you're taking care of yourself.*

He didn't respond right away, and she hadn't expected him to. Having said her piece, Isla lay down on the couch and didn't move until well past dinner, forgetting about the kettle and the tea. She let herself feel low and alone for as long as she could stand it. When it came time to pick herself back up, she had to force it, ramming her shoulder against the door of her functioning brain hard enough to dislodge the jam that had trapped her outside it for hours.

She washed down her medication with water, then stood for a long time in the middle of the kitchen, her mind blank and unable to envision what to do next. Her insides were as hollow and fragile as bird bones. There were a dozen things she could be doing—laundry, tidying up, reading, painting—but she could not muster the energy to do any of them. She didn't even want to.

Isla forced herself to shower and went through the motions slowly, as if the blue bathroom were indeed underwater and she was moving dreamily and unhurriedly through its currents. After wiping condensation off the mirror, she stared at her reflection.

Her face was made up of the components of at least three different women. The shape was too angular and made her high cheekbones look more alien than attractive. Wide-set eyes under a large forehead, thin lips, a weak chin, teeth that were still crooked here and there because she'd never worn a retainer after braces, and freckles that dominated her face like a heat rash, dark brown against her pale skin and all the more noticeable for it. They had been a constant companion on her face since she was a child. Granted, they'd been downright adorable when she was a kid, but as an adult, compounded with everything else that had gone wrong on her face after hitting puberty, it completed a picture that Isla never felt at home in. Staring in the mirror was the equivalent of staring at an odd-looking, homely stranger. Someone who should just stay in the house rather than inflict themselves on other people. Someone no one would look twice at, nor had they in a long time. Ewan was better off without her anyway.

She was so tired of feeling this way about herself. So unbelievably tired. But she didn't know how to stop. It seemed inevitable, and all the facets of her life pointed to that truth instead of refuting it.

We see what we want to see, she reminded herself. Hadn't a therapist once told her that? We find evidence to fit our worldview and our view of ourselves.

But all the rational thought in the world couldn't touch how ugly *felt*.

She didn't know what to do with all of the bad, tar-like thoughts sticking to the inside of her brain except let them sit there while she dried her hair. It had gotten so late that she didn't even want to make dinner, so she didn't eat.

Isla didn't look at her phone again until she crawled into bed.

Oh, Isla, he had texted. *Don't worry about me. I want you to take care of yourself. You are so very important to me and to the other people who love you. Believe that.*

Then, an hour later, when she hadn't responded: *Have you found a new therapist yet? To help with your mom?*

No, she responded. *I need to get on that, though.*

Promise me.

I promise.

*　*　*

Isla's emotional state leveled out a week later. At Ewan's encouragement (after she stopped ignoring his texts because she'd stayed in bed until three), she made tiny daily steps that helped. A walk outside; a load of laundry; a five-minute pickup session in each room; an actual meal that she ate out on the back porch, even though it was just mac and cheese.

By Monday, she still wasn't ready for work, so she called off. Isla felt raw and new again, too easily flustered, breakable, and couldn't bear the thought of interacting with anyone or trying to focus on work. She slept early and often that week, forcing herself to check in with Ewan every night because he was worried and it wasn't fair to leave him in the dark. It was hard to tell herself that he didn't care when he was being so kind and patient with her.

She found a therapist who specialized in anxiety disorders and depression after a stressful search for the *right, most perfect* therapist, because what if she found a bad one and had to go through canceling appointments or keeping them to save face and just enduring them and then she'd have failed at this too . . . God, shut up, brain.

Her first appointment was the day before her Hannibal tourist trip with Janelle and Eleanor. It stunned her when the women didn't cancel and even presented her with lunch options on Friday, arguing over which place had the best bar food—"but Isla, it's ultimately up to you, where do you want to go?" Shyly, Isla defaulted to the one within walking distance of the riverboat area, where they planned to get on one of the steamers. Isla cautiously allowed herself to get excited over the day they had planned but kept the possible cancellations in her back pocket in case she needed to be prepared for the disappointment.

By the time she reached the high-rise downtown that housed the psychiatric group, her palms were sweating and her heart raced. Sweat dampened her armpits, and she tugged at her top uncomfortably as she checked in. In the waiting room, Isla clasped her hands together and held them tightly, willing her heart to slow down as the pressure in her chest mounted. She took long, slow breaths. Nope. Not working.

She fished for her phone and scrolled through the exchange she'd had with Ewan before she left.

E: *It's tonight, right?*
I: *Yeah. I'm so nervous.*
E: *Just talk honestly and let the conversation go where it wants to. I'm proud of you for doing this, Isla. Be proud of yourself.*
I: *I'll be super proud if I vomit in her office.*
E: *It probably wouldn't be the first time that's happened.*

It distracted her until Dr. Nowicki came in. The older woman had a broad, kind face and graying blond hair, and her handshake was firm and warm. Isla drew comfort from that as she sat in an armchair across a coffee table from the therapist.

65

"Well then, Isla," the doctor said as they got settled. "Let's talk about you. Let's find out why you came to me and what you'd like to accomplish here. Does that sound all right?"

"Yes," Isla replied, after a hesitation.

"You seem nervous," Dr. Nowicki observed, her eyes drifting to Isla's defensive posture and her tightly clasped hands. "A little on edge. Coming here was scary, wasn't it?"

The "yes" came out on the exhale of a held-in breath.

"But you did it anyway. That's a good sign. I'm glad you went through with it, even though it scared you to death. It hasn't been the first time you've done something like that, and it won't be the last."

Dr. Nowicki gave off a maternal vibe that satisfied a deep need in Isla, and by the time the first session was over, her body had relaxed and her mind had quieted. She could do this. It wouldn't be easy, but the alternative was suffering quietly at home, at the mercy of her emotions. And now that her rent wasn't astronomical, she could actually afford regular therapy sessions again.

I like her, she told Ewan later that evening. *I think I'll keep this one. How are you doing?*

As long as I'm talking to you, I'm hanging in there, he replied.

That's not at all sad and depressing. Go take our dog for a walk. Treat yourself to a donut for breakfast tomorrow.

Mmm. Boston creme.

That is disgusting.

Fondant is disgusting, but I don't give you grief about your love for barely edible decoration.

The fact that he knew that and she had never once mentioned it surprised and pleased her. *More for me, then.*

All of it for you, you fondant-loving weirdo.

She curled up in bed and let his teasing warm her, like sitting by a firepit on a cool evening. She liked it when he forgot himself and just talked to her like a normal person and not this overly concerned version of himself. Not that she didn't appreciate that concern, but it was nice when he took off his counselor hat and put on his husband hat. Or even better, his friend hat.

Sometimes she wanted to tell Willow that she was talking to someone and not go into detail about who he actually was to avoid the "time travel" discussion, which would go smashingly, she was sure. But then Willow would want a picture, and Isla would have to admit they hadn't met yet. She could lie and say she'd met him through online dating, but she didn't want to get hung up on questions she couldn't answer, and then the whole thing would turn awkward.

So she kept Ewan to herself. A secret just for her. He was a line from an E. E. Cummings poem: *Here is the deepest secret nobody knows.* She carried him in her heart, and that was where he would stay until she had a real person to touch and talk to.

Isla fell asleep talking to him, learning more about him as she pulled information out hand over hand, like heaving up an anchor from an ocean floor. He'd broken his ankle falling out of a tree when he was six. During his goth phase, he'd dyed his hair blue for a while. He could cheerfully die facedown in a tub of guacamole. His dream vacation was to drive around Alaska or Iceland and camp. He was cursed with resting bitch face, which made everyone assume he was in a bad mood all the time (and his sarcasm didn't help). *Not when you smile,* she thought, bringing up the only photo she had for the two hundredth time. *When you smile, your whole face fills with sunshine.*

She'd gone and fallen in love with him, and the present version of him didn't even know it.

CHAPTER SEVEN

Please cancel. Please cancel. Please cancel.

Isla walked along the busy sidewalk on Main Street, phone in hand, stomach in knots. She had gotten up too early, nervous-cleaned, put on a long, loose, shell-pink skirt with a white top to make herself feel better, then gotten worked up all over again when she didn't hear from either Janelle or Eleanor as she left to meet them. They had confirmed they were coming the day before and agreed to meet at eleven for brunch.

But still.

She stayed relatively close to the restaurant and kept an eye out for them, but as the minutes ticked closer to eleven and she still didn't see them, she was both terrified they'd ditched her, which would make it awkward at work next week, and ready for the sweet relief she knew she'd feel if she could just go home for the rest of the day.

"Hey!"

Eleanor, dressed in a gorgeous lemon sherbet sundress that draped her like a lady in a Rubens painting, stood behind her, massive round glasses shielding her eyes from the glare of the sun. Next to Eleanor, Janelle waved, dressed for the heat in shorts and a loose sleeveless tee.

Both women looked happy to be there as they sat down to eat and chatted excitedly about the boat and mansion tour. Since the Mississippi River pier was right in town, they walked down to the boats after lunch to spend a portion of the afternoon on the water.

Isla had dreaded how this would go all week, and of course her brain had made a mountain out of a molehill and catastrophized what would turn out to be a wonderful Saturday afternoon. The only times Isla felt twinges of trepidation were at Janelle and Eleanor's insistence that they take pictures. Isla wanted to flinch away from the camera lens, but she smiled gamely and promised herself she wouldn't look at the pictures they posted later.

When it came time to tour the mansion she had run away from, Isla felt more confident walking in with two other people. The mansion was charming and old, floorboards as cranky as an old woman with arthritis, large Persian rugs cast over wooden floors, chandeliers and leather couches and beautiful artwork. They took their time, enjoying the air conditioning, and quietly razzed some of the decoration choices.

I don't want this to end, Isla realized as the afternoon came to a close. It surprised her. She was having a genuinely good time. When her coworkers—no, her friends—indicated they needed to drive back home for dinner plans, Isla's farewells were sincere, and she hugged them both a little tighter.

"Thanks for coming with me," she said, hoping they could hear the truth behind the words. "I had a really great time."

"This was a good idea," Janelle agreed. "Next time, stay in the city and we'll take you bar hopping."

Isla waved them off, then stood by the office where Mark Twain's father practiced law, hugging herself. God, she wished she could bottle these warm, happy emotions to take out later when she needed them. For now, she would enjoy the feeling while it lasted.

The green of the tree leaves looked soaked with chlorophyll, vivid green and alive to Isla's eyes. The breeze was more fragrant, the sky a deeper, hard blue. She fell in love with the road home again, adoring its gentle swells, the worn pavement, the swaying trees and wildflowers and horse farms.

The urge to paint came on so strong that tears stung her eyes. As soon as she got home, she changed into sweatpants and an old T-shirt, then pulled out her drop cloth and set it out on the back porch with her easel. Isla painted outside, letting her hand make the shapes she saw in her brain. The picture only suggested concrete images through her use of broken, blended color, bold and vivid brushstrokes, and a palette knife, but Isla was more concerned with capturing the feeling of happiness and contentment. For once, she didn't care whether it was a perfect representation of her mind's image of it. She wanted whoever looked at this to feel the same way she did right now, and that was enough.

By the time the drive to paint was through with her, she was losing light as the sun set. Her stomach rumbled, giving her another warning to stop, and Isla reluctantly brought her work inside and let the paint dry. She checked her phone.

How was it? Ewan asked.

Amazing, she replied. *I had such a good day. I just finished another painting. What did you do today?*

Not a whole lot. So you're feeling okay? Therapy is good, work is good, you're painting again, making friends. Is there anything else going on you haven't told me about?

Isla frowned. What an odd question. *I feel fine. Why? Am I doing things differently than you're aware of? Should I be?*

No, I think you're okay. I'm . . . looking for something, and I think I know what it is, but I don't want to say until I know for sure.

She regretted the direction this conversation was headed. The positive feelings from the visit and from painting were wilting like a sun-starved houseplant. Isla didn't like to think about the unexplainable aspects of their communication— how it was possible, why it was happening, what was supposed to come out of it. She knew that she died in his future, but he wouldn't say when it happened or what kind of death he was trying to prevent. She didn't understand why that wasn't readily apparent, unless it was an illness where personal choices mattered very little.

Then why did he say he was still looking for something?

Ewan, maybe I could help if you give me more information. There. She'd addressed it head-on. *Not knowing what you're looking for or what's going to happen is just as stressful and distracting as knowing. Let me help you.*

No response.

What are you afraid of? she asked. *No-judgment zone, remember?*

I've been trying to draw this out for as long as possible, he confessed. *I wanted to just talk to you for awhile. I didn't want all of our conversations to revolve around that one terrible thing.*

"What terrible thing?" Isla asked out loud. The room got colder, and she was suddenly trembling as her body tried to protect everything vital inside her by retreating to the heart of it. *Is it an accident? Cancer?* The impossible occurred to her, and the revelation made her gasp. *Does someone kill me?*

He shot that down immediately. *No. It's not cancer either.* Granted, Mom's colon cancer had been a first, even though milder gastro issues ran in the family. The thought that this was her future and a potential end for her wasn't a pleasant one.

Then what are we dealing with here? she asked. *Colonel Mustard in the library with a candlestick?*

Silence.

Half an hour went by. *I knew it*, Isla added, hoping to prompt a reply in case he'd put down his phone.

An incoming call came through.

A call from Ewan.

"Oh my god." Isla gaped at her phone. And just like that, her heart was a thoroughbred horse at the Kentucky Derby, sprinting at the fire of the start gun. "Ohmygodohmygodohmygod." It kept ringing, and she wanted to answer it, but oh god, was she really about to hear his voice? Were they really going to confirm this impossible connection and talk to each other?

She swiped to take the call. Placed the phone to her ear with a trembling hand. Took in a breath. "Hello. Isla speaking." Her voice came out breathy and unsteady, tightrope walking from a high, high place.

There was a faint noise on the other end of the line; a scruffy sound between a laugh and a gasp for air.

"Isla."

She shivered as he spoke the two syllables of her name. His voice was soft and deep, quiet as a cathedral, reverberant through time and space like so many church bells pealing. It should be impossible. But here it was anyway, and his voice set something free once trapped inside of her.

"Ewan." Isla held her breath, afraid of scaring this moment away. "Hi. I didn't know if you'd ever call."

"I . . ." He paused, and the sound of him clearing his throat raised gooseflesh on her arms. "I didn't know if I would ever be ready. It's . . . so good to hear your voice." His tone changed as he spoke, wavered and roughened with emotion.

This had to be so hard for him. So very hard.

"It's good to hear yours too," she said, softening her voice to match his pitch. He always sounded so confident in their text exchanges. Sure of himself and ahead of the game, navigating their situation far better than she. This was a different Ewan. This Ewan sounded sad and tired and . . . *wistful*. She had to handle this Ewan with careful, steady hands. She whispered playfully, "Isn't this so crazy?"

His husky laugh almost undid her. "So crazy," he repeated. She heard his quiet breathing and remained motionless to catch every tremor of air. "You sound the same."

She stayed silent, letting him gather his thoughts to say what he needed to say.

"The same and yet . . . not. You sound happier."

"I'm talking to you. That always makes me happy." She hesitated. "Was I not happy?"

"I can't answer that," he said.

"How long has it been, Ewan?" she asked kindly. It was remarkably easy to set down her burdens and pick his up. Being a solid, kind presence for him took nothing and meant everything.

This time, his short laugh had a hitch to it that brought tears to her eyes. "Three months."

"Oh, honey." Isla put her hand over the ache in her chest. "I am so sorry."

"Can you . . ." He cleared his throat, his voice deepening. "I haven't heard you say my name in a long time. Can you say it again?"

It was an innocent yet intimate request, and she found that she would do just about anything if he asked her like that. "Ewan. Of course. Are you okay with this? Do you need a break, or . . ."

"No," he said quickly. "Stay on the line. I'm fine."

"Are you really?"

"As much as I can be, sweetheart. But the most important thing is whether you're okay."

Isla sighed. "I wish I knew what that meant, Ewan."

"I know, I'm not helping," he said regretfully. "But based on everything I've talked about . . . I think you're already doing the work to help. It's an ongoing process." She didn't say anything, didn't know what to say. He added, "I'm not ready to tell you yet. I know it's not fair, but I'm asking you to please . . . please . . . be patient. I *will* tell you when you need to know."

She couldn't sit there and argue with the plea in his voice. He wasn't doing this to be difficult—he truly felt like he couldn't open that Pandora's box yet. As frustrated as she was, she knew she needed to recognize that this was a weird and unsettling situation for him too. He was talking to his dead wife on the *phone*. And there were no written rules regarding communication across timelines. Every sci-fi movie and novel about it taught her that unintended changes and actions could have disastrous consequences. Though she doubted she, with her little life, would make huge ripples if she decided to do something radical like take a road trip out of state or get a dog.

Then again, the *Titanic* had sunk in part because the watchman had forgotten to hand over the keys to a locker that stored the binoculars used to look out for large obstacles, like an iceberg. The butterfly effect didn't apply just to people on the world's stage. Sometimes it applied to ship workers and graphic designers.

"So what you're saying is," Isla started slowly, "someone drops a piano on me."

Ewan snorted, then laughed, rich and warm and a little rusty in her ear. This man's laugh would be the thing that killed her dead. "I . . . yes. It was an anvil. Horribly tragic."

"In pursuit of a small, flightless desert bird?"

"I tried to warn you. They're crafty."

There, that was better; he sounded less sad, more amused and engaged. "Well, future man, in your infinite wisdom with your special future knowledge, is there anything broad and not specific I should know? Lottery numbers, future world series games I could bet on?"

She heard a rustle of fabric in the background, as if he were shifting his position. "I would never let you abuse that power."

"Are you sure? Don't you want to retire before eighty? How about the Derby?"

"I have never paid attention to the Derby," he admitted. "I'd never even tasted pecan pie before you introduced me to it."

"Verdict?"

"Mmm, not a fan."

Isla gasped. "Ewan, I'm afraid this relationship is over before it even started."

"I could have said that when I found out you hate sushi, but I stuck around," he shot back.

They talked. About idle, unimportant things, and then about hopes and dreams they'd held as children. Ewan would casually drop knowledge not many people knew about her, reminding her of how very extraordinary these conversations were.

And then it had to end, because both of them had lives, and neither life had much to do with the other on the surface.

"Can we do this more often?" she asked before they hung up.

"Yes." She could hear the smile in his voice, and it was like the first bite of cold, delicious ice cream. "Good night, Isla."

"Good night, Ewan."

Isla barely slept, and instead sat up in bed and sketched ideas for other paintings, his real voice reverberating in her head.

* * *

"Your dad."

Isla groaned. "No, please don't ruin this perfectly nice conversation."

"I know you're not close," Ewan continued, as if she hadn't spoken. "I kind of got the hint after you met my father. You guys got along like a house on fire. You told me you never knew it could be like that. Why is that?"

She didn't want to talk about this. It was a gorgeous Friday evening, hearing Ewan's voice was still new and shiny, and she didn't want to sully it with all these old, uncomfortable feelings. But he seemed determined to press onward with picking out aspects of her life that were difficult snarls, as if talking about them enough would untangle them. Isla sat outside on the patio with her chamomile-and-lavender tea.

"It's not that we don't get along," she started. "We do, sometimes. We have good moments. But he was a hard man to get to know and be close to growing up. He worked a lot. We didn't understand each other, and he used a measuring stick that was always too high for me. It made me a nervous wreck."

Especially when her anxiety had turned into full-blown panic attacks in high school. She'd miss school, he'd get angry, her grades would slip, he'd get angrier. What was wrong with her? Why couldn't she just go? "Sometimes . . ." She hesitated, not knowing how to say it, or if she should say it at all. "Sometimes he made me feel like I wasn't the child he signed up for. Like he wanted someone more like him and he got this meek, quiet, awkward-looking girl instead. I always felt like a disappointment."

And when she had tried to make herself disappear and they found out, there was no sense of shock, or relief that it hadn't worked. There was just more disappointment, except quieter this time, accompanied by a distance that even her mistakes couldn't breach. As if she'd died anyway. After she came back from a seventy-two-hour stay at the hospital, they never really talked about it, and she'd been too chickenshit to try again, so she kept enduring. Her parents were ultimately more concerned with their crumbling marriage than anything else.

The divorce had been such a relief.

"Listen to me," he said firmly. "You are not meek. You're just shy, baby; there's nothing wrong with that. You're not a disappointment. If he thinks so, really thinks so, then he's never seen you for who you are. And awkward looking? No."

"Truth," she countered, her heart still cartwheeling over *baby*.

"Not a bit. Your perspective is skewed. Remember what we talked about? Would you say that about your friend?"

Isla squirmed, uncomfortable with even an indirect spotlight on her looks. "I . . . I don't know."

"Probably not. Be kinder to yourself," he admonished gently. "Believe me when I say, because it's the truth for me and you can't tell me otherwise, that I *am* attracted to you. Isla, by the third date, I couldn't wait to have you to myself." His voice pitched lower, a deep purr in her ear. "Shall I tell you the things I wanted to do to you? The things we've done together?"

Isla's face was a flash fire. When she put her hand to her cheeks, she was pretty sure she was running a fever. Instead of enduring the usual barrage of naysaying her brain indulged in like a competitive sport, there was ample space and desire to . . . envision it herself. *Want* it. Instead of scoffing at him and calling him a liar, she believed him and felt an answering heat flood her entire body. She wanted to ask him what things he alluded to. Then hear him say it. Never in Isla's life had she been more acutely aware that the only person who had ever truly satisfied her had been herself.

She had a feeling he would change that. Because future her would let him in.

"I took that too far," he said in the silence. "I'm sorry if it made you uncomfortable."

"You didn't," she replied breathlessly. "On the contrary. I think I needed to hear that." Still blushing furiously, she added shyly, "I *liked* hearing that."

"Good," he said. "Get used to it."

She had no idea what to say to that. God, she was absolutely terrible at this. "Um. I . . ."

He chuckled. "Cat got your tongue?"

"Shut up," she shot back with a smile.

"Nerd," he said affectionately. "I'll spare you and change the subject to something you'll hate. I want you to try to work on this thing with your dad. Talk to him, or talk to your therapist about it. Just try, for yourself. You'll feel so much better."

Isla sighed. He was like a dog with a bone. "I don't want to. It's hard and scary."

"A lot of things worth doing are hard and scary."

"Ugh, stop it. I'm an adult. I pay taxes and my mortgage and contribute to the economy. If I say it's hard and I don't want to do it, I don't have to do it."

"You're right," he agreed. "But if you don't, then you'll just use this as ammunition against yourself later. *I'm a coward*, you'll say. *I give up too easily. I'm too weak.*"

Damn him. It was endearing that, say, Will knew her really well because they'd met in the fifth grade, but being seen like this by a man was an altogether new experience.

"I feel personally attacked," she said.

"You should."

"You are The Worst."

"On the contrary, Buttercup, I think you like me a little."

"I really don't," she lied.

"Now, Isla," he said, amused, "we agreed to be honest. This is how kittens get punched in the face."

Isla laughed into her hands. "I agreed to nothing; you just did this." As soon as she said it, she wanted to take it back. "Er . . . you know what I mean. *You* didn't, but . . ."

"My text got through," he finished. The reminder sobered them both, and the line went quiet.

"How are you today?" Isla asked. "Are you eating, getting enough sleep?"

"I have more better days now that we're talking. I'm eating. Not sleeping well. That *is* mostly your fault, you know. I can't stop reaching out to you."

"I'll take the blame for that," she said softly, picturing that poor man racked with insomnia and grief, walking around during the day like a zombie. Drifting through the motions of life. She remembered it well. "But you need to sleep. Go to bed. I'll be here."

"Promise?"

"I promise."

CHAPTER EIGHT

"How did you feel when you returned home from the hospital after your suicide attempt?"

Isla stared at her therapist for a long time while she formed an answer. "Invisible," she finally said. "No," she corrected. "Noticed, but only because I had done something horribly wrong."

"And why were you wrong?" Dr. Nowicki asked. She recrossed her legs, then wrapped her hands around her knee. "Why do you always make yourself wrong, Isla?"

The question startled her. She wanted to refute it, but she couldn't.

"Why couldn't it have been what it was?" Dr. Nowicki's voice was gentle. "An attempt to make the hurting stop. And to make what else stop?"

Oh god, she hadn't known she'd have to *voice* it. Isla looked down at the floor, saw her fingers latch on tightly to her skirt and bunch the material in her grip. She couldn't look at that kind face when she said it. "Hating myself. Being full of . . . despair. All the time."

She felt more than saw the doctor nod. "It's exhausting, isn't it?" the woman asked, still impossibly kind.

As Isla nodded, hot tears slipped down her cheeks. She was appalled by them.

"What if you didn't have to feel that way?"

"I don't know how to stop," Isla choked out. A tissue appeared in her line of vision, and she took it with a shaky thank-you.

"I think we can work on that. Let's start by recognizing that the inner voice telling you that you don't belong anywhere, that you're unlovable and ugly and no one wants to be around you? That voice isn't you. That's not who you are. It's a shadow self, and frankly, it's terrible at giving advice."

Isla laughed through her tears.

"Challenging it is going to be hard work, but I know you can do it. I don't think you can really see how strong of a person you have to be to put up with those feelings and the extreme reactions your body puts you through and then live in the world anyway. Yet you do it every day. That is commendable, Isla. But we're going to work on making it easier, more manageable.

"And we're going to start with forgiveness—for yourself. Do you think you can have empathy for that little girl who tried something to make the hurting stop that didn't work? Do you have a little forgiveness for her?"

Isla cried.

*　*　*

She called her dad when she got home from that session. She didn't know what she planned to say, if she'd say anything about what they'd discussed in session, but it went to voice mail anyway, so Isla went straight to bed. Her heart felt like an open, throbbing wound. Her phone lit up with texts from both Willow and Ewan, and she ignored them.

The next morning, Isla got up and realized she had told a real live human being she'd tried to kill herself all those years ago, and the world had not ended. She had not imploded. She had not been judged.

She was still here.

Isla looked around her house and loved it once again for its blue walls, its clean, wooden counters, its trinkets and knickknacks. She let herself think she was proud of her interior design, and for once, nothing negative countered it.

And she knew what Ewan wasn't telling her.

She hoped she was wrong, but a part of her knew now. So many little things he'd said would fall into place. The way he *grieved*.

It took her almost all day to work up the courage to bring it up. She avoided it by cleaning furiously and painting the beginnings of a colorless, snow-laden landscape that matched the mood she was trembling on the precipice of.

After forcing herself to eat something, she asked him. *What do I die of, Ewan? Tell me.*

To her surprise and irritation, she got nothing in return. She almost angry-texted him but stopped herself. He didn't have to be glued to that phone. He could legitimately be busy. She still had no idea what he did for a living, what friends he had, what obligations he needed to fulfill. He didn't exist just to talk to her, even though it felt like it sometimes.

So Isla forced herself to wait and be patient and ignore her phone until the ping of another text came through.

It didn't happen until eight thirty, when Isla was ready to climb the walls until her fingers bled.

Isla . . .

I think I know. She headed him off. *I think I know, but I don't want to guess. Tell me. Please. I can't wait any longer. We've been talking for almost two months.*

The typing bubble appeared, then disappeared. Appeared, then disappeared.

8:42 PM: *You died by suicide.*

8:43 PM: *I'm not trying to save you from something external.*

8:44 PM: *I'm trying to save you from yourself.*

The only sound in the room was Isla's own quiet breathing. She nodded slowly, reading it, then rereading it. Unable to sit, she stood, then paced, then sat again. That hideous, familiar pressure returned like an anvil on her chest. Her arms were too weak to shove it off. She leaned forward and wrapped her arms around her legs until her forehead dropped onto her knees. Blood rushed to her ears. She didn't move as crashing ocean waves filled her eardrums.

Isla listened to the night noises outside. Katydids. Trilling birds. Croaking frogs. The breeze through the chimes on her back porch. She could see all of her belongings in the dim, dull light cast by the moon slanting into her windows. The windows were still open, so the curtains fluttered dreamily.

A curious numbness spread outward from the center of her chest.

It's not true, she thought. *I would never do that again. I told myself I would never try again. On my worst days, there are things I love about living that are greater than the relief of dying.*

Most worst days.

And if it was true, it meant she found the love she'd wanted all her life and it didn't even matter. Love cured nothing. She had thought the feelings of worthlessness would evaporate if someone just loved her. Made her their priority. She would be better, feel better about herself, knowing she was loved and lovable.

But it wasn't true.

It didn't matter.

She did it anyway.

For one long, horrible moment, Isla didn't feel real. She was a figment of Ewan's imagination. Already gone. A ghost, wandering the last place she was remotely happy.

Her whole life amounted to nothing. She would die as she had lived: utterly unremarkable, talent wasted, a disappointment to her family, her friends, and her future husband. She would let down the one person who loved her not because he was related to her and therefore obligated to, but of his own free will.

What was the point? What was the point if she was just going to decide to end it so soon? If she was destined to die young, by her own hand, no matter what she did?

Shit, she might as well just do it now. Spare Ewan all that pain and grief. Just walk right into the Mississippi with weighted pockets and sink down. Ewan would be better off. He could go find someone less broken. He deserved better.

"No." The word startled her, as if someone else had spoken it. It was spoken firmly, as if she wasn't crumbling on the inside. She shook her head, then dragged her fingers through her hair and pulled on the strands. "No," she said again, more desperately.

She loved Ewan. She loved her art and Willow and beautiful fonts and vintage clothing, and she wanted to visit other countries and try more vanilla lattes in new cities. She didn't want to leave. It wasn't destiny, and it wasn't inevitable. Free will was a real thing that she had exercised time and again. It would be easier to think it was out of her hands, but this was in her control. If she stayed on the path she had started on, there was a way out. There had to be.

Ewan's very presence in her life was proof of that. Because wasn't there also something else at work here? Some weird, inexplicable, *magical* thing neither of them could explain? His ability to reach out across time to set her on a path that wouldn't lead to that one decision?

Isla could lie to herself all day and say she didn't understand how she could do it, and on good, amazing, wonderful days, maybe she really couldn't. But she knew. Too many days in succession, one after another after another, of numbness, of despair, of hopelessness, of the intolerable feeling of living inside her own skin . . . that would do it. She knew that soul-crushing headspace. And she also knew that nothing Ewan could say would make a dent. Her worst and darkest self would shunt his words and gestures off to the side with the skill of the best goddamn goalkeeper in the world.

But she was not dead yet. And right now, Isla wanted to live. She walked back to her bedroom and picked up the phone.

Listen to me, Isla, Ewan had written. *I promise that you are already making good, positive changes that are important for you to make, to help you manage and cope better when things get bad, but there is one thing that makes it worse one day, one thing that I know contributed to how you felt about yourself and your place in the world. I know how we can prevent it, so you can keep growing and learning until you know, really know, how wonderful you are and how much you have to offer the world.*

She had no tears for herself, but a well of them rushed up at the frantic tone of his message.

Isla called him. "Ewan?"

"I know what will help," he said, picking up the thread of his text message. The same plea she'd seen in his words was in his voice. "I didn't want to believe it and I kept fighting it, but I don't think there's another way."

"Ewan?"

"I think this is the only option, on top of—"

"Ewan, it wasn't your fault."

He went quiet.

"I don't know how many dead people get the chance to tell the people they left behind this"—and oh god, this was a real conversation she was having—"but it *wasn't your fault.* There was nothing you could have done, because if I was set on doing it, or if it was a rash, spur-of-the-moment reaction, nothing would have stopped me. And it's not because you didn't reach out enough or pay enough attention. It's because I suffer in silence *well.*" Isla's laugh was brittle. "I'm fucking great at it. I rarely tell people how I really feel, so it all just festers. I know this about me; I've *met* me. I told myself for a long time that I didn't know how to be any other way, but I don't think that's true. I think it's just a familiar headspace for me to be in, and I'm scared of how hard it will be to change. I'm terrified of change. And if part of that is opening up to people and being vulnerable, I'm scared of that most of all. Can you . . . hold on a minute?"

Isla put down the phone and curled up in a ball on her bed, rocking herself gently for comfort as the onslaught of self-loathing and grief over her mother and a lifetime of exacerbated fear ran through her like a burst dam. Purging all of that, giving it a voice, was the equivalent of launching herself off a cliffside and free-falling. She wasn't even scared of the impact—it was the fall. It was a long, long way down.

She picked up the phone again. Closed her eyes. Let the truth spill out of her like spilled ink. "I did it to find relief," she whispered. "Not from you. Not from anyone. From my own head. Because there was no other escape. I'm sorry. I'm sorry, I can't talk on the phone anymore." Before he could say another word, she hung up. She knew she owed him the chance to talk, but she couldn't face his grief and anger and disappointment at the way she'd left him.

Ewan wasn't done: the text messages started to come in. She didn't read them at first, but then forced herself.

I should have known, buttercup, I should have known anyway. I know you, I knew what you struggled with (I thought I knew and now talking to you I didn't know, I didn't know all of it) but I sometimes didn't take it as seriously as I should or I didn't understand sometimes it frustrated me and I feel so fucking guilty for ever assuming your reactions weren't entirely justified but I thought I could FIX it, I thought if I told you I loved you enough you would believe it and you SEEMED okay a lot of the time except when you weren't and Isla I'm so goddamned sorry, I love you and miss you so much I wanted to be what you needed I wanted you to stay so badly.

She dropped the phone and gave in to deep, quaking sobs, curling up on her side and letting them overtake her. The sorrow was huge, and she was powerless against it—just like she was powerless against every negative emotion her mind pummeled into her if she made the slightest misstep. Isla let herself feel all of it until she was cried out, alone in her house with a distant, impossible tether to the man on another end of time.

When she responded, she didn't just tell him what she knew he needed to hear—she meant every word. *I love you, Ewan. You loved me enough. I don't think I loved myself enough. And you didn't know everything because I didn't want you to—I was afraid for you to find out. I know better now. You're helping with that, I promise. I see now what you've been doing and I appreciate it from the bottom of my heart. You have no idea.*

I didn't listen enough, he insisted. *I'm not perfect, Isla, I just have hindsight. You have to MAKE me listen.*

Okay, she consoled him.

But there is one thing that will help.
What is it?
You can't go to Chicago for your birthday.
Isla's brow furrowed.

You HAVE to stay in Missouri. In fact, don't drive anywhere on June 22nd. Just stay home. Because you get in a car wreck when you're there. You were on Lake Shore Drive, northbound. Somewhere near a hospital or Navy Pier, I think.

Northwestern, she filled in for him silently. The hospital her mother died in.

A car merged on too fast and rammed right into you. You sustained a traumatic brain injury that affected the nerves in your hands. You could use them, but only for so long before you had hand tremors. You couldn't paint anymore like you used to. Eventually, you stopped trying altogether.

"Oh," Isla whispered. *My work?* she typed.

You kept working, but you dropped down to part-time. That was also in part because of the headaches. You started getting more frequent migraines. You survived three years after the accident.

It sounded devastating. Painting, even when she was self-critical, gave her the greatest joy of her life. To have to give that up, and then have both stomach issues *and* migraines *and* depression *and* an anxiety disorder?

That sounds . . . unbearable.

Don't underestimate yourself, he replied. *You tried your damn best to keep a positive outlook, even though it wore you out. You were dealt a shitty blow and you did everything you could to get back to normal so you could paint again, and I admired that tenacity. You pushed yourself. I know you've got it in you, Isla. But I think things start to break down when you don't ask for help or tell people how you're really doing.*

Isla rubbed her hands, her fingers aching with sympathy pains. Given the choice, no, she would rather not lose the ability to paint or to work without pain, at least not until old age.

I'll stay home that weekend, she said.

Thank you. And maybe . . . maybe just don't drive back to Chicago at all this summer? And be extra careful on the roads. Wear your seatbelt, don't drive at night, the deer come out en masse after dark.

I know, my dear, I'll watch out. I can't avoid the highways forever. But Lord, she'd worry about it now. His paranoia, while sweet, was also contagious.

Another question occurred to her, and she hesitated to ask it, afraid of what she would hear—in fact, just as afraid for him to lie to her as to hear the truth. She asked anyway.

Were you ever happy with me? Did we make each other happy? It sounds miserable, Ewan, I'm not going to lie.

I don't regret anything and I would choose you and love you all over again, he replied. *I was happy. You made me so happy just by existing. I think you were happy, too. You worried a lot, and you were very shy, but you were so much fun to be with. My life is better because of you. And I want you to have a chance to make a different choice for your life, one that will allow you to keep creating and not live with chronic pain. Even if it takes you away from me.*

It won't, she immediately rejected. *It shouldn't.*

He didn't reply.

She couldn't let it go. Isla stayed up, trying to piece together this future life, both wonderful and terrible for the things it would bring her and the things it would take away. None of his revelations had disclosed how they'd actually met. They couldn't possibly have met before the accident, if the accident was June 22, which was in two weeks.

So they met after. How soon after, she didn't know, but Isla had a feeling it would be sooner rather than later.

Then another thought occurred to her, introduced by the snake that lived in the grasses of her mind. *He noticed you because he felt sorry for you.*

Isla didn't even consider censoring herself on this one. Tonight she was too laid open for that, like a frog in a science lab, her insides picked apart and examined by forces beyond her control. *When you met me, did you just feel sorry for me? Was that it? You felt bad for the injured girl with a truckload of mental illnesses and then stuck around?*

It was probably hurtful. Hell, she knew it was hurtful. But she hurt, and she needed to know she wasn't some charity case that he'd taken on and then just gone along with because it was easier.

I don't know what to say to that, he responded. *What is it that you want to hear, Isla? Do you want confirmation for how you feel about yourself right now?*

Tell me.

Would you believe me?

Isla let out a watery laugh. God, she was so sick of crying. *No.*

Too bad. I didn't feel sorry for you. In my line of work, I see people with far worse injuries, far sadder cases than yours.

He might as well have slapped her. *Wow. Thanks.*

You jabbed at me first.

The queasy guilt in her stomach agreed with him. *Are you a doctor?* she asked.

No, not in the way you're thinking. And I didn't feel sorry for you because you didn't let yourself feel sorry for yourself about it, at least not that I saw. You tried so hard to adjust to your new normal and find a way to do the things you wanted to do. I don't feel sorry for people like that. I feel proud of them.

Now he'd made her feel like an asshole. But she wasn't ready to apologize yet. The emotions swirling around in her were strange, some directed at him, some at herself, some at God and the world in general.

Isla changed the subject and didn't care whether he wanted to talk about it. She didn't want to talk about it either, but here they were. *Was it my only attempt?*

That I know of.

And he would be right. After high school—after moving out of her mother's home and never going back to Dad's unless she had to, after getting the space she needed to finish school and get help for her panic attacks, she'd gotten better. She no longer thought of suicide as a desirable option. She liked her work, she liked Chicago, and her anxiety had been fairly well managed until Mom got sick. Knowing that it would all make a reappearance made her so unbelievably tired.

How did I do it?

Please don't ask me that.

Isla realized, too late, how callous of a question that was. Morbid curiosity for her—a reality for him. More than likely, Ewan was the one who'd found her. Her mind wanted to go down that rabbit hole, wonder how she might have gone about it. When she was fifteen, it was her wrists. If she had sustained an injury that gave her access to pain medication, it was probably an overdose in the future. An endless sleep.

I'm sorry, that was low, she said. *It's a lot to take in.*

I know. Can you do me a favor, Isla? Talk to me. Talk to everyone about how you're doing. I don't mean this as a way to help ME, but for you to get more comfortable being honest with people. You hid from me and I didn't even know it. It's not your fault, it's just the way you coped.

Oh, yes. Tell everyone how utterly fragile and broken she really was. The thought was so terrifying she very nearly laughed in his face. *I'll try,* she wrote back.

There is no try. Do. Or do not.

Okay, Yoda.

It's *Obi-Wan*.

Isla reluctantly snorted with laughter.

I have the wisdom of hindsight, he repeated. *Don't be surprised when present-day Ewan has no goddamn clue what he's doing.*

I'll go easy on him. Isla didn't want to find him cute or funny tonight. What she really wanted was to hold on to him, another human body, and draw comfort from him. She wanted to sleep for years. *I have to go to sleep,* she told him. *I love you, Ewan.*

I love you, Isla.

CHAPTER NINE

It was the road. Her road. A frost had set in, sugarcoating the dead grass in frothy, sheer white, the dark earth a vague memory underneath. A fence post, old and warped with rain and weather, stretched down a length of the road like jagged teeth. The house had one inviting light on, one tiny square of yellow in a canvas of blacks, grays, and white. Gradients of colorlessness.

The landscape was dismal, bleak, and beautiful. It put a face to the landscape of Isla's mind.

A series of them, she thought. Sparse, rural winter landscapes. Looking at them would feel like loneliness, the muted quiet of a snowy winter's night, and the anticipation of warmth, if one could only get out of the chill. A crow on one of the fence posts; the frostbitten grass; the road meeting the dark, naked trees.

Isla worked until her back ached. When she surveyed her work in progress, she was satisfied. It looked the way she felt. That was all she asked for.

When she wasn't painting, she was researching online, contacting old college friends about their freelance businesses.

How had they gotten started? What were the best platforms for selling their work? She visited the Instagram page she had started to show some of her work and scanned through each photo to find out which paintings had gotten the most attention.

People were actually asking where they could buy prints. She'd had no idea, because she could never bring herself to read the comments, too afraid of the harsh criticism so rampant online.

At work, Isla jumped at the chance to help out with more website rebranding projects to learn as much as she could and supplement what she knew from her own forays into website design. She asked Janelle and the other developers for advice on setting up a general e-commerce site, and they were generous with their time and advice. By the next weekend, she had a pile of resources from the developers, and she went home straight after work to do more research on the proper techniques for photographing artwork. She checked out one of the DSLR cameras and a tripod and bought a studio lighting kit that made her wallet cringe.

After obsessively trying to get the angle of the lighting as perfect and glare-free as possible, Isla spent hours photographing each painting she wanted to sell prints of, then editing every one of them until they were mirror-perfect digital versions of the originals. By midnight on Sunday night, she had a splitting headache and she wasn't even close to done, but at the same time . . . she felt amazing. Tiny starbursts of pride kept her motivation high.

She called Ewan to tell him about her progress, and as excited as he was for her, a somber note threaded through his voice, thin as a sewing needle and just as sharp. "Ewan," she said. "Are you okay, love?"

He hesitated on the other line.

"That road goes both ways," she reminded him. "If you want me to talk, you get to talk too. No bottling it in."

"Sad," he admitted. "Happy to hear from you. Waking up alone every day is something I'm not used to yet. But having you right here has helped."

Isla wished her arms could reach such an unbreachable distance. He'd spent so much time looking after her, checking in on her, that she forgot sometimes. How he'd lost a wife.

"We'll fix it," she assured him. "You made that happen. You told me what to avoid. And even if it happens anyway? I want to get better. Just by knowing . . . I can work on this. Having your support has meant everything. Future me didn't have that."

"No, she didn't," he said sadly. An urgency kicked up in his voice when he added, "But you'll still stay off the road next Saturday, right?"

"I'll stay off the road." Isla hadn't canceled on Will yet, afraid of disappointing her, but she had a fib in her back pocket: a work assignment, or an illness, or a delivery. The truth was too outrageous. "When do I meet you?" she asked.

"Soon," he promised.

Since he'd brought it up, Isla bit the bullet and called Will to cancel the trip. Willow was understandably upset, which ordinarily would have been enough for Isla to cave and go anyway. She couldn't stand disappointing people, especially people she loved. She'd rather cut off a least favorite body part than deliberately upset someone.

But no. She'd promised Ewan, and disappointing him was even worse. He would feel like everything he'd tried to do was for nothing if she ignored him. Willow didn't know how important it was for her to stay put. And so Isla made apologies and promises to visit later in the year.

It was done. The trip was off, and the accident wouldn't happen. But the more Isla thought about it, the more she wondered if the accident was the sole thing that caused her to take her own life. And the answer to that was no. No such accident had prompted the first attempt. So while preventing the accident, in Ewan's mind, would probably help stave off an attempt, it wasn't guaranteed.

That was up to Isla.

So what could she do differently? Because she couldn't live in constant fear of what future her might do someday. Or live with the conviction that it was inevitable. But was suicide inevitable the way death by a heart attack or an aneurysm was inevitable? A fatal car crash? Would destiny ensure it happened anyway?

"Nope," she said out loud. If the universe wanted to kill her in a freak piano accident or because she had the damn unfortunate luck of being on the highway when a car hit her, fine, whatever. She already lived her day-to-day life with an extra dose of fear of *everything*, and she was not going to add one more thing to that pile. But if the universe was somehow insistent that no matter what Isla did, her end game was to take herself out early? The universe could fuck right off. "I decide," she declared to the room. "And I can decide not to do it."

The very idea that it could be predestined insulted her. That was *her* decision to make, no matter if it was prompted by brain chemistry or a headspace she couldn't suffer anymore or whatever would drive her to seek out that relief again.

But she didn't want to live a life that she needed an escape from. She wanted a life she wanted to *live* in. And she couldn't have that if she did nothing but fear everything and everyone, even herself, now could she?

After the divorce, when Isla was sixteen and she and Mom had gone to live in a two-bedroom apartment in Park

Forest, Mom had tried to explain why it had taken so long. Why she'd waited, even though the signs had been there for years. "I kept waiting for it to feel like the right time," she said, on some long car ride they were taking for the hell of it, probably to Indiana Dunes. Yes, that was right; Isla had been wearing her bathing suit under her clothes.

"It had to be the right time," Mom repeated. Her brown hair had more wisps of gray then, which she would eventually cover with hair dye in defiance of aging. "But then I realized that time had already passed. The right time was when I was sick and tired of being sick and tired. We'd long passed that stage."

Isla was sick and tired of being sick and tired.

"Thank you, Mom," she whispered. She let herself miss her mother, let the grief grip her good and tight. There was no shame in it. She was allowed those feelings, even though it had been a year and a half. *Only* a year and a half.

So no. She wanted to reject that fate. And the only way to do it was to be proactive. There were too many things Isla wanted to do that she had been too afraid to do, and it was time to change that.

Nothing like a second chance, before the first one even terminated, to shock you out of complacency.

Isla dared to hope.

* * *

It had been a hell of a Friday for the entire office. One client had a conference the following weekend, and it was all hands on deck to finish their signage, posters, event app, and a dozen other things that involved every department. Isla briefly mourned staying in on her unofficial birthday weekend instead of the original plan to go see Will. The long drive would have helped her wind down.

"A drink, Isla?" Janelle asked as they packed up for the night.

"Promise me somewhere with food, and I'm in," Isla said. She marveled at how much easier it was becoming to say yes and mean it, and to leave when she'd run out of spoons and needed to go home.

They carpooled downtown and parked near the iconic St. Louis Gateway Arch as it reflected fire back into the sunset on its graceful curve.

"I don't get tired of seeing that," Isla said out loud, pleased with the week, the company, how settled she felt.

"Have you been up it yet?" Olivia, the agency's admin assistant, asked. The entire group gasped when Isla shook her head.

"Oh, we have to go now," Eleanor insisted. "They're open late. We're doing it, right now."

"Are you serious?" Isla stared up and up and up at the Arch. "They let you in there?"

"All the way to the top!" Bobby, one of the copywriters, grinned at them all. "Let's do it. Then we get food."

Caught up in the moment and genuinely excited to go up the Arch, Isla followed them across one of the city parks and watched the Arch loom taller and taller. It was much wider around up close than she would have thought.

The inside of the Arch was cramped, narrow, and hot, with exposed metal inner workings all around them. Isla didn't love that part, but she did love going on a mini adventure with her coworkers, doing a thing she had never done before, and feeling like a part of their group. The lonely, outcast girl inside her basked in the moment.

They rode to the top in a little tram car, and Isla forgot about being sweaty when they looked out the long, narrow windows at the top of the Arch. All of St. Louis sprawled out before them, aglow with lights and the setting sun beyond. Isla leaned on the padded incline that led up to the windows for a better look, sharing the space of her window with Janelle.

"This never gets old," Janelle said quietly.

Isla smiled. She used to feel that way about driving along Lake Shore in Chicago, any time of the day or night. The skyscrapers and architecture, the tree-lined streets, the lake . . . it never got old. Not that she would be driving along there anytime soon. This view would have to do for now.

Afterward, Olivia took them to a tapas place nearby, and they grabbed a round table out on the patio, under reams of string lights. Isla lost track of time while they chatted about weekend plans, work, and department gossip. She didn't feel uncomfortable participating in the conversation; she didn't feel excluded.

By the time Isla got back home, it was almost midnight. She thought her chest would burst in its effort to contain its shades of happiness.

The house was dark when she got in, and Isla flooded it with lights as she kicked off her flats and changed out of her work clothes, leaving her socks and pants and dress shirt strewn about in a trail as she went, promising herself she'd pick it up later. Full of good food and wine, Isla curled up on the couch and selected Ewan's thread, her wine-muddled brain amazed all over again by the signal that connected her to however many years in the future, where Ewan sat in a house somewhere, talking back at her through time.

And promptly fell asleep, a half-written text sitting in draft.

When Isla awoke, the early-morning sunlight—along with every light she'd left on—provided no escape for her pounding skull. She whimpered all the way to the kitchen for a glass of water to wash the headache medicine down with, then retreated to her bedroom with the phone, where thicker drapes lived to help her banish the sun from her presence. She'd missed one text from him.

Please contact me as soon you get this, sweetheart, I have a few things to tell you.

She called him.

"You sound tortured," Ewan said, amusement deepening his voice.

"Red wine gives me headaches," she confessed. "What did you need to tell me?"

Ewan sighed, muttered something to himself that sounded like "out with it," and then said, "I put this off for as long as I could, but now you need to know. The accident is how we meet."

Isla sat down hard on her bed. "Oh," she whispered.

"I'm a physical therapist, Isla. Your doctor sent you to me for physical therapy because of your TBI—your traumatic brain injury. I helped you rehabilitate."

There was no reason on God's green earth for that to make her want to cry, but her emotional response system was well and truly defective.

"I worked with you for six weeks, three times a week." He laughed a little. "You took me by surprise. I loved our sessions. You always dressed so cute, always greeted me with a smile even though I knew you were in pain and you were frustrated. When your therapy was over, I didn't like the thought of never seeing you again."

"What did you do?" she asked, her mind racing to catch up with this other life she'd never live being laid out for her.

"Asked if you'd be willing to take me on a Mark Twain tour of Hannibal. I lied and said I'd never been. I have most certainly been there; I attended Missouri public schools, I'm pretty sure a field trip to Hannibal was a requirement." They both laughed. "We spent the whole day together and finished with dinner on the Mark Twain Riverboat."

Isla couldn't tame her grin despite the kaleidoscope of emotions rioting through her. He sounded nostalgic and happy. "You probably had me hook, line, and sinker."

"Ehh, you were pretty suspicious of me in the beginning. You kept believing I just wanted to be friends, so we hung out for a while, every weekend, until I asked to kiss you. You looked so horrified that I thought you felt sorry for *me* and agreed to hang out just to be nice."

Oh god, he wasn't wrong. She would be dumbfounded at such a beautiful man's request to willingly kiss her. "That is the opposite of the truth," she told him. "You're a stone-cold fox, Ewan."

"Thanks, Buttercup."

She let out a deep breath. "So no accident, no physical therapy." Isla couldn't believe she was putting this into words. Like the death knell of a relationship that, in her timeline, had never happened. "No Isla and Ewan meet-up."

"No," he said softly. "That doesn't mean we won't meet another way. But it does mean that history is very clearly being rewritten in . . . about two hours. If the accident doesn't happen—and it *shouldn't*," he said, with a warning tone, "then, as far as the timeline is concerned, we never meet."

Somehow this possibility had never occurred to Isla. Before their conversation, she'd never once linked their meeting with the accident, and why should she? He'd said they met in St. Louis. She worked there, for crying out loud. She'd pictured running into him on the street, at a museum, at a show. Some beautifully mundane location. Not in the aftermath of a tragedy.

Because now it fell to Isla to find present Ewan. The mere thought of it took shears to her confidence and cut it to ribbons. "How will I ever convince you to give me the time of day?"

"Don't underestimate my interest in you," Ewan replied, his voice soothing. "Just be persistent. *Talk* to me, Isla." His voice turned hard and firm. "And for god's sake, *do not* turn around and get in your car. Stay put. I don't care if the path of least resistance is just to let it happen and you think you'll be fine. I can't risk it. I can't keep losing you."

Isla squeezed her eyes shut. Took one breath, then another, and another. "Tell me everything I need to know to find you."

She learned more about Ewan Park in two hours than she had in two months. Where he'd grown up (Creve Coeur), his birthday (March 15), and his Korean name, which he used as his middle name (Sung-ho). The more she learned, the more she panicked. How on earth could she approach him? How could she achieve any sort of connection to make up for the lack of what they would have had? She kept grilling him for additional information, like a bona fide creeper. Where did he like to grocery shop? What kind of car did he drive? Had he gone to any concerts or bars or other places right around the time they would have met?

She wrote everything down to reference later, since relying on memory alone would be a mistake. This was too important to mess up. Every detail would help her feel more prepared to step into an unknown future, a departure from the one previously written for her and Ewan.

"It'll be different," he said. "Your version of me won't know you like I know you now, but I'll be here to help you. Don't be scared, sweetheart. Don't make yourself small anymore. Take up space, Buttercup. It's yours to take."

"I'm afraid I'll mess this up and it won't work," Isla admitted. "You'll move on to someone else or something will happen and I'll never get to meet you."

"Don't think like that. Have a little more faith in yourself!" The warmth and affection in Ewan's voice soothed her as if he'd reached out and stroked her hair. "We'll just take a different path to get to each other. There's a reason I've been able to reach you. Something beyond our understanding got involved, and I have to believe we're meant to meet no matter what. I'll help you make sure of it. I know you can do this."

"I'm glad one of us is confident," Isla said.

"Soon it will be both of us." Ewan paused, and when he spoke again, she heard the smile in his voice. "It's almost your birthday. Happy—"

The line went dead.

CHAPTER TEN

"Ewan?" Isla pulled the phone away from her ear. The call was gone. Did it drop?

Her pulse fluttered madly in her throat as she went to her recent calls to redial him.

Ewan's number wasn't on there.

Isla nearly dropped the phone with her fumbling, shaking fingers. She went into her text messages.

The thread had disappeared.

"No," she whispered. She scrolled, read every thread, every name. Went into her contacts: no Ewan. Her pictures: the wedding photo was gone. The saved screenshots . . . all of it. Nothing involving him saved.

He was gone. As if he had never been there.

A hole in the earth opened and Isla fell down and down and down, waiting for an impact that wouldn't come. Her body kept free-falling. She rocked, pressed the heels of her palms into her eyes.

The accident never happened. She didn't go, and it didn't happen, and so the timeline changed. She would never go to physical therapy for an injury she didn't have, so their story was rewritten.

Time had already begun the rewrite.

How could it never occur to you, she thought as the fluttering wings of a panic attack quivered through her chest, down into her stomach, that the house, or the connection, or whatever it was would not continue to let you speak with the man you undid meeting?

Silent tears coursed down her cheeks. She curled up into a ball while she concentrated on slowing her breathing down, to stave off the worst of the panic and the horror and the grief.

"He's not gone," she whispered to herself. "He's real and in St. Louis right now. He just doesn't know you exist."

But that wasn't it; it wasn't the source of her pain. She mourned the Ewan she knew, had built a bond with over the past three months. That Ewan was lost to her forever, as surely as future Isla was lost to that Ewan forever. Even if he didn't remember it now, even if she had never happened to him in the first place. The man she had just spoken to on the phone? She could never reach him again.

Her Ewan was gone.

*　*　*

The rug was unforgiving under her cheek, but the discomfort was the only thing keeping Isla fully present, rather than falling off the edge of the earth and into a place that would make purgatory look accommodating.

Nothing had felt like this since her mother died.

How much can there be? she idly wondered. Her fingers ran over the bumpy ridges of the rug, and the sensation of the coarse material on her skin gave her the same cottonmouth aversion that nails scratching on denim did. How much pain can one body hold in it before bursting like a water balloon? When did the universe say, *We've done quite enough to this one?*

There didn't seem to be a finite amount, physically or emotionally. And to the brain, she knew, the difference between the two was splitting hairs. Emotional pain registered as physical pain because the brain could not categorize it any other way. If something hurt, that pain had to register *somewhere*.

Right now, it radiated through her like debris from a nuclear explosion.

The need to cry consumed her, but she was afraid to let it happen, because it would break her. Just shatter her into a thousand pieces.

She wanted her mother.

Tears welled up into her eyes, and through sheer force of will, Isla held them back. She had never wanted to hear her mom's voice again so badly. She wanted a blanket and a cup of tea handed to her by her mom, and she wanted to feel Caroline's hand on her forehead as she pushed back her bangs and kissed her temple like she had when she got sick as a child. "Rest up, honey," she would say. "Everything you need is right by the bed. Holler for anything else." She always knew exactly what to do when Isla was sick.

Isla didn't want to move. She didn't want to do anything but grieve.

The doorbell rang.

"Really?" Isla said testily. Who the hell would she know who'd come this far out in the country to knock on her door on a Saturday morning? And if they were local, she certainly didn't want to bother with it.

Ignore it.

The doorbell rang again.

Isla stubbornly didn't move.

Knocking. Oh, wonderful, now there was knocking. Sighing dramatically, Isla stood up, took stock of the fact that she was still in pajamas, which were presentable but wrinkly, and stomped out of the bedroom.

She flung open the door, prepared to deliver the coldest resting bitch face of her life.

"That is a *look*," Willow said. "I'm actually impressed. You are terrifying."

"Will?" Isla asked dumbly. Her best friend stood in her doorway, as if she'd teleported from Chicago. But she hadn't—a familiar SUV sat next to her car in the driveway. Willow's parents stood by it, looking around. Emilio Sanchez was hauling a cooler out of the back, and Zara Sanchez stood in the front yard, gesturing to the giant oak trees and their wide canopies, pulling out her phone and taking a photo. The sight of them alone was the equivalent of at least ten hugs.

"Surprise!" Willow grinned.

"What are you doing here?" Isla could not catch up to the situation.

"We figured we'd bring the birthday celebration to you, since you couldn't make it." Willow slung an arm around Isla's shoulder and squeezed. "Lucas sends his love; he has a show tonight. Can't spend your birthday weekend alone, can you?" Her pleased expression faded to concern. "Honey, have you been crying?"

Isla burst into tears.

"Oh, oh, okay." Willow gathered her into a hug.

Horrified with herself, Isla buried her face in her friend's neck, breathing in the comforting smell of Will's shampoo. She felt Willow gesture something to her parents, and then her best friend led them both inside, closing the door behind her with her foot.

She led Isla to the couch, and Isla held on to Willow and cried herself out. The sobs that racked her body were close to snapping the fragile bones inside her chest. It was the day her mother died all over again. It was selecting a casket to hold her mother's body, it was her father removing himself from the arrangements so Isla had to bury her alone, it was years of staying small enough to escape attention before anyone else could notice all the things wrong with her. It was finding the love of her life and losing him.

When she could think again, she realized Willow was rubbing her back and shushing her softly, as if she were a newborn. Isla had never loved her more. "Thank you for coming," Isla said weakly. "And letting me cry on you. I love you."

"I love you." Willow kissed her forehead. "Now go take a shower and brush your teeth, I can smell the wine from last night. I'll bring Mom and Dad in and show them around. Then you can tell me all about it."

The shower was glorious, and Isla stood under the spray until her fingers were prunes. A part of her wished she had the chance to use the entire day to just shut down and mourn the unexpected loss of her Ewan. Play dramatically sad music, weep over her coffee, sleep the day away, and lie around like a broken doll. She wanted to feel sorry for herself and she wanted to do it in solitude.

So no, not real thrilled that her day of solitude was taken away from her. But it was a lovely gesture on Willow's part, and she adored the Sanchezes. If there was an acceptable alternative to wallowing in seclusion, being surrounded by people who obviously loved her was it.

She could hear them all in the kitchen when she snuck out of the bathroom and into her room to change into a long, mustard-yellow summer dress with a small white floral print.

Isla had decided a long time ago that if she was going to feel bad about herself anyway, she might as well dress cute to take some of the sting away.

"I'm sorry I wasn't ready," Isla apologized when she joined them in the kitchen. "Thank you for being patient. It's so good to see you!"

"Oh, Isla, you look splendid," Zara cried, abandoning her fruit salad to collect Isla in a hug. Zara framed her face and kissed her cheek. "What a beautiful little ranch you found."

"Your paintings are out," Emilio remarked as he gave her a hug. "Are you finally selling?"

"Soon," she confirmed. "Part of . . . part of the reason I couldn't come this weekend was because of it. I'm digitizing my portfolio to sell prints too."

Zara clapped her hands excitedly. "Have you found a gallery?"

"Oh no, no, not yet." The idea of networking, attending gallery showings, and engaging with different gallery owners sounded terrifying. Isla wasn't ready for that yet. Willow handed her a glass of water, and she gladly took it. "What did you bring? What's our theme?"

"Carnitas," Emilio announced, giving the word a few extra syllables in his excitement. "We'll put these on now, let them cook all day. When the meat's on, mis hijas, take me to the nearest grocery store and we'll get a few more things. One of you drive; I plan to start drinking by noon."

Despite running on no sleep, despite everything that had happened and hadn't happened, Isla enjoyed their visit. Being around Willow and her family was like wearing her favorite warm sweater in the dead of winter. They ate, drank, reminisced, and the Sanchezes asked Isla to show them around St. Louis the next day. Isla didn't even mind it when she sent pictures to her dad to show him what a nice surprise she was having and he never responded.

When Isla fell asleep with her head on Willow's shoulder, Zara gently shook her awake to say good-bye for the night. "We're heading to the hotel," she said softly. "We'll meet you girls for breakfast, nine thirty?"

Isla nodded sleepily. "Drive safe," she whispered.

Like they were twelve, Zara kissed their foreheads, and she and Emilio walked out to the car, hand in hand. Isla leaned against Willow, who looked like she'd been dozing herself. "You won the parent lottery," Isla said drowsily.

Will smiled. "I really did. Except when they remind me that *sommelier* is just a fancy term for *wino*."

Isla's own laughter took her by surprise. "They're proud of you. They just don't fully understand what you do."

Willow looked over at her, brown eyes sharp and assessing. "What was wrong this morning?"

Isla let her head fall back to stare at the ceiling. She could probably get away with telling Will some of it, just omitting the "never met him" and "he was talking to me from the future" parts. She just had to frame it correctly so Will didn't ask her questions she couldn't answer.

"My anxiety was really bad this week," she admitted. "Finally selling my art had been hitting all my buttons, and it's scaring me even though I'm excited to do it. I hadn't slept much at all last night, and it was so amazing to see you guys that I just kind of . . ."

"Cracked."

"Yeah. And I . . ." Hoo boy, here went nothing. "I met this guy. Ow!"

Willow shook her shoulder where she'd slapped her with delight and surprise. "Shut the front door!"

"He lives in St. Louis. I met him through work." Isla rubbed her shoulder and glared at Willow, who gleefully ignored her expression.

"Tell me everything," Willow insisted.

"There's not much to tell." There was way too much, and Isla had to be careful about gushing. No impossible questions. "His name is Ewan. He's sweet and funny and kind to me. But he doesn't see me in that way yet." Or at all, since current Ewan had never laid eyes on her. "I really like him, and I want to try to get to know him better, but I'm *so bad* at this, Will. I don't know how to approach guys. I'm so awkward it hurts."

"You are only awkward sometimes," Willow amended, "but it's a really endearing thing about you. The worst he can do say is no, babe."

Oh, and that would be the worst possible scenario, Isla thought. "I don't even know what to say to him. How to even approach him."

"Casual. Don't put the cart before the horse. You get all up in your head about any prospects because your brain moves too fast. Within, like, sixty seconds you've plotted out the whole trajectory for a relationship, all the way to its grisly end. Don't look so shocked, I've seen you do it. Relationships don't have to start out so *heavy*."

"I don't know how to stop doing that," Isla said.

Willow looked her dead in the eye. "Quit obsessing over the future. Let yourself be present with this guy. Ask him out for coffee. Tell him you're new and you don't know St. Louis very well. Does he have any recommendations? Things to do? When he tells you, ask him if he'd like to go with you, like a guide. Keep it friendly. It's definitely a speed you'll be comfortable with."

"But then what do—"

"Nope." Willow put her hand over Isla's mouth. "We are not worrying about it. If you really dig this guy, just start by spending time with him. Feel it out. And feel free to throw all of your panic in my direction so I can tell you that you're overreacting."

Isla sighed. It did feel better to confess some of this out loud. At least someone else finally knew a part of it. "Thanks," she said. "I wish I was better at this."

"It takes practice, and you haven't had a lot of it."

"Willow, I'm not like you," Isla said quietly. "I don't have the kind of face that draws much attention."

"You have a beautiful face," Willow countered. "And I love it like I love you. You have the kindest, sweetest soul and you would give people the shirt off your back. Anyone who can't recognize that is a fool and not worth your time. And I wish you didn't think you have to go around apologizing to people for not looking the way you think you should . . . for *them*. I wouldn't change a thing about you."

"That's *not* what I'm doing."

"Maybe not consciously, but girl, your body language says it all." Willow demonstrated by laying her hands on Isla's tense, drawn-in shoulders, then tracing her finger down the hunch in Isla's back from her defensive posture. "You close in like a clam when you're nervous. People react to that. I have to watch my posture and my expression in my line of work, because relaxed, confident body language and an approachable expression earn me more tips. It also makes everyone else relax. If you're not relaxed, then they're not. See what I'm saying?"

Isla consciously relaxed her shoulders, rolled them, and then sat back instead of leaning forward. It occurred to her that she did this in her therapist's office too, or at work before giving a presentation. Hunched into herself, shoulders up and tense. No wonder her shoulders ached all the time.

"I'll work on it," Isla finally agreed.

"Good. And send me pictures of this guy. I want progress reports on these dates."

CHAPTER ELEVEN

Isla had gone to RISE for coffee every week she'd come into town for the past two months and missed a chance encounter with one (1) Ewan Park by twenty minutes. All this time, they had loved and frequented the same café and she'd never known it.

Now she had to find him.

Not to approach him. Not yet.

This was a reconnaissance effort. A confirmation that he did indeed exist in real life.

Ewan had said he came in on random weekdays, but always between seven and eight AM. He stayed for about thirty minutes, and he usually read or met one of his friends for coffee. She hadn't come by every day and only once last week, but frankly, she had needed to wallow in self-pity and feel low for a few days before she put on her big-girl pants.

Plus, she needed a game plan. She couldn't approach him out of the blue. That wasn't how Isla rolled, and if she tried, she would choke and make a fool out of herself. She would sabotage her own efforts if she approached this with someone else's tactics; someone more confident, more savvy, more comfortable carrying on a conversation with someone who was a romantic interest.

The other version of her had been able to handle someone like Ewan because their visits had been structured. There was a nonromantic, practical reason to be in his company, so it allowed her to relax and be herself. No pressure to perform or act any differently, because he was just her physical therapist. By the time Ewan asked her out, other Isla would have spent weeks getting to know him.

She had to recreate that dynamic.

But before she could do that . . . she had to at least see him. Not engage. Just . . . creep in the corner like a stalker and discreetly stare at him while he broke her heart, none the wiser.

If he would just show up.

Isla sighed, took a sip of her latte, and checked the time. 7:40. Maybe today would be the day he'd just run in and grab something to go, which was why she'd parked herself in the corner between the front windows and next to the barista's counter. Every new person through the door drew her eyes up.

None of them were Ewan.

Her eyes wandered away from the door, checking out the decor once again. Halfway through her sweep, she finally noticed a staircase. Oh. The café had a second floor. Two months coming here and she'd never noticed it had a second floor. That's some real effective reconnaissance-ing you've been doing, you idiot, she chided herself.

She shut her laptop and took herself and her drink upstairs. The second floor was just as charming as the first; books hung from the walls and ceiling, pages open midflip, elegant paper butterflies in flight. Airy rooms, wooden floors, cozy reading chairs. Isla wandered, taking her time as if trying to find the perfect spot while distracted by her phone, casually scanning everyone in the room.

Her eyes passed right over him at first. Then he registered, in the blue armchair tucked away in a corner, underneath a bookshelf and next to a window. His head of dark hair was bent over a book, and a cup of something sat on a table next to his elbow. Black-and-white gingham-patterned slacks with a black blazer thrown over the back of the chair, a white Henley pushed up to his elbows. He wore a watch with a black leather strap and a braided leather bracelet nestled next to it. She watched him scoop his hand through his hair, then turn his head to look out the window, which gave her a perfect view of his profile.

This was the man from the wedding photo. Same strong jawline, same smooth, light golden skin, same beautiful face with its graceful masculinity. She had expected Ewan to be on the leaner side, based on the photo, but had not expected the muscle definition that the Henley helpfully exposed. He was *toned*.

Oh god, she was staring. And she was still standing in the center of the room. Before he could spot her leering at him like a mouth breather, Isla turned and sat diagonally from him on someone's old dining room chair at a nearby table. The chair partially faced him, so she could keep an eye on him and work from her laptop at the same time. Her heart knocked as loud as carpenters on the roof of her rib cage.

Ewan Park was real, and he was ten feet from her. The past version of the man she had spoken to every day for over three months. Who hiked and wanted to go to Alaska and was a secret goth and a self-described Luddite. She knew that to be true, because when she'd looked him up online, she'd found a very small social media presence. The one account he had was set to private, and there was one lone photo on his company's website. Which had been designed in-house a good ten years ago and never touched again, judging by the use of Flash graphics, the lack of color contrast that made it hard to read some of the text, and Times New Roman, as if the entire thing were some kid's high school English paper. It wasn't the worst she had seen, but it was not doing them any favors.

Isla couldn't pay him too much attention without feeling her cheeks grow hot to the touch, so she paid more attention to her work email than it needed, finishing her latte in the process, and remained hyperaware of his every movement, which included:

- Turning a page
- Crossing a different leg
- Taking a drink

Somehow, the most boring, mundane actions became the most captivating one-man show she had ever seen. He never once checked his phone. He had great posture. And he was a slow reader. She couldn't tell what he was reading from her vantage point, and she was dying to know.

When he checked his watch and got up to leave, Isla's knee-jerk reaction was to follow, but she quelled it. No, eager beaver, you cannot follow him to his place of employment like an *actual creeper*. He would be well within his rights to call you a stalker, and that is not how we start relationships, Isla Abbott.

She had seen with her own two eyes that Ewan was a real boy, and now she could commence with the only plan she had in her back pocket to talk to him face-to-face.

That god-awful website.

* * *

Isla almost chickened out and emailed first, but she decided it would be too easy for that to go unnoticed for weeks. His office's admin staff might just bookmark it to get to later, and then she'd be forgotten about.

She had to go in person. And talk to actual people. She'd have to *pitch* herself to them, and she'd probably only have a minute to sell herself as the freelancer they needed to update and redesign their website so it could join the rest of the world in the current decade.

It was going to be a nightmare.

Isla stood in front of the unassuming building that housed West End Physical Therapy, and because it was July 7, it was about a hundred degrees outside. She felt like wilted lettuce left out on the counter for two days.

Armed with her expertise in graphic and web design (and a dose of Xanax), Isla stepped into the chilly air conditioning of the office. The waiting room was pleasantly, if plainly, decorated with linen-shaded lamps, potted plants, and a low table sporting coffee and tea. A few baby steps above a hospital waiting room. She ignored the empty waiting area and headed for the front desk. The admin assistant was an older, plump woman with paper-white skin and gray-peppered curly red hair, glasses on a chain, and an embroidered ribbon in the shape of a watermelon on the front of her shirt. Her wrists had a thousand gold bracelets on them.

Isla liked her instantly.

"Hello, darlin'," the ribbon lady greeted her. "Got an appointment?"

"I don't, actually." Okay. Okay. Here we go. Isla took a cleansing breath and urged her pulse to stop tripping all over itself in a race it should never have entered. "My name is Isla, and I work as a graphic designer for a local ad agency. I thought about contacting West End through email, but that lacked the face-to-face communication I like to start out with, so I thought I'd drop in."

Ribbon Lady watched her steadily, nodding along, and Isla almost fragmented under the probing eye contact, as if Ribbon Lady could see every crack in her ceramic. "I'm . . . I'm looking to build up my freelance career as a graphic and web designer, and I've been specializing in assisting small businesses in refreshing and redesigning their websites. It's given me a lot of practical experience outside of the work I do for my company, and it's helped them bring in more business. I started perusing local business websites that I thought I could extend my services to and, well . . . here I am."

She handed her business card to Ribbon Lady and prayed the woman didn't notice how her hand trembled. That entire speech had shaken her like a bag of Goldfish in the hands of a toddler. She glanced down at the name plaque off to one corner of the desk. "Barbara, is there an owner present today that I could speak to?"

"Barb, honey," the woman said absently as she looked the business card over, then looked Isla over. "Isla, is it? I like what you're selling. Our website looks as old as I am, and I keep telling Jeff we need an overhaul. But I'll tell you right off the bat, we're not rolling in the kind of money it'd take to bring in a professional."

"I'm relatively new on the freelance end," Isla countered, "so I could negotiate a much lower rate to get started—lower than an agency might charge, with an agency's skill level."

Barb hummed and then went silent, tapping the business card against the desk. Isla fidgeted. "Let me talk to Jeff," she said. "He's the owner. He's not in today. Got anything I can give him?"

"Yes." Isla handed over a written statement of everything she had just told Barbara, or Barb, honey, as well as a short list of services she felt the website needed and reasons a professional web designer was the right route for them to take. "The website on my card also links to my online portfolio. I want to expand my clientele base, and I'd love to do it with local businesses. My company's office is right downtown, so I would be easily reachable."

Barbara took the papers and gave her a warm smile. "I think you may be the ticket that'll get me off website duty indefinitely. I hate updating that damn thing. Got young kids in this office that can't even pull it off."

Isla laughed politely, her heart blipping at the vague reference to Ewan, and then asked where the restroom was. Barbara pointed her down an adjacent hall. As Isla walked down, her body wanted to curl protectively over the contents of her queasy stomach, as if it could hold everything in by assuming just the right position. Her hands shook as she opened the door, locked herself in, and threw up in the toilet.

After purging it all out, Isla slumped on the cold tile and trembled in the aftermath of holding herself together so tightly her springs had broken. She'd done it—she'd actually gotten through that spiel with a complete stranger. She felt a little gross now, but much better.

Isla washed her hands, sipped some water from the sink, and didn't leave the bathroom until her face no longer looked like death. When she exited, she nearly took someone out with the swinging door.

"Oh!" she gasped. "I'm so sorry."

"It's all right."

She knew that voice.

That familiar, deep, masculine voice mere feet from her as she shut the door partially so he could move, then reopened it to slip out. She inhaled sharply when she saw the white Henley and gingham dress pants. She hadn't expected to run into Ewan-mother-loving-Park, so sure, let's add "flustered and flushed" to "pale and sweaty" and "just threw up from nerves."

She looked up and got a glimpse of gorgeous dark-brown eyes gazing right at her before she shied away like a horse, apologized again, and took off. God, she could not look at him right now. Not when he used the voice she knew and had lost. He was so unnervingly good-looking (and good-smelling; Jesus, this man smelled like a crisp morning in the mountains) that it made her . . . well . . . second-guess everything.

What on earth had someone so sharply dressed and so handsome been doing with her? How could she ever hope to get his attention if she wasn't able to see him like the other version of her could see him, without that common thread linking them? Even if she started freelancing as their website designer, what were the odds she would actually see him and talk to him? All of that work could be done remotely. They'd only need to meet with her for check-ins, if that.

She was a bundle of nerves all day, checking her phone and her personal email to see if Jeff from West End Physical Therapy contacted her, then reminding herself that he was out today and there was no way he would respond to her that quickly, get a grip, Isla.

Now she just had to wait and see whether they were interested.

*   *   *

Jeff from West End Physical Therapy never got back to her.

After the two-week mark and one follow-up with an unresponsive Jeff, Isla didn't know what to do. She couldn't force the man to be interested in hiring an unknown free-lancer to refresh his company's website, and it was a pipe dream to even think it'd be that easy.

Isla furiously tried to distract herself by prepping her personal website and business page on an e-commerce site to sell prints of her work. She picked her top-ten favorites and concentrated on finishing their digital versions in order to put them up. There was no point in overwhelming herself with trying to put up the entire catalog, so she decided to chunk it in manageable deliverables—just like a project at work. She found that if she mentally framed this as a work project, it felt less personal and, therefore, less overwhelming and scary. As far as her brain was concerned, she was showcasing someone *else's* art and not her own.

By the time the first print options appeared on her website—*her website*—it was one in the morning and the center of her upper back burned like fire. Isla stood from her computer, stooped like an eighty-year-old, and took herself to the living room to do some yoga and whine pitifully during every painful stretch.

When she finished, her knee-jerk reaction was to check her phone for a text from Ewan. That pull had tugged at her at least three times a day for the past two weeks, and although the accompanying burst of sorrow had lessened as the days passed, it left behind a concave hollow in the center of chest. As if she'd dug and dug with her bare hands to uncover something precious she had hidden away for safe-keeping, only to find the hole empty. And every time, she was compelled to check the text thread, just to be sure, and Ewan's name was still missing from the list. All their conversations still spirited away.

It no longer seemed like a guarantee that she'd have those conversations back someday. Ewan's boss clearly wasn't interested, so Isla wouldn't be able to recreate a safe, neutral environment to interact with a Ewan who didn't know her.

Now what?

*   *   *

She had no idea. Ewan had told her to be brave—don't be afraid to approach him, it will work out—but that advice relied heavily on her ability to initiate. She'd gone back to the coffee shop four more times now, and had so far done nothing but steal furtive glances at the unsuspecting physical therapist while he sipped his coffee and progressed in his book. He had no clue she existed, and Isla didn't know how to fix that.

Except to talk to him, like a regular ass human being did when they were interested in another person.

Trust that you're supposed to meet, Isla reminded herself, even as her heart banged a war drum at the very thought of approaching a handsome man in a public space. The more time you waste, the harder this will be. She stared at him from across the café, the heat of excitement and terror and dread flushing her body until sweat prickled her forehead and the back of her neck. If she waited too long, she'd work herself into a panic attack and have to leave. Just go up to him. There is nothing wrong with approaching someone.

Ewan got up and left before she worked up the courage to leave her seat.

Coward.

The next time she went to the coffee shop, he wasn't even there—a kid had taken the blue chair and settled in with a smoothie and a tablet. The crushing relief of being spared the crisis warring inside her (how to approach? what to say? *what to say??*) was so huge it made Isla light-headed. She let out a slow, trembling breath and sank down in an available corner seat of a long worktable to while away the time with a book on her phone.

"Excuse me."

Isla looked up into a pair of direct dark-brown eyes, black strands of hair falling boyishly over them. Ewan Park looked down at her with an apologetic air about his gorgeous person.

Oh God, no. I'm not ready.

"Do you mind if I sit here?" He gestured toward the lone empty chair next to hers. "My usual seat's been taken."

She cleared her throat and desperately tried to think quickly through the situation her brain was stuck on like slogging through molasses. Ewan Park was standing in front of her, talking to her. Now *talk back*. She glanced past him at the blue chair once more. "You've been usurped by a tween, I see."

She realized it was a stupid thing to say as soon as the last syllable passed her lips, because his brows shot up in surprise as he looked back at the chair he always sat in. Nice one, Isla—now he knows you've been staring at him long enough to mark his favorite chair.

Ewan laughed a little. "I plan to duel for my rightful seat on the blue throne later."

Thank you for not asking why I knew that. And thank you for not remembering that I was the sweaty girl you ran into at your work's bathroom. "Well then, yes, you can sit here with the common folk instead."

"Thanks."

Isla became aware of her own body in a deeply uncomfortable way now that it was in close proximity with Ewan's. She could not relax with him there, and so she held herself as carefully as she did when she was stuck in crowded places and overstimulated, as if she could disappear if she were small and still enough. She didn't want to disappear in this case, but she also didn't know how to relieve the gnarled knot of feelings he stirred up in her. She was mildly horrified to feel tears burn at the back of her throat.

Do not cry in front of him, she commanded herself as he sat next to her, completely oblivious and engrossed in his book. This was Ewan. Who had loved her and mourned her and teased her and flirted with her in a not-so-distant future past. Who wanted nothing more than to help her save herself.

Sitting next to him in a coffee shop seared her like being too close to the sun, and they'd barely exchanged more than four sentences. And she still hadn't said *anything*.

"Hey." Isla startled herself with the sound of her own voice. Ewan looked up from his book, and her heart lurched. "I'm new to the area, and I . . . don't know it very well. Do you have any recommendations for good lunch spots downtown? My work isn't too far from here." What paltry, ridiculous small talk after everything they'd shared. Every word undervalued what he meant to her.

"I do, actually." Ewan rattled off the name of a few restaurants that Isla absolutely did not write down, because she couldn't take her eyes off his face. He wore early mornings well, his eyes as bright and alert as a sunrise. ". . . has great crepes. You should try their matcha mint latte, too."

"I will," she said faintly.

Panic unfurled its petals as Ewan gathered his things to leave. Oh nonono. What if this was *it*? "Would . . . would you be interested in—" She stood at the same time he did and took a step forward.

Right as he lifted his coffee cup.

She accidentally jarred his elbow and sent the cup flying. Isla watched in horror as the lid popped off and coffee splattered all. over. his. white. shirt. "—going with me?" she finished in a breathless, high-pitched rush. "I'm so sorry!"

The flash of pure irritation in his eyes, coupled with his sharp inhale, internally drove Isla into hiding like a turtle shoving its head into its shell. He'd thrown up his arms and was staring down at the screaming stain, as if he could not believe this random woman had just thrown his own goddamn coffee at him. She frantically searched the table for napkins and found two poor, thin excuses that he immediately took to blot his shirt.

"I'll get a . . ."

"It's fine," he said on a sigh.

"No, no, I'll get a rag," Isla insisted. She had to make this right. She had to. Her face felt like it was the color of a fire engine. It was a thousand degrees in this café. She might very well pass out in front of him.

"Really, you've—it's fine."

You've done enough.

Isla's breath shuddered out of her. "I'm so sorry. Can I . . . can I make it up to you somehow? Lunch?"

She didn't think he even heard her. He sighed again to himself as he dabbed fruitlessly at the dark stains. "I'll have to change in the office," he murmured, eyebrows drawn down, his fingers curling tightly around the crumpled, useless napkins.

"Please let me buy you a new coffee at least. I feel so bad." Isla could feel something precious slip away as he gave her nothing but a distracted glance that went right through her.

"It's okay, it was an accident. You don't have anything to make up for."

She could hear him trying to stay patient and keep his irritation below the surface. His word choices made her realize he had heard her earlier—he just didn't want to acknowledge that she'd asked. Maybe, to him, it was the politest way to say no.

He walked away, a stranger.

CHAPTER TWELVE

"You know what I'm going to ask next."

Isla grimaced. She regretted telling Willow about Ewan, because Will had found a way to ask without directly asking about him over the past few weeks, and Isla had never had a satisfactory answer for her. It was sweet, but every nudge toppled Isla over an edge and into a mess of mortification, grief, and shame.

She had failed, and there was no fixing it. This Ewan knew her only as the creepy woman who'd spilled coffee on him, and there was no coming back from that.

Isla distracted herself with the sights, sounds, and smells of the pet store she'd moseyed into after finishing a store run next door. She smiled at every dog she came across in the aisles and studiously avoided eye contact with their owners.

A bird squawked from a few feet away, and Will asked, "Are you . . . in a pet store?"

"Maybe."

"Finally getting a dog? That was like one of the major moving perks you gushed about."

"I'm thinking about it."

"Then you don't need the dog toy you're probably carrying around."

Isla stared down at the soft, squeaky, porcupine-shaped toy in her hand. "That's really creepy, Will."

"I heard you squeaking it a moment ago. So have you talked to him?"

Isla sighed. "I tried. It didn't go very well. I, uh . . . spilled coffee all over him."

Willow snorted.

"It's not funny!" Isla cried.

"Babe, it's a little funny."

"I wanted to die. He was so mad. I pretty much blew it."

"I think you're blowing it out of proportion."

"I asked him if I could make it up to him, and he wasn't having it."

"Because you just spilled coffee all over him." Willow laughed at Isla's aggravated sigh. "Catch him again when there's some distance between the coffee spillage and the next time he sees you; when he can laugh about it and really notice *you* and not the scalding coffee. It's not the end of the world, Isla."

She sighed, letting her eyes settle on a colorful parakeet cleaning its wings. "It feels like it. He's probably already completely dismissed me."

"You won't know that unless you try again."

I *am* trying, she wanted to say. I'm doing so much shit out of my comfort zone, Will, you have no idea. I threw up in a *public bathroom*.

"And then if he's really not interested, then it's not meant to be."

Was it even possible for their relationship to never be . . . meant to be? Could the universe really undo their bond because they didn't meet the same way as the first time? Could this Ewan just hate her forever and that was that? The thought was so distressing that Isla slipped into the adoption center for cats just to pet them for comfort.

When Will started gushing over her website and all the paintings she was finally letting people see and buy, Isla felt a little hope and pride worm their way past her brain's need to point out that these milestones weren't all that impressive compared to what other people had accomplished, despite how miserable she felt about Ewan. But those things were impressive for *her*.

She was allowed to be proud of herself. And when Willow talked about how this was the start of her art career, she allowed herself to believe in that version of Isla too. Because it was as real as the anxiety-ridden version. She *was* an artist; she just had to make some special accommodations for her anxiety disorder so she could get on with her life and be one anyway.

"I've got to go," Willow said, after a long, and very satisfying, chat. "I'm meeting Anne and David at Lincoln Park Zoo's after-hours shindig."

Isla sighed with nostalgia and envy. "Have a good time."

"*You* have a good time. Promise me you'll do something this weekend. And put down that dog toy. You don't own a dog yet."

She guiltily shoved the plushie onto the nearest rack.

*   *   *

Hello Ms. Abbott,

I had an interesting conversation with Barbara, our receptionist, about your visit last month. I am intrigued by your offer, and impressed with the credentials and samples I found online. We are, in fact, overdue for an overhaul of the website, although it's not a particularly pressing need at the moment. Would you have time to meet this week?

Best,

Jeff Hammond
President and Director of West End Physical Therapy

Shit.

"That doesn't sound like good news."

Isla looked up at Eleanor, who stood by the entrance to an art exhibit. She shouldn't have checked her email. It had been such a nice, relaxing Friday up until a minute ago. Their office was right by the Contemporary Art Museum, and the museum was free and open late on Fridays, so a bunch of them had headed over after work to spend the evening wandering the museum.

Both alone and with her coworkers, Isla had been slowly tiptoeing around St. Louis to get to know it better, paying particular attention to Grand Center and all it had to offer. Venturing out on her own was still uncomfortable, but in a way that felt like pulling on an itchy wool sweater versus wrapping herself in a blanket of needles. She'd gone to a concert by herself the weekend before, and cried with joy at hearing one of her favorite songs live. The progress, though it came in fits and starts, was encouraging.

"It's nothing," Isla said, slipping the phone back into her pocket. That was a complete lie, but it was too complicated to discuss. She should have been over the moon to get this close to scoring the freelance gig, but after she'd completely destroyed Ewan's first impression of her . . . now she wasn't sure. If she got it, she'd do the work, of course—extra money and experience was always welcome—but could she work with Ewan? Did she have it in her to try this again?

She honestly didn't know. It was cowardly to admit, but she didn't want to go where she wasn't welcome, and she clearly wasn't his favorite person. There was no guarantee she'd get it right if she tried again. Her Ewan had enjoyed the luxury of thinking out his responses and editing them before sending those messages. Isla sucked at editing the social awkwardness out of her speech: see coffee shop debacle. All her spoken words were first drafts, hastily thrown together at the last minute to be judged by the world. She was still an artless, naïve college student in her speech; on paper and online, she could deliver dissertations.

This is exactly the line of thinking that'll help you be less weird in front of Ewan if you see him again, she thought sarcastically. Remember what he said? Would you be this harsh with a friend? No. You would be kinder.

Be. Kinder.

"Let's check out this exhibit," she said to Eleanor. "I've heard his work is really amazing." She would email Jeff back later.

And try one more time.

*　*　*

Normally, Isla loved silences. She could think in silences, organize her thoughts, lay them out in a coherent fashion. When there was too much noise, too much stimulation, her thoughts scattered to the four corners of the earth, and she found it hard to participate in conversations where too many people were talking. It became harder to express her opinion because, if no one asked for it, they clearly didn't want it. So she didn't talk. People who could sit in silence with her were people she felt more comfortable with; they gave her the space to talk when she was ready. Willow was like that. Her parents had never really been like that, which made silences at home uncomfortable and threatening. Mom couldn't stand the silence, and Dad's silence usually meant something was wrong.

This silence was terrifying.

Jeff Hammond was a tall, big-boned man going bald, with a ginormous smile and even bigger hands. His hand had swallowed Isla's up when they met and he ushered her into a seat. His office was filled with medical-themed paperweights, files, a charming bronze elephant statue in one corner, and walls covered in human body charts and his degrees. Isla had tried to mentally distance herself from herself in order to get out her spiel again, focusing on the importance of redesigning the website as a marketing tool to help sustain and bring in more business. It was easier to fall into the rhythm of the language she heard and used all the time at work; she was comfortable with it. And since Barb's reaction had been positive, it bolstered her to deliver it one more time.

But now Jeff was quiet as he looked over her materials. He kept scratching his faint beard scruff, his gaze averted from her to inspect the mock-up designs she'd created to show him what a finished product might look like. The possibility of a denial was very real, and it cramped Isla's gut painfully. If he didn't say yes, she didn't have another plan. This was the only comfortable way she could think of to be around Ewan, and if this avenue was closed to her . . .

Please say something, she encouraged silently. *Please don't make me break the silence. I don't want to seem pushy. But I need you to say yes. If you don't, the only Ewan I'll ever know is a Ewan from the future who married another me in another life that I may never get to experience, and that hurts more than I can say.*

"I like this second mock-up."

Isla snapped to attention. "That's a very clean, user-friendly interface."

"I agree. But I'd like to make a few changes to it."

Her palms started to sweat. "Everything in there is negotiable. We can design to your preferences while making sure the user experience is prioritized."

Jeff gathered the materials and aligned them together with an efficient snap of the paper against the desk. He smiled brightly at her. "I'm excited about this. The rate's fair; the timeline, with a few adjustments, works for me. You've got yourself a gig."

The center of Isla's chest lit up like a Christmas tree. "Wonderful! I can put together a contract."

They chatted more about the stipulations of the project: deadlines for deliverables, reviews and feedback, and other aspects of the redesign that would require her to work with a few of the therapists to revise some of the content, like updating the staff page. Every time her mind brushed up against the possibility of working with Ewan, it flinched away.

When they met again, she hoped he didn't remember her.

* * *

Ewan Park sat across from Isla in the outside patio of Café Osage, and she could barely look at him without her face burning. He looked incredible; that black hair parted to the side, styled to fall on either side of his dark-brown eyes, the strong jawline, and softly angled eyebrows that gave him a continuously attentive, inquisitive air, which was both attractive and unnerving. His smiles were quick, inviting flashes of joy. All the while she fervently prayed he wouldn't recognize her, and every time she caught him giving her a longer, thoughtful stare, she held her breath and wished him a faulty memory that couldn't place her. Nope, you've never seen this woman before. This person definitely did not throw coffee at you last month, no sir.

Ewan's coworkers were Erica Schumaker, originally from Des Moines, who had moved to St. Louis when her husband needed to relocate for a new job, and Derrick Thompson, born and raised in St. Louis and expecting a second child soon with his wife. Ewan Park spoke in a voice that was soft and deep, quiet as a cathedral, reverberant through the patio like so many church bells pealing. Hearing him again sent more thin, spiderlike cracks through her brittle ceramic. It mended and broke her heart, and she grieved anew for her lost Ewan. This was harder than she'd thought it would be. She wanted so badly to talk to him like she used to.

Today he'd told her he was born and raised in St. Louis, that his father was a professor and his mother an event planner. And that was the last thing he said directly to her.

Isla passed out the project packets she'd printed for each staff member, then walked all of them through the website redesign and what she would need from them.

"I think it's important for your potential patients to see you at work," she said between bites of a delicious savory crepe. "See the facility, put faces to names, and come in armed with that knowledge on their first visit so they feel that much more comfortable. I'd like most, if not all, of the website's visuals to come directly from your office. I can schedule some time to come in to take photos of the facility, as well as all four of you, Mr. Hammond included, at work helping patients. You can all select your favorites afterward."

"Do we need image release forms of some kind for our patients?" Derrick asked.

Isla nodded. "It might be helpful to ask them ahead of time if they would be okay with having their photograph up on the website, and then you can let me know who's willing. I can schedule my visits around their appointments."

By the time lunch was over, she had a good feeling about working with all of them and a set game plan, but she had zero confidence when it came to Ewan. He was polite. He talked to her, but he talked to everyone, and would sometimes lapse into silence, listening, occasionally meeting her gaze with that searing directness but not contributing to the conversation. As if she were just a temporary blip in his Saturday morning. A spilled coffee, irritating and quickly forgotten.

Because that's exactly what she was.

*   *   *

It was raining, so Isla splurged on RISE's vegetarian hash for a hearty breakfast. She'd gone out in a long-sleeved, Peter Pan–collared shirt and a skirt with tights—a little fall-ish, but it was one of her favorite outfits. She claimed a table upstairs in order to get a solid hour of work on the new project before heading to the agency. She deliberately timed it so she wouldn't see Ewan. She had work to do and no bandwidth to be around him, so she settled in with her hash and a latte. She left her headphones off to hear the patter of the rain and the soft clink of utensils on plates, the coffee grinder whirring downstairs. The airy, crisp sounds of people waking up to begin their day.

"Good morning, Ms. Abbott."

Isla's hand flew to her heart as she looked up and saw Ewan standing by her chair.

"Sorry to scare you," he said. His hair looked damp, as if he hadn't prepared for the rain, which was completely unfair, because the mildly disheveled look was way too appealing. Today's outfit was navy slacks and a gray dress shirt.

"It's all right," she finally said, her heart still racing, still affected by the sound of his voice. "Good morning, Mr. Park." What are you doing here? Why did you deviate from your schedule?

"Just Ewan, please. You know, I kept thinking all through that lunch that I've seen you before."

"You haven't," she said immediately.

He leaned his hip against the table and folded his arms in a casual gesture that tripped up her pulse. "I think I have."

"No," she replied in a full octave above her normal register.

Please don't say it. Please let my embarrassment die a quiet death.

Ewan rapped his knuckles on the table that had witnessed the entire failure of an exchange. The only thing that kept her from bolting for the bathroom to get away from him was the hint of amusement in his eyes. "You spilled coffee on me."

"I did not do it on purpose," she protested, the temperature on the entire floor rising to sweat-inducing proportions.

"I believe you," he replied, a smile trembling on the edges of his lips. "That was my favorite shirt."

"Don't wear white in coffee shops," Isla retorted, instinctively relapsing into the way she talked to future Ewan when he sassed her.

His laughter surprised her. "I didn't come here to make you feel bad. I just wanted to confirm that my eyes weren't playing tricks on me."

Isla frowned, plucking nervously at lint on her skirt. "It was not my finest hour. I still owe you a coffee."

"You're doing my company a big favor; we'll call it even." He tapped a knuckle to the table again. "Enjoy your breakfast, Ms. Abbott."

"Isla," she said faintly as he walked away to his preferred blue chair in the corner. He didn't hear her.

She left before he did, and since his nose was in his book, she didn't bother him. That hadn't been . . . the worst exchange. Will was right; he had a better sense of humor about it with some distance from his shirt being ruined. Some of her mortification exited stage left, and now she could remember The Coffee Incident without writhing in a pool of her own humiliation.

She was learning the hard way, since her Ewan had disappeared from her life with a change in the timeline, that nothing was guaranteed. And she couldn't expect it to be. Isla had no foolproof plan for how to even become friends with Ewan, so she would just do what she was now being paid to do: work on his company's website.

And pray that lightning would strike twice.

CONTACT

CHAPTER THIRTEEN

It was raining again.

Ewan sighed as he stared out into the misty gray rain drizzling down to the pavement. The cloudy sky leeched the color out of everything, like a blue tint in a movie designed to make everything look dreary and vaguely ominous. He preferred the sound and fury of a proper summer thunderstorm over this November-like rain.

He wouldn't be jogging in the park today. He'd done it despite the rain yesterday, but the break from the heat, the cool rain on his skin, and the wide-open, empty paths had lost their pleasure after an abrupt downpour soaked him through.

No thank you.

It was a day to just stay inside, but he had patients to see from nine to two; a short Saturday, to be sure. Then he could come home and watch a movie or take a nap.

His phone pinged, and he walked away from the windows facing Memorial Plaza to pick it up from the breakfast bar in the kitchen.

It's raining, his mother announced. *All day. Don't come tonight while the roads are wet. You know how people get.*

Had it been a normal Sunday dinner, he wouldn't think twice about not coming, but tomorrow was Umma's birthday. No doubt a part of her wanted him to come tonight anyway.

But it *was* raining.

Crazy drivers, he agreed.

A little rain and they forget how to drive, she added.

I'll see you tomorrow, bright and early, he wrote. *It's not every day a young lady turns 25 again.*

Ha. Drive safe.

Ewan pocketed his phone and grabbed his keys and an umbrella. He passed the mother-of-pearl jewelry box he still needed to wrap for her birthday to replace the one that had broken last year when his parents repainted their house. Umma had tried to shrug it off, but both he and Appa knew how devastated she was. He liked looking at it, and it had taken a godforsaken amount of time to arrive from Korea, so he was waiting until the last possible minute to wrap it.

He left early enough to have some time to finish the newest Erik Larson book with coffee at RISE, but he still had to park farther away than normal. It was, after all, a rainy Saturday morning, which called for coffee indoors.

After ordering his espresso, Ewan made it upstairs to find someone else in his favorite blue chair *again*. A petulant part of him wanted to ask them to get up—didn't they know? He *always* sat there. But the person in the chair was also about ten, and assigned seats were not a thing, so he would have to suck it up and sit somewhere else. Sighing again, he glanced around to find an open seat.

Ahh, look who'd come back to the coffee shop today. The nervous freelancer who'd splattered him with coffee sat at one of the small tables, laptop open. He couldn't remember her first name. Had she told them at their team lunch meeting? He guessed it didn't really matter. Shoulder-length brown hair, even bangs brushing up against straight eyebrows. She had the darkest freckles he'd ever seen on someone with such fair skin: concentrated along the bridge of her nose and her cheeks, then fanning out to the rest of her face like a scatterplot graph with outliers along the edges. She wore a green polka-dot tunic tucked into a black skirt and tights with tidy little camel boots. It was an adorable outfit.

He had to say hello, if only just to fluster her again. He wasn't mad about the coffee incident anymore (keyword *anymore*; he'd been hot for a few days over the ruined shirt), but her reaction made a bit of teasing worth it. And coincidentally, there was an open seat next to her. Ewan moved forward, close enough now to see the look of concentration on her face as she typed. He cleared his throat to announce himself, remembering how he had startled her yesterday.

She looked up, and he suppressed a grin at the instant wariness in her eyes.

"My usual seat's been taken. If I sit next to you, do you promise not to throw coffee at me?"

He watched half a dozen emotions cross her face as she attempted to gather a response, like a ticker rolling past pie slices on a spinning wheel. It landed on indignation. "This is a toddy cold brew. I'm not going to waste it on your shirt."

The freelancer had some quips hidden up her sleeve. "Fair enough, Ms. Abbott."

"Isla," she said, after a moment's hesitation. "Please."

He settled into the chair next to hers. "Isla, then. I won't bother you while you work."

She shook her head, her bluntly cut hair sweeping her shoulders with the movement. "You won't be a bother."

Isla Abbott shot a smile in his general direction and then went back to work, so he opened his book and read. Or tried to read. He kept sneaking glances at her. She really did have an unusual face. Wide-set eyes, nose a little too small, lips a little too thin. But there was something refreshing about the unconventional lines of her face, especially when paired with pretty gray eyes and a pleasing smile. He couldn't decide if he found her conventionally attractive, but she had a face he wanted to keep looking at.

Ewan realized almost too late that he'd run out of time before his first appointment, and he shut his book and stood up. "Don't work away your Saturday," he told her, then almost walked away before remembering to ask her about the photographs she needed for the website. "Ms. Abbott—Isla. I did speak to a few of my patients, and I only had two decline the use of their image. Can I contact you later with some times for a photography session?"

"Yes, of course," she said. "Text might be best, in case either of our schedules change at the last minute."

"I can give you my number now."

Isla's expression grew pinched, like a rain cloud passing over a blue sky, before it smoothed out and she agreed. Ewan didn't know what to make of that, so he shrugged it off. He handed her his phone to type in her number, then sent her a text to confirm.

"Thank you," she said. "Enjoy your weekend."

"You too." Ewan left, but his eyes lingered as she hunched over her work. He inwardly winced for her back. That defensive posture was typical for people who did a lot of close computer work. God knew he'd seen enough desk workers come in complaining about upper back and neck problems, tension headaches, and knots the size of baseballs.

His Saturday appointments went smoothly, and Ewan settled back inside his apartment afterward for the duration of the rainy weather, parking on his couch and letting the rain and the low drone of the television lull him into a nap.

When he woke up and checked his phone, he found a missed text from earlier in the day; Isla's reply. *Hi, Ewan, I received your text. Thanks again.*

Jeff had mentioned something about the freelancer that resurfaced; she painted too, apparently. Curious and bored, he looked her up on his phone and found her website. He scrolled through whimsical, dreamy paintings, brushstrokes of color that formed a hazy rendering of real life. He wasn't an artist, but he knew one when he saw one, and he knew she was good. A few weren't as cheerful, invoking instead the bleak and colorless day outside. A frosted field, an icy road, a black forest, a raven on a fence post. He hadn't expected work like this from a graphic designer, but then again, he knew nothing about graphic design. And people certainly fell into careers that might not align with their passions but with their skills. After all, he'd harbored dreams of starting a metal band, even though he had no musical talent whatsoever. And his parents would have killed him.

Then one painting caught his eye. Ewan sat up, eyed the painting more closely, then grabbed his laptop to bring up a larger picture.

That was a *very* particular spot to choose for a landscape. Ewan had to bring up pictures of the actual trail to make sure it didn't just vaguely resemble the view he knew so well from his childhood.

The side-by-side view was identical. He was looking at the summit of the valley below the Ulsanbawi Trail in Korea. That hike, and that view, had made him a hiker. The summer he turned eight was his first trip out to Korea, and the first time he'd ever visited his grandparents instead of the other way around. A week into the trip, they took the train to Gangwon-do Province and stayed at a hotel next to Seoraksan National Park. Harabeoji woke him up just before sunrise, and they drove to the Ulsanbawi trailhead.

The three hour hike up to the top required frequent stops, but resting along the trail gave Ewan ample time to soak in the view: sheer rock faces rising out of the ground that made him think of landscapes from *The NeverEnding Story*. He expected Rock Biter to emerge from the tumble of rocks at any moment. The stairs up to the top were steep and the air grew warmer as the sun rose. When they made it to the top and the valleys spread below them, hazy with mist the sun hadn't yet burned away, Ewan had never seen anything more beautiful in his young life—and he hadn't since. Nothing he'd ever experienced could touch hiking that trail, sitting at the top with his grandfather and sharing a snack, hearing Harabeoji tell him stories about his father's childhood in Daegu. When they finally hiked back down, they stopped for ice cream at one of the shops along the trail. He'd had a mango-flavored Melona ice pop.

Ewan happily lived in that memory for the next few minutes, its reconstruction so vivid it burned his throat like hot delicious tea. It had been weeks since he'd last called Halmeoni and Harabeoji—he needed to fix that.

And he needed to buy that painting. Harabeoji's birthday was in November, and he could mail it to him as a gift. It would be astronomically expensive to ship, but Harabeoji still talked about that hike as much as Ewan liked to relive it, to this day. It would mean the world to him. Ewan would bring up the painting when the freelancer came in to take pictures.

Hi Isla, he typed. *I looked at my schedule, and some of the best times next week that work for my patients and your schedule are Tuesday or Wednesday after 5 p.m. and before 7:30.*

Her response of *Let's call it Tuesday from 6–7 p.m.* came through while he was staring blankly at the pitiful state of his kitchen cabinets. The weather was too shit for another store run. He could make an omelet, but that didn't really sound appealing.

The next text saved his food dilemma.

What are you doing

Tae never punctuated his texts, unless it was excessive exclamation points. *Napping*, he replied back.

Come for tacos

It's raining, Ewan wrote.

Will you melt? Like the witch from The Wizard of Oz?

Yes, I will melt.

Liar, tacos now

Ewan sighed. Tacos did sound good. And they were probably from Seoul Taco, which had delicious spicy pork burritos.

Already ordered

He dialed Tae's number. "Too late," his friend said smugly. "Food is on the way. Come over; it's gross and boring outside."

"Which is why I'm *inside*," Ewan countered.

"Alone, loser. Come over." Tae hung up.

Ewan snorted, then with a resignation he hadn't known set in at the ripe old age of thirty, grabbed his black rain jacket, wallet, and keys and left the apartment. He had grown used to Tae's last-minute invitations and hastily thrown together outings at the whim of his overactive brain. Luckily, Ewan almost always had a good time. Tae was just incapable of planning ahead.

He drove to West End in the pouring rain and scored a spot right in front of the old rehabbed red brick house, which had been a steal thanks to a foreclosure. A wrought iron staircase attached to the left side of the house led to a bedroom that Tae used to rent out as an Airbnb before it became his boyfriend's studio space. Ewan ran through the rain to the covered porch, which was cluttered with a porch swing and a few cushionless chairs. He knocked and waited.

"Got nachos too," Tae announced with a wide grin as he opened the door.

"That's it? Are you allergic to vegetables?"

"We have kimchi. It counts," called a different voice from the kitchen.

Ewan took off his jacket and hung it in the hall closet. "Hey, Jun-su."

"Hi, Obi-Wan." Jun-su waved without turning around, choosing instead to concentrate on divvying up the tacos. The house had originally separated the living room from the kitchen with a wall, but Tae and Jun-su had knocked it down and turned it into an open floor plan, broken only by a low wall with a breakfast nook. Ewan loved the shit out of their house. The wall behind the fireplace was exposed brick, and the rest of the house was a lot of wood browns and slate blues, with interesting little decor touches, courtesy of Jun-su, and a veritable forest of plants in every room, courtesy of Tae. A couch rested against the low wall and faced a TV turned to some random cooking show on Netflix.

Jun-su eventually came around, holding two plates of tacos and burritos. He handed one to Ewan and kept the other.

Tae raised an eyebrow. "Where's mine?"

"In the kitchen," Jun-su shot back, but he laughed when Tae took a swipe at him, dancing back and balancing his plate like a server in a restaurant.

"Can you make it tomorrow?" Ewan asked as he and Jun-su got settled with their food.

"Of course," Tae scoffed as he came back and shoved his way between the two of them to fit on the couch, his knobby knees jutting up to balance his plate. "It's Umeoni's birthday."

"Just stay the night and we'll leave together in the morning," Jun-su said, using his inside voice as usual, which was all the more noticeable juxtaposed to Tae's habitual speaking-to-an-auditorium voice.

"We are watching Food Network," Tae informed Ewan.

"That looks like Netflix."

"Cooking shows on Netflix," Jun-su clarified. He switched to Korean to ask Tae if he'd remembered to move laundry from the washer to the dryer, which devolved into a pseudo argument of no, maybe he forgot, but who works a real job around here, hmm? The horticulturist who has to show up at work every day or the artist who sleeps in until ten? Ewan stayed out of it, both because he would end up siding with Jun-su, since his art career wasn't anything to sneeze at, and because Ewan's spoken Korean wasn't that advanced, even though his parents had enrolled him in Korean language school for a good six years and he'd spoken it at home as a kid. Passable, sure, but he was more comfortable decoding it over speaking it these days.

Tae was bound and determined to trick Jun-su into moving the laundry to the dryer, as if it wouldn't take him all of two minutes to do it himself. His protests made Jun-su laugh and made Ewan want to playfully punch Tae in the face, like he'd wanted to the first day he met him.

Ewan had come home after his first year at the University of Denver to find a tall, gangly Korean guy standing in *his* bedroom, hands in his pockets, looking around. When he spotted Ewan, he bowed and shook his hand, then grinned and said, "I am your replacement."

Tae hadn't stopped teasing Ewan by saying he was the "replacement son" ever since. It was Ewan's own fault, really, for going away to college in Denver instead of graduating from UMSL like he was supposed to. If he had stayed, his dad wouldn't have gotten involved in the international exchange student program at the university. Wouldn't have seen that a foreign exchange student from Seoul was coming in to complete his undergrad for horticulture and biology. Rather than let a student put himself in further debt with on-campus housing, Professor Park had offered to house the foreign exchange student, and thus Min Tae-seok, Tae for short, had come to live with the Parks for eight semesters.

Ewan had tried to be irritated with Tae, because at the time it still felt like his parents were punishing him for needing to strike out on his own for college despite how deeply discounted tuition would have been at UMSL. Tae-seok— such a proper Korean "son," not the rebellious American son they'd gotten. But Ewan couldn't keep up the dislike. Tae became the brother he never had.

Fingers snapped in front of Ewan's face. "Where is your brain?" Tae demanded.

"Head," Ewan corrected absently. "Where is my head."

"Well?"

"Not watching a cooking show. Did someone move the laundry yet?"

"You could do it," Tae said.

"No. Put on a movie."

"I have a better idea," Jun-su said. "There's a show at Red Flag tonight, and the rain has stopped. Want to go?"

Jun-su had found the one thing that would get Ewan out of the house after ten PM. "Who's playing?"

*   *   *

The bass took up residence inside Ewan's chest, recalibrating the beat of his heart until it matched the booming, rhythmic thumps. His eardrums were bleeding from the screeching guitar, begging for a reprieve, and the band knew just when to give it; as soon as it become unbearable, the tempo switched, slowed, turning into a melodic rat-a-tat-tat of the snare and a dreamy sequence of chords.

He lived for this.

Live music pushed everything negative out of his life and left only enough room for the things that got him out of bed every day. Here he could wear the clothes that felt like an extension of him: the long tailcoat frock jacket he loved, the brocade pants. No one mistook him for a tourist in his own city, even though he was pretty damn sure he and his friends were the only Asians who came to shows like these. They didn't give a shit. It was about the music.

Jun-su was always game to dress the part like it was Halloween, which really meant putting on leather pants, a black T-shirt, and boots, but Tae acted like grunge was making a comeback and wore his usual plaid. He was also fanatically into it—not so much the music itself, but the energy that so perfectly matched the energy levels living inside him. He enjoyed anything that allowed him to let his inner Muppet out. Tae head banged with the best of them, grinning like he was having the time of his life. Ewan opted to lean against the bar and nurse his drink as he let the music flow through him.

Ewan needed these shows at Red Flag like his patients needed therapy to heal their muscles and tendons. The band tonight was good; instrumental sludge metal. No lyrics to decipher, just heavy guitar riffs, distortion and postindustrial synth, and one hell of a good drummer.

One of the few women at the show—truthfully, it was a sea of white dudes most of the time—kept glancing Jun-su's way, and he would pointedly not look in her direction lest his eye contact send the wrong message. Ewan didn't blame her. The man was simply beautiful. His hair was currently dyed an ashy blond, which made his already guileless features look angelic. And then Tae slid in, an arm around Jun-su's waist, putting his lips to his ear to talk as Jun-su let out a husky laugh. Tae didn't dare kiss him because none of them knew how LGBTQ-friendly this crowd was, but it was intimate enough that the lady admirer's face fell and she turned her attention back to the music. Neither man noticed. They had such an easy, effortless way with each other and such obvious affection, which Ewan found sweet and enviable.

They made him painfully aware of his single status. But that was a choice; he hadn't actively dated anyone in over six months. No real reason for it other than focusing on his work and enjoying some solitary time. Plus, meeting people organically was annoyingly difficult, because (1) he didn't frequent many bars anymore, and if he did, it was a gay bar to hang out with Tae and Jun-su, and (2) he absolutely hated dating apps. He didn't have a lot of social media accounts and preferred to stay off them, so online dating was intimidating and sounded like more work than it was worth. His social circle was small, and he rarely ventured out of it. He went to metal concerts, sure, but it was a solitary thing. He liked his life the way it was, even though it meant spending a lot of time alone. Dating in college had been far easier, but the women he dated had ambitions that took them out of state, and more often than not, it was a difference in life goals that ended the relationships. Ewan didn't want to be far from his parents or his friends.

Disgruntled with his own thoughts, Ewan went to the bar and ordered another beer.

* * *

He'd had no intention of staying the night afterward, no matter what Jun-su said, but when Ewan woke up, he was definitely not in his apartment. He lifted his aching head and peered blearily around the predawn living room, then sighed and dropped his head again.

And didn't move until footsteps shuffled into the living room.

"Why do I always end up out here and not in the guest bedroom?" Ewan mumbled.

"We offer and you always say no," Jun-su said. Ewan heard the crack of the fridge door opening, then shutting. The rattling of beans. He hissed when the whir of the coffee bean grinder assaulted the air and his skull.

"Warn a guy," Ewan called. Jun-su laughed.

They stopped by Ewan's after they headed out so he could change into a fresh pair of clothes and retrieve Umma's birthday gift, and then they drove to the outskirts of St. Louis and into the neighboring town of Creve Coeur.

Umma greeted them at the door with the understated flair and poise that made her such a successful corporate event planner. Mrs. Ahn oozed competency, which Ewan hadn't realized until he was an adult was an act as good as his own. Instead of feeling duped, he remembered feeling relief . . . and admiration. Ahn Nari had busted her ass to perfect her English with private tutoring through Appa's linguistic colleagues, traveled internationally for corporate events at least three times a year, and did pro bono event planning for the Gateway Korea Foundation in her spare time. Umma was like a lovely bespectacled shark; if she stopped swimming, she just might stop breathing. He couldn't remember a time she hadn't been involved in something and bringing him along to the events she ran, whether they were out of state as an impromptu vacation opportunity or within the city limits because his parents couldn't afford childcare at the time.

Those were some of his best childhood memories—doing homework at the venue, hidden away from the client and slyly fed catered event food and desserts by Umma's staff, then whisked off to dinner afterward at fancy restaurants, comped by her company. A day to themselves when it all wrapped up, a chance to explore whatever city required Ahn Nari's expertise. It was Ewan's first exposure to the kind of work that didn't feel like work, and he'd tried to follow that path himself: helping people while still staying close enough to medicine to make his parents happy.

Seeing her now, in her frosted pink blazer, flowered top, and dress pants—on a Sunday, for crying out loud—Ewan felt a pang of homesickness for the woman right in front of him. He regretted choosing not to stay overnight. They lived barely thirty minutes away and he had no excuse. He tried not to notice how her whole countenance lit up when she saw that Tae was with him. Umma kissed their cheeks. "So tall," she sighed as she ushered them in and they took off their shoes. Then, with a poke at Tae's side, "Too skinny."

She clucked at the sight of the gift in Ewan's hands, fussed and waved it off as she took it from him. "You didn't have to," she said in a finger-wagging tone, even as her fingers curled around the floral paper possessively. "I said no gifts."

"It's not a gift," he clarified. "You'll see."

When she'd turned her back to bring it into the living room, Tae shot Ewan an alarmed look. "She said no gifts," he hissed. "I didn't get her one."

"She never means it," Ewan murmured, in case she could hear them. "That's just something she says."

"Show-off," Tae muttered.

"I *am* the real son."

"Gentlemen." Jun-su shot them both a warning look, which melted into a heart-stopping smile when Umma reappeared. She hid it well, but Ewan knew that smile flustered her to no end. "Ajumma, let us take you to lunch," Jun-su suggested in Korean.

"Your favorite place," Ewan added with an eyebrow waggle.

Her eyes widened, as if the suggestion of her favorite guilty pleasure was scandalous. "We should wait until your appa is home."

"He doesn't like that restaurant," Ewan said. "He'll never know."

"Bacon and eggs," Tae said enticingly, dangling the words like a carrot on the end of a stick. "Potatoes. Waffles."

Umma's shoulders slumped. "Fine, yes. It's so terrible for you."

"It's your birthday; you're allowed," Ewan consoled her.

Greasy American breakfast food was Umma's weakness, and they loaded her up on fried everything with the reckless abandonment of hungover college students. They were not college students; they were, however, hungover.

"I appreciate the gift," Umma said to him as she tucked into her waffles and scrambled eggs. "But you know what gift I really want."

Ewan schooled his expression to a practiced chagrin. Aw, shucks, you caught me. "I'm sorry I wasn't able to gift wrap a girlfriend for you, Umma."

"You know I want you to be happy," she countered. "You are thirty now. You get set in your ways the older you are. Keep it up and you'll be alone forever."

She'd given him that spiel every year since he turned twenty-five. "Thanks, Umma. I just don't have time for dating." Or the inclination. Usually. It only snuck up on him when he saw the way Tae and Jun-su looked at each other, as if the answer to the universe lay in the eyes of the other. He knew she just wanted that for him, but it was easier said than done.

"You make time, like anything else." Umma looked pointedly at Tae and Jun-su.

When they finished eating and went home, she focused on Tae: how was work? The lavender he'd given her earlier in the spring was blooming nicely. She wanted to plant a cherry tree in the backyard, could he show her? They switched to Korean for the conversation, and although Ewan was able to follow it, he no longer felt comfortable responding when they really got going. He knew his Korean wouldn't measure up to their smooth, fast, and fluid cadence. Every time he had to answer in English and interrupt their flow, embarrassment burrowed deeper.

And whether he liked or not, carbonated bubbles of resentment floated up to the surface. Umma loved nothing more than to chat with Tae in a way she couldn't with anyone else, except Appa and a few of the friends she had through the Gateway Korea Foundation. He didn't begrudge her the connection. He really didn't. He just resented that, when it came down to it, she had clicked better with Tae than she ever had with him. And of course, he could never let on, because he couldn't begrudge Tae a mother figure either. Tae's parents back in Seoul had made it known he wasn't welcome in their home after he came out. He needed a Nari.

But Ewan needed a Nari too. He just needed to come to terms with no longer being an only child. Jun-su had gotten drafted by proxy—the sunny, adorable Cindy Brady with the avant-garde career. Which made Tae the Marcia.

Ewan hadn't expected to end up as the Jan.

* * *

By the time Tuesday evening rolled around, Ewan had done preliminary research on what the Ulsanbawi painting might cost, since Isla hadn't listed a price for the original. And then built an argument for why he needed the painting in case she didn't want to sell. Most people responded positively if you mentioned grandparents, so he figured it would work.

He was with Jimmy Sanderson when Isla came into the therapy room. Jimmy was recovering from a motorcycle accident that had fractured his leg and arm. The old man possessed the long white beard, rosy cheeks, and twinkling blue eyes that made him the de facto Santa Claus of St. Louis, so much so that he volunteered as Santa in children's hospitals every December. When Ewan asked him if he'd mind having his picture up on the website, he'd smiled wide and said, "Son, I'd be damned pleased for people to see that Santa's got to work on his exercises too."

Jimmy was in the middle of hip rotations when Ewan saw Isla approach. With her dark hair pulled up in a ponytail, cropped leggings underneath a robin's-egg-blue floral dress, and a DSLR camera in hand, she looked like a college student fresh out of class.

"Hi," she greeted him.

"Hi, Isla. Jimmy, this is Isla Abbott, the freelancer redesigning our website. Isla, this is Jimmy Sanderson."

"How do you do," Jimmy said as he shook Isla's hand. "Before you ask, yes, Santa is currently receiving physical therapy for a nasty fall he took out of the sleigh." He winked at her and added in a low, conspiratorial voice, "Shouldn't have taken it out for a test run in mid-July."

Isla laughed, a fresh, light, happy sound that zinged through Ewan in a way he wasn't expecting. "As long as there wasn't alcohol involved in that unfortunate accident." Jimmy gave her a hangdog expression, and Isla looked appropriately scandalized. "Mrs. Claus won't be too happy."

The old man laughed delightedly. "Honey, what makes you think Mrs. Claus wasn't right there with me?"

Laughing, Isla asked about his injury, and Jimmy fell into that easy, slow cadence of his that Ewan always liked. He never could tell if looking like Santa was the thing that put people at ease around Jimmy, because damn if that man didn't have an actual mischievous twinkle in his blue eyes, or if it was the fact that Jimmy spoke as sweet and slow as molasses poured into a cup. Either way, Isla responded to it the way most people did, settling into a comfortable stance, giving him her full attention as they chatted.

She ended up asking more questions about Jimmy: his grandkids, moonlighting as Santa, his year abroad in China—Ewan hadn't even *known* that. How had she gotten that out of him? He looked a little closer at Isla Abbott. She was an active listener, and she gave Jimmy enough nonverbal space to speak his thoughts without interjecting too much. The smile on her face was genuine instead of humoring; she was enjoying the conversation as much as Jimmy did. Ewan normally didn't pay this close attention to the interactions of other people, but he couldn't remember the last time he'd paused long enough to converse in such a way with a virtual stranger. He was busy, everyone was busy—Isla was too, but nothing about her demeanor suggested that Jimmy was wasting her time. It didn't feel transactional. It felt honest, and terribly sweet of her. It made him think of his grandparents. He appreciated anyone who made time to listen to the stories of the elderly.

. . . but they *did* have jobs to do.

"Okay, you're not off the hook with your exercises just because a pretty girl's talking to you, Jimmy," Ewan teased. He didn't miss the way Isla's cheeks flushed the color of the pale-pink chrysanthemums in Tae's garden, but she just instructed them to continue with the exercises while she hovered and took pictures.

Occasionally, she would have them pause in a movement and adjust their stances for an optimal photo. After about fifteen minutes, she lowered her camera to look at some of the pictures, then declared the photo session finished.

"Thank you for participating, Jimmy," she said warmly. "We'll have you look at the final photos too, so you can select the ones you like best."

"I look forward to it, Miss Isla."

"Take care of that leg—no more joy riding on the sleigh, Mr. Claus."

Jimmy chuckled and waved her off like they were old friends. And Ewan didn't remember to ask her about the painting until after she left. He made a hissing sound of disappointment.

"What's wrong, Doc?" Jimmy asked.

"I forgot to ask Ms. Abbott a question. She's a painter too, and I wanted to purchase one of her paintings."

"A painter too," Jimmy repeated slowly. "Cute little thing, Doc. Real sweet."

Ewan shot him a cautionary look, but Jimmy only chuckled.

"A single man could do worse."

"Leg lifts next, Jimmy."

CHAPTER FOURTEEN

All it took was a fragrance.

Someone in the office walked by her desk wearing a twin perfume to the one her mother wore all the time. The familiar smell sent her back to high school, sick with strep, her mother brushing back her hair and feeding her ice cream to soothe her throat. To college, when Mom helped her move into her dorm, fussing over whether she had enough to eat and if she'd ever leave her room. To two years ago, when Mom spritzed on her favorite perfume before chemo because it made her feel normal.

Isla made a beeline for the bathroom, but the tears were already blurring her vision. She sat on the toilet and could do nothing but let it come, like a nosebleed intent on gushing itself out, with nothing on earth to stop the flow until it was good and ready to quit.

It took her forever to come out of that bathroom. She felt tender again, overly sensitive, a living nerve. Even the lightest touch caused pain. There was no way she could work like this. Once the tears stopped and she tried to calm her breathing, a headache crept along the sides of her head, nestling behind her eyes and turning the bathroom lights into high beams.

When she got back to her desk, head bowed so no one looked too closely at her, she took her medication, drank some water, and then walked into her boss's office.

"Hey—whoa." Jeremy sat back and got a good look at her face. "You okay?"

"Not really," she admitted. "I just . . . had a bad moment today. Can I take the brochure project home and wrap it up tonight?"

"Client needs it by six, kid. Could you get it done in time? If you need to hand it off, that's fine; I just don't want you stressing about it and then we haven't had it reviewed before sending it off."

The reminder set off a maelstrom of panic. He must have seen it in her eyes, because he rose from his desk.

"No, no, I can stay and get it done." The promise of tears waited in the wings, ready to take her down at the least provocation. She could not let it. She would not let her boss down, and she would make this deadline. "It's only about an hour and a half's worth of work."

He watched her face for a moment, nodded, then said, "Finish it, then go home. You look beat."

She only got through it because focusing on the work took her mind off her complete failure to remember the deadline and the lingering, gut-punch grief, as if Mom had died in front of her during lunch. When Jeremy blessed the brochure as excellent work—*sure, Jeremy, this is me believing you, because it was a garbage rush job*—she hightailed it out of there at four thirty and brought her laptop with her to work from home the next day.

Isla carried all that negative shit inside her the whole way home and managed to top it off with a dollop of frustration over her inability to connect with Ewan. It wasn't as if he owed her anything, because he most certainly didn't, but it was both a blessing and a curse to know they had fallen in love and married in another timeline. She was tragically already in love with him, and he was not interested.

When she got settled in at home, she did something even dumber than freak out and cry at the office and almost blow a deadline.

She called her dad.

He didn't pick up.

That was fine. That was what she'd expected. It was only five thirty anyway; he probably wasn't home from work. Sometimes, she thought, it would be nice to talk to him when she wanted to commiserate about Mom.

She wished she could talk to Ewan.

A wholly different kind of grief flooded her, and Isla was just . . . done. With herself, with her brain, with how much her emotions weighed. Enough to buckle her knees.

Isla put on the most depressing music she owned and took a bath, intent on soaking and shutting her mind off. But of course it wouldn't quit. She opened her eyes and stared at the pool tile ceiling of her bathroom. She had to carry these feelings for this man inside her, alone, while he carried on with a life she could only touch the edges of. The possibility of him slipping away was real and terrifying, because she wanted the life Ewan had painted for her. The good parts of it, at least. And then the things she could do differently now.

She had to stop thinking of him in these cataclysmic terms. He was a person who was nice to her, and she just had to be nice back and pray he was, or would be, interested in her as a real friend, and then maybe something more. And if fate or destiny didn't want to give her a second chance, well . . . shit, that would suck. More than she could put herself in touch with. But it wouldn't kill her.

She had survived worse things.

* * *

Friday was fired from the moment it started. This entire *week* had been having a field day with her. The upcoming thunderstorm gave her a morning headache, and Isla was tired and cranky. She just needed coffee and eggs; that's all she asked. And maybe a paper bag. RISE obliged her on the former, but at this point, she didn't even want to see Ewan. She just wanted to put on headphones and tune out the entire coffee shop.

But then he walked in. He looked disgustingly put-together, and she almost resented him for it. Black slacks, a white shirt, and an off-white cardigan pushed up at the elbows; warm for July, but then again, she'd felt the AC at his office, and it was a force to be reckoned with. The leather bracelets were back on his wrist, and his hair was swept back from his face like he'd stepped off a runway.

When he looked her way, his face bloomed into a smile that still held that teasing edge, as if their first meeting endlessly entertained him now and he thought of it every time he saw her. Great. She smiled weakly and waved back.

"Good morning, Isla," he said as he approached. "I received your email. I'll go over them with Jimmy next week."

"That's great. Thank you. I enjoyed meeting Santa."

"He's one of my favorite patients." Ewan sat next to her without asking, and when it looked like he was permanently parking there, Isla tried not to squirm with nerves. Outside, thunder grumbled under its breath. "Can I ask you a question not website related?"

Don't read too much into that, she warned herself. "Sure."

"I found your website, and I see that you paint." He looked a little unsure of himself and apologetic, as if he'd been caught staring into her bedroom window instead of viewing the website she'd put out there for everyone to see.

"That's technically website related," Isla pointed out.

His uncertainty morphed into an amusement that put an endearing sparkle in his deep brown eyes. "Yes, technically." He shook his head, a smile quirking his lips. "Anyway. Your work is gorgeous. I saw one in there I recognized, or rather, I recognized the place you painted. Have you ever been to South Korea?"

"I haven't," she confessed. "You're referring to the trail, aren't you?"

"Yes." His face lit up. His honest joy hurt Isla's heart, like looking into the sun hurt your eyes. "I hiked that trail with my grandfather when I was young. It means a lot to me; that day, the memory. I couldn't believe you'd painted it."

I painted it for you, she thought, her throat growing tight, wishing she could tell him that she knew how important that memory was to him and how much he loved and missed his grandparents . . . but she couldn't. "A friend told me about it. I thought it was so beautiful that I had to paint it."

"You did a wonderful job. It perfectly captures the beauty and serenity of that summit." Ewan said it so sincerely that heat flooded her cheeks. "I know you sell prints online, but I was wondering if I could buy the original from you. Name your price, I'll pay it. I want to give it to my grandfather as a gift."

Isla blinked. "Oh, I . . . well, I've never actually sold any of my originals before."

"I would love to be your first customer."

She laughed, mostly in disbelief. She wanted to just give it to him, but that would be too weird. People who sold artwork did not give away paintings to people they barely knew. She had a feeling it would start them on the wrong foot too.

"Can I get back to you on a price? Pricing the prints was far easier than the works themselves. And you're the first person to ask, so it won't be going anywhere."

"Sure, take whatever time you need. I'll let you get back to work."

"No, it's okay." Isla shook her head, tucked her hair behind her ear self-consciously, and made herself look at her screen instead of him. She didn't want to stop talking. "I'm ahead of schedule."

"I have to head in anyways."

Oh. Isla forced a smile as Ewan left, trying to ignore the little voice whispering its *I told you so*s at the perceived dismissal, slyly reminding her that he was only interested in the painting and this was purely transactional.

She remained behind after he left. Her breakfast had gone cold.

* * *

Isle figured out a price for the painting that night. It still felt like too much to charge him, so she applied a twenty percent discount. She emailed him the amount and a screenshot of the actual painting out in her living room.

His response came through almost immediately. *Sold. I can pay you right now.*

There's no rush, she replied, *but if you'd like, I can drop it off to you this weekend.*

Perfect, he replied back, then gave her his home address.

When Saturday came, Isla carefully wrapped the painting and loaded it into her car, along with a few other prints that online buyers had purchased, which she'd printed out and framed and now needed to ship. Orders had been slowly coming in, usually by people who'd found her website through her Instagram, and the sales were padding her savings quite nicely. The extra money gave her extra room to breathe.

Ewan's apartment, as she remembered him telling her, was in front of Memorial Plaza. The Arch curved gracefully between the buildings to the east of his home. She parked in the parking garage next door and called him.

"Hello," he answered. "Is this Isla, by chance?"

"It is," she said with a smile. "I'm out front with your painting."

"Wonderful. I'll be right down." His voice was like rich, creamy, melted caramel. As sweet and warm as it had been when they talked on the phone . . . before. Isla waited in front of the apartment complex, the sun hugging her skin with barely a breeze to relax its tight embrace. Because it was the weekend and she'd felt like it, she'd chosen a floral sundress and sandals, with lemon-yellow sunglasses that made her feel vaguely retro and cute. When she dressed like this, sometimes she could even forget how much her face disappointed her.

Ewan came out in a T-shirt and hiking pants, with a black corded necklace around his neck that made Isla think of baby goth Ewan. Luckily, her smile at the mental image timed itself to match Ewan's smile of greeting and his cute little wave.

"Hi! Thank you for bringing it over. I like your shades."

"Thanks. They're zesty."

His burst of deep laughter made her toes curl.

They got the painting out of the car together, and she helped him carry it up to the fourth floor. After they set it down in his living room, Isla looked around curiously. Ewan's apartment was uncluttered, filled with the contrast of dark and light: black walls, pale wood countertops, brass knobs, bright wooden floors, creamy rugs, plum-purple accents, plants with waxy green leaves hanging from the wall or spilling onto the window ledge. It was a soothing space with a mildly sensual vibe, like how water felt against naked skin.

"Your place is beautiful," she said, forgetting herself and walking in farther. "I didn't expect darker colors like this to feel so inviting. It really opens the room."

"That was the idea."

It was so . . . orderly. Even the clutter looked deliberate, like the off-white cardigan she remembered from earlier in the week thrown over the back of a chair and a pair of motorcycle boots by an ottoman that looked like the *Beauty and the Beast* ottoman that turned into a dog. Or the ottoman that was originally a dog. There was an intentional theme, whereas Isla's decorating sort of fell into a haphazard theme after years of collecting things she liked.

When she spotted the mural on the far wall, she gasped. "Is that a Woo original?" The street artist's style was distinctive: dark backgrounds, bright splashes of colors, and figures swimming out of the darkness, with *Woo* written in Hangul at the bottom right. This one depicted a golden cage on a black velvet backdrop, and a bluebird sat on a swing inside its bars, staring out at some distant point of freedom. Woo's work often showed up in the dead of night in cities all over the world. A few of his murals hung in contemporary museums across the country.

"It is," Ewan confirmed, coming to stand next to her. "We know each other."

Isla turned to gape at him. "Get out."

"All Koreans in America know each other."

She eyed him suspiciously, detecting the sarcasm. "Sure, sure. Like a Korean directory."

"You're not supposed to know about the directory." His serious expression broke into a grin. "I really do know him, though."

"Well, now I really don't believe you."

He laughed, and it was one of those deep belly laughs you couldn't fake. *She* had made him laugh. Isla imagined that little bluebird in the cage breaking free and soaring into the sky.

"I promise, Scout's honor—and I *was* a Boy Scout. That's an original, not a replica. It was a gift for something I helped him with, and I asked him for a work based off a favorite poem of mine."

"'Bluebird,' by Bukowski?"

Ewan's gaze grew less amused and more thoughtful—*assessing* her—and she felt that change inside her like a key turning. "Yeah, that one. Not a fan of the man himself, but I'm a fan of the poem."

Isla quoted the last stanza of "For Jane," the only Bukowski poem that so completely captured her grief. "I took a lot of comfort in that poem," she said, to distract herself from the thrill of the small spark that flared to life deep within her.

"Who did you lose?"

Isla hesitated as she prepared to let out the thing she really didn't like people to know unless they had to, since so few here in Missouri knew. The thing that had irrevocably changed her relationship with so many people back in Chicago. Big deaths, sometimes, ushered in so many little deaths. "My mother."

The instant shock and sympathy on Ewan's face made her want to hide from him. "I am so sorry. When?"

"Last year. It was cancer, and after a few months at stage four, in the end you're just relieved they're not hurting anymore." Too much, too much, too much, she censored herself.

People's will and ability to care was very short, especially if they were strangers, unless they'd experienced the same thing. "It's part of the reason I moved here."

Ewan nodded. "Are you seeing a grief counselor or a therapist?"

She nodded, wholly uncomfortable under the glare of his undivided attention. "I have good days and bad days, but my therapist helps me get through it."

He looked so sad that she almost wanted to comfort *him*. "Is that why you work so much?"

Isla had to think about that. "Do I?" She supposed she did. Between her actual job, the freelance website redesign, and her painting, it didn't leave room for much else, did it? "I guess it does keep me from dwelling on everything that happened. I don't mean to jam my schedule so full, but it's almost like I can't help it at this point." The tactic felt second nature, because she did the same for her anxiety—keeping her mind and body preoccupied. Except when she went overboard and it backfired on her. Which was all the time.

She shook her head, feeling like she had overstayed her welcome in his soothing downtown apartment. "Anyway, I should go. I hope your grandfather loves the painting."

"He will." Isla was pulling her keys out of her purse when he said, "I know I paid for it, but I can't overstate how much this painting means to me. Do you have a free weekend coming up soon? I'd like to thank you for it by doing something fun. And so you could get a break from work."

Oh, so this was a pity thing. Isla looked down at the rug and prepared to settle for crumbs. She tried once, twice, to do the thing she always did: bury her feelings and go along with the flow because it was easier.

She couldn't do it. Not when it felt this bad. She didn't want his attention when it was born of feeling sorry for her because she'd lost her mom. When he would just check that box after it was done and drift out of her life.

"My weekends are pretty full while the redesign project is still going, but I should have some free time when it wraps up. I'll let you know, because that sounds nice."

Ewan easily accepted that answer, which only affirmed Isla's suspicions.

It didn't really mean anything.

CHAPTER FIFTEEN

Three days a week.

Ewan saw Isla at the coffee shop on Tuesdays, Thursdays, and Fridays. He learned that she normally worked remotely but had made an adjustment to her schedule for this gig. He'd taken to changing seats to chat with her about the progress on the website and anything else that came up. It would be rude to do otherwise. Plus he genuinely knew nothing about designing websites, and it was a little fascinating to watch her work. She had endless patience for what were probably very stupid, basic questions, and he appreciated that she didn't make him feel like an idiot when he asked.

For whatever reason, those three days became his favorites. He liked the freelancer's company, even when they said nothing and all he heard was the quiet clacking of keys as she worked. And maybe it was because of that. They could sit in the quiet and it still felt like a full conversation. The world was already so loud, and she knew how precious quiet could be.

Today was one of those days. He didn't have a patient until nine thirty, so he was in no particular rush, and his current read was a damn good one. He sensed more than saw Isla lean over, and she politely hovered her hand near his book to get his attention, as if she were ready to turn the page for him.

"Can I help you?" he asked seriously.

"I finished updating your bio section," she said. "Can you read over your summary and let me know if you want changes?"

"Sure." Ewan leaned in as she turned her laptop for him to read the text. The page was in draft mode, or whatever it was called, and he quickly read through the summary she'd written based on the interview they'd done the week before. His brain idly noted that she smelled nice . . . honey and cinnamon, warm scents that made him think of winter. "This is good. Can I see what the page looks like?"

Isla hit the preview button, and what he saw was a drastic improvement over West End's previous bare-bones employee page. She'd taken their company colors, black and orange, and used them on the page in a way that wasn't as in-your-face and distractingly vibrant; less like a tangerine and more like the soft reddish orange of the sandstone formations in Colorado's Garden of the Gods. She'd paired each physical therapist's summary of their credentials and specialties with flattering, professional photos and placed individual appointment buttons under each name to encourage patients to schedule with their preferred therapist.

"This is great," he said, which was kind of an understatement, and he hoped she heard the sincerity in his voice. He started clicking around the pages and found descriptions of different types of physical therapy, information on the services West End offered, and lists of patient resources. "I know you've explained what you're doing, but I still don't know how you made it look this good. Jeff will love this."

She clearly didn't know what to do with praise, because she looked away to hide her flush, which was endearing. "I just, ah, keep the user in mind. If I were in pain and looking for a physical therapist to help make the pain stop, I need as much information as I can get in a short amount of time to make my decision. What services do they offer? Will my insurance cover it? Can I afford it if I *don't* have insurance, and what options do they have for me? Who will be treating me? How do I get an assessment and make an appointment? They shouldn't have to go hunting for that information; it should all be at their fingertips. The design and the colors reinforce your branding, make it memorable, and make it aesthetically pleasing as well as functional."

"It's a lot less cluttered than our old home page."

"You don't want to overwhelm a new patient. Keep it simple and make this as easy as possible to navigate. White space is really important; it makes what content you have easier to digest, balances the whole page, and removes distractions. It draws their eyes where you want them to go." She traced her finger over to the Request Appointment button and the Services menu bar. "They shouldn't have to scroll to get what they need. All of this helps turn a visitor into a customer, or in your case, a new patient. It sounds very calculated, but good design helps establish trust and makes for a better and easier experience for your patients. And after all . . ." She shot him a quick smile that made her gray eyes sparkle with diamond chips. He'd never noticed that before. "I can help get them in the door, but you all carry that promise through and do the work that helps them live better lives."

He loved listening to people when they spoke of their passions, and every word of that design crash course told him how much she loved what she did. It completely transformed her from a shy, hesitant wallflower into an engaged, animated authority in her area of expertise. It made him want to get her talking about painting. If she was anything like Jun-su, she'd talk about technique and other artists well into the night. He wanted to go to an art museum with her and let her loose.

Isla cleared her throat, her eyes flitting away from him as she closed the preview page. "Anyways, that's . . . yeah. I design things for the internet, and that's some of the psychology behind it."

"It's fascinating," he said. "I mean that." He must have done something to make her self-conscious, because she couldn't meet his gaze anymore and didn't seem to know what to do with her hands. He knew how to fix that. "Can I tell you how I do some of that work once those patients make appointments with me?"

She visibly relaxed as the focus shifted off her. "Of course."

"When I do evaluations, I don't just ask where the pain is and when it started. I try to get a complete picture of how their day-to-day might be inadvertently contributing to the injury. Not all injuries come from a singular event; many develop over time. I see a lot of patients with back pain or shoulder pain that they can't find a point of origin for until we really start to dig into their repetitive behaviors. You know what a common one is?"

Before she could answer, he traced a finger down the slouch in her back. Isla straightened her spine immediately, inhaling quietly at the unexpected touch. He paused at T5 in her thoracic region, near the bottom edge of her shoulder blades. His fingers traced bone and muscle on a daily basis, assessing, manipulating, massaging, all in an effort to help his patients overcome their injuries and gain as much mobility and pain reduction as possible. A feather-light touch should have felt no different; a calm surface of an alpine lake.

It rippled those waters.

"Poor posture," he said. He'd wanted to tease her about the way she hunched over her laptop, but found he couldn't summon the right tone. "Sitting at a desk all day for work is harder on your body than you think. Do you get headaches?" She nodded, her eyes quietly, steadily on his. He cleared his throat. "It could be contributing. I can show you some simple exercises to do that would help."

"Will I have to make an appointment?" she asked.

He let out a breath, grateful for the hint of humor in her voice. It broke whatever strange hold he'd been in. "This one's a freebie. And speaking of freebies—the offer still stands for a fun outing as a thank-you for the painting."

"I didn't think you were serious," she replied, after a beat.

Her disbelief tripped his hurt wire. She really thought he'd been lying? He had been totally sincere. She'd lost her mom recently and had moved here all by herself and she was overworked. What about that offer rang insincere?

Did she think he'd offered just because he felt bad for her? And was that entirely untrue? Ewan shifted in his seat, uncomfortable with the level of introspection this mental trip down memory lane was giving him. He *did* sympathize, but that wasn't the only reason he'd offered. And he was going to prove it to her.

"I meant it," he said. "If there's anything fun you've wanted to do but haven't made time for, name it. I never need an excuse to go exploring in my own backyard."

Isla mulled that one over. "What is your definition of fun?"

"You pick."

She narrowed her eyes. "What if I pick something you hate?"

Ewan shrugged. "I couldn't hate anything if you were keeping me company."

Her cheeks went charmingly pink. "Well . . . I've heard there's some pretty cool caves in Missouri, but I haven't been able to check them out yet. Would you be up for something like that?"

No way had this woman just casually tossed out one of his favorite annual activities. He hadn't expected her to suggest anything outdoorsy, since she didn't seem the type, but that was also a ridiculous stereotype to hold just because she liked to wear dresses and skirts. A pleasant surprise indeed. "Isla, you have made my day with that request. Yes, absolutely. Can I pick the cave?"

"Go for it."

Holy shit, his birthday had come early. "Great! Yes. This is perfect. I'll text you the details and get the tickets for a tour." He sensed the argument in the crease of her forehead before she even voiced it. "No, no—it's on me. I don't want your money."

Isla leaned back in her chair as if to get a better look at him. "You're too excited for this. Why am I nervous?"

"Don't be." Maybe. But what he had in mind was so much fun, and he worried that if he gave her too much information up front, she'd back out. If she wanted to see caves, she was going to see *caves*. Ewan Park did not do anything halfway. "I have plans to make. Go enjoy your Saturday." Isla's face absolutely did not believe him. "Trust me, you'll love it."

He was determined get this wallflower to do some living beyond work.

*   *   *

Isla expected a normal guided tour through a beautiful local cave system, because that's how these things worked, didn't they? Caves were dangerous, wild things, and the sensible way to enjoy them was on a clear path with guardrails.

Ewan, it turns out, did not *do* sensible when it came to nature.

She should have figured that out when he texted her. *Wear comfortable, sturdy shoes, long sleeves and long pants. Things you wouldn't mind getting dirty in. Oh, and bring a change of clothes.*

Why? she asked. *These are guided tours.*

Trust me.

The more you say that, the less I do.

Because Isla was a rule follower, she wore long sleeves, long pants, and running shoes, and brought a change of clothes that sat in the back seat as she drove to meet him at 300 Cave Hollow Road, just south of Hannibal. All she knew was that their tour was for the Cameron Cave and then maybe, if they had time, the Mark Twain Cave.

She met him in the parking lot of the gift shop/visitor center and tried not to notice how his long-sleeved athletic shirt lovingly wrapped around his biceps and hugged his abs as he got out of his car. Jesus. This was a punishment. Someone, somewhere, was laughing at her.

"Full disclosure," he said. "It *is* a guided tour, but there's no electricity in Cameron Cave. It requires flashlights."

Isla waved it off. "I know, I have Google, and it's fine. I'm sure it will be beautiful." She was looking forward to having the cave surprise her with the arc of a flashlight, its formations rising out of the dark and exposed to the light. She didn't know if Ewan's goal had been to shock her with a more "authentic" nature exploration just to see how she'd handle it (even as she thought it, she knew it demeaned him, but she couldn't always control where her mind wandered), but if it *had*, she wasn't backing down from this. A cave didn't require much socialization—this was a structured activity with a guide. She could handle it.

"Yeah, but did you find the off-route tour they offer?"

Isla frowned.

Ewan grinned.

"It's safe," he stressed. "But it's a bit physically strenuous. I brought you knee pads and elbow pads."

"What have you done?" she wondered.

He patted her on the shoulder, and the imprint of his fingers left a heat map along her skin. "Let's get some adventure in your life, Isla Abbott."

* * *

Isla thought she'd experienced darkness before she entered the cave.

Without the head lamps on their helmets, the darkness here was . . . total. It ate light like the center of a black hole. Cool, velvety nothingness swallowed her and everyone around her whole. It hid the cave's wonders from the eye, promising a whole new world if only one had a light to illuminate it.

This mazelike cave was so far out of her comfort zone that she would have expected to feel like a baseball knocked clear into the stands, free-falling and praying someone would catch her. But so far? She *was* scared. She was also . . . excited.

Isla ran her fingers over the jagged limestone walls on either side of them as they walked a narrow passage, everyone's shaky head lamps lighting the way, their ears attuned to the jovial guide clearing the path for them. Ewan walked behind her, and she almost forgot about him as they carefully navigated their way down and in. Her head fell back to catch a glimpse of the sparkling mineral deposits streaking along the rock the guide called gypsum.

"How are we doing?" Ewan asked from behind her.

"It's so pretty," she said. "This is . . . I have never done anything like this."

"That was the point. It's going to narrow up here soon. Just remember to take it slow and easy."

Isla's breathless excitement to even be doing this overrode her normal anxiety response. When the path narrowed to the point where she had to squeeze her body between the uneven limestone walls, she did as he said, placing her feet mindfully on the rock and slowly squeezing through. She misjudged where to place her foot at one point and slipped, letting out a quick gasp as she lost her balance. Ewan swiftly grabbed her hand, squeezing and pulling to help steady her.

"Easy," he said, his tone nonjudgmental and patient. He braced a hand against her upper back. "You okay?"

"Yes." Isla's heart pounded more from his close proximity in the dark than from her fumble. "This may come as a surprise to you, but there's not a lot of light down here." One of the other tour attendees laughed. "You do this on the regular, huh?" she asked him as they continued.

"Every year. Missouri has a lot of caves."

"I'll admit I usually stay aboveground. I get my nature from gardens and conservatories, where the light is," she replied. Isla admired how the rock undulated like waves, to the point where she could not have understood how a human would be able to pass through if she hadn't seen the woman in front of her do it. She gamely moved between the immovable waves, breathing in slow and deep to keep her body calm and relaxed. "I go to botanical gardens to get ideas for paintings."

"One of my best friends works at the Missouri Botanical Garden." He was annoyingly not out of breath. "You should check it out. I can let him know you're coming if you want a tour. He's the reason I have so many plants in my apartment—and why I'm able to keep them alive."

"By keeping them alive, do you mean you . . ." Isla huffed as she carefully stepped/slid down where the path dropped a few feet. ". . . or him stopping by to water them?"

"Hey now," he shot back. She caught the flash of his smile in her head lamp's arc. "He might, ah, ask for proof of life on occasion and make me send him pictures to see if they're dying."

As they traversed the cave's winding path, he told her about Tae and how they'd met in college when the young man had come to live with their family. When Ewan talked about his friend, Isla almost forgot that he'd brought her out here only as a thank-you for the painting he liked. He didn't outright say how hard he and his family had worked to make sure Tae could stay and work in the States, but she could read between the lines. It was an exhausting and expensive process to gain citizenship, which she'd learned from friends who worked for immigration and ESL centers in Chicago. Tae was lucky to have had a built-in support system to help him emigrate, and Ewan's pride in him emanated from his voice.

A ripple of real panic moved through her when she found out they had to crawl to get through a low, low portion of the cave. The rock sandwiched the open space into what amounted to a basement crawl space, and Isla had to pause to collect herself as she watched the others ahead of her slowly crawl through, chatting merrily among themselves, laughing at their own nerves as they went. It helped that it was a shared kind of fear; they were all in this together.

Ewan came up behind her and gave her shoulders a quick squeeze of encouragement. "Easier than it looks."

"I did not sign up for this."

"You are correct—I signed you up for this."

"Did you take me here to kill me? Is this actually payback from the coffee stain?"

He laughed. "I am not punishing you for the coffee spill." He appeared in her line of sight, serious now, and added, "Are you really nervous? Even without the guide, I know the way; I've done this a number of times. I won't let anything happen to you."

Isla huffed out a breath, eyed the low clearance, and rolled her neck. "No, I can do this." She dropped down and slowly crawled along the rock and dirt, feeling the ceiling of the passage scraping along the top of her helmet. Nerves and exhilaration fueled her forward. "I can do this," she whispered to herself.

And then she saw the little hole they were supposed to pass through to clear it.

She became Alice in the White Rabbit's house, nibbling on the wrong cookie and growing so large that she burst through the roof and the windows. Only she couldn't burst through this roof. Isla's house was solid rock and it constricted both her and her lungs, freezing her in place. There were no shutters to open that would allow her to breathe, because no fresh air circulated down here, under the earth.

She heard Ewan crawl up next to her. "Isla?"

"Too tiny," she said in a voice that matched the adjective.

"It only *looks* tiny from here."

It was fifty-seven degrees, and she was suddenly slick with sweat. "Did I mention," she said slowly, taking deep, measured breaths to slow down her trapped-bird's pulse, "that I'm prone to panic attacks?"

Ewan was silent for an eternity. "You did not," he said slowly. "But that's okay. Do me a favor and take off your helmet."

"It'll get dark." Isla hated the edge of fear in her voice.

"I'll keep the light on you."

She did as she was told, and the relief from removing that compression off her head was instantaneous. She heard him murmur something to . . . she didn't know who, the other tour people or the guide, but she didn't care, and couldn't hear them anyway over the roaring in her ears. Isla rested her forehead on her hand and dreaded the mounting panic weighing down each limb. Dear God, please no. Not down here. Not in this tomb.

"Isla." Ewan's voice was soft and calm, deep and intimate in the dark. She focused on it like the beam from a lighthouse. There was no guarantee her ship wouldn't crash on the rocks anyway, but at least she had that beam to focus on. "What you're experiencing right now is extremely common, especially for people who have never done this before, but it passes. Keep taking deep, even breaths."

She nodded.

"You are so close to getting through this part of the tour."

"I can't move," she whispered.

"You don't have to right now. Take all the time you need."

"Can I . . . can I have some of your water?"

"Of course you can." Ewan shifted, and Isla unfroze long enough to grab the bottle. She spilled an absurd amount of water trying to choke it down, then shakily handed it back to him. She jolted when she felt his hand on her back, and bit her lip until it bled to keep from crying at the simple kindness of his hand rubbing wide, slow circles across her upper back. "You're doing great," he kept saying. "We can hang out here all day if you want to."

"I don't want to."

"It's naturally air conditioned."

Isla's laugh could barely stand on its own two feet. She was crying—she could feel the cool tracks on her cheeks—and she was grateful for the darkness as she struggled to keep her breathing deep and even.

"Want to hear something cool about this cave?" he asked. She nodded into the dirt underneath her fingers and focused on the feel of Ewan massaging the tight knots in her neck. "This cave wasn't discovered until the 1920s, when the owner of the Mark Twain Cave opened up a sinkhole and started exploring. A whole world down here that no one had seen. Its inhabitants are typically bats. How do you feel about bats?"

"I like them," Isla admitted faintly. "I've never met one outside of a zoo, but I think they're beautiful." And bats navigated the dark like pros: fearlessly, adaptive to their environment. If a tiny little bat could do it, Isla could do it too.

He told her about the different species of bats that lived in these caves, one of them charmingly called little pips, and Isla felt the breathing exercise start to work, her heart rate slowing, her fear subsiding just enough to bring her back to her surroundings. She risked turning her head to look at Ewan.

He lay on the cave floor next to her, looking content to sit there until Isla was ready to move. "How are you doing, Isla?"

"I want to get out."

"You got it. Hey, Luis? We're ready to go."

Isla had forgotten about the rest of the tour and was prepared to start apologizing for holding up the entire procession, but the other members had nothing but words of encouragement, stories of their own about being nervous or getting scared. Nevertheless, her fingers trembled as she crawled through the hole, one elbow after another, one breath at a time, until the ceiling opened up and freed her.

She stood, light-headed and slightly disoriented, and almost didn't register Ewan pulling her in for a hug. "You did great in there."

"I did not. I had a panic attack."

"You weren't the first, and you won't be the last," Luis the tour guide said. "The good news is that we're not going back that way."

"Best news of the day," Isla said through a dry throat.

Ewan laughed, giving her shoulder another rub. "Come on, adventurer. Let's conquer this cave."

A low level of lingering fear nipped at her heels for the rest of the tour, but Isla was able to turn it into background noise thanks to some genuinely beautiful limestone formations, products of water and time, that her head lamp pulled from the darkness. Stalactites hung like jagged icicles above them, forever frozen in time, and stalagmites formed an almost alien landscape around them, glistening and roughhewn in the light. She and Ewan fell into the rhythm of teamwork, although he needed less help than she did, particularly over one large boulder that he all but lifted her up on with a show of strength that sent her heart fluttering. She laughed with delight when a few bats flew past and disappeared almost as soon as they swooped past their lights.

By the time they reached sunlight again, Isla felt better, but she had a hard time looking Ewan in the eye after quietly losing her shit. She also felt kind of gross and dusty. Naturally, Ewan's version of gross and dusty just made his hair look artfully disheveled, because nothing was fair.

"You did that!" He raised his hand for a high five, and Isla weakly returned it. "Ready to shower?"

"Are there showers here?"

"Yes. I'm going to take one, but it's up to you if you'd rather wait until you got home."

"I'll . . . I'll wait." Isla stripped off the knee and elbow pads and handed them back to Ewan, and they both sat down on the curb next to their cars. The need to be alone now was overwhelming and beginning to leech out all the wonder and joy she'd felt even in the parts of the cave after the crawl space. But there was no graceful way to immediately exit, so she just endured. "I think I'm more cut out for hiking."

Ewan wiped some of the dust off of his forehead, then sneezed. "I think you're cut out for both. You handled that like a champ."

"It was fun, but challenging," she admitted.

Ewan's expression grew solemn. "Isla, if I had known you had panic attacks or issues with small spaces, I wouldn't have suggested this. In hindsight, I should have asked, and I'm sorry for that."

Do you regret this now? Isla wondered, the thought scraping off all that fragile, newly healed skin to reexpose the wound of the cave panic attack. Did I drag you down? "It's . . ." She never talked about this, ever, and she didn't have the appropriate words now to explain herself. "I really did love it, I just got scared. I didn't know how it was going to affect me because I hadn't done it before. I didn't mean to ruin it."

"You didn't ruin anything," Ewan insisted. "You were brave in there. It scared you and you did it anyway."

Isla needed out of this conversation like she'd needed out of that crawl space. It was nothing he'd done. The whole event took every shred of hope she had and hoarded it back in the cave like hidden treasure. She hated that she couldn't just enjoy something without her issues putting all these hidden clauses on the Fun Agreement that inevitably altered the whole experience. Ewan didn't deserve that. He clearly loved stuff like this, and if she couldn't participate without a melt-down, then she had no business even going. "Thanks. I'm just going to shower at home."

Ewan rose after she did. "I'm glad you came, Isla."

She smiled tightly. "Me too."

CHAPTER SIXTEEN

Isla didn't show up at the coffee shop for a week.

It threw off Ewan's mornings the way burning your toast or ruining a shirt with spilled coffee did. He got only one reply back from his check-in texts: that she had a new work project that demanded early-morning hours at the office and she had to adjust her schedule to accommodate it and the West End work. He understood that, but it didn't feel like the complete picture. She'd given him the subplot but not the main arc.

Had it been the cave tour? Ewan couldn't make sense of it. She'd gotten scared when she had to crawl, but he didn't blame her at all—Tae had cursed him in Korean, English, and Japanese when they'd reached that portion of the tour a few years back. Isla had been game for the whole thing, and he admired the grit she'd demonstrated during each leg of it. She'd pointed out every bat they'd spotted with a childlike sense of wonder, and even tried to get closer for a better look when she could.

Yet it felt like she'd been avoiding him ever since.

It was a muggy day on the cusp of autumn when Ewan parked his sour ass in his blue chair instead of at the table they usually shared. He had not heard from his freelancer in over ten days, and Barb had pitched the curve ball of the year at him yesterday when he'd asked about her. "Honey, she wrapped up the redesign last week. Ms. Abbott's finished up, and that website's a beauty."

It was. He was scrolling through it now, and the professional polish Isla had put on their business would no doubt help increase their new-patient numbers.

She didn't have ties to West End anymore. Did that mean she didn't have ties to him either? Every morning he came to their café and Isla was still not there was another morning his chest hurt the way it did when he heard beautiful, sad music. A longing and an ache. He'd never expected her to just . . . not come back.

He hated the way her absence made him feel. More than that, he hated the suspicion that he'd been the cause of it somehow.

Ewan left the second floor empty hearted, pitching his empty coffee cup in the trash and trudging down the stairs. This bad mood was going to splatter all of his coworkers like cooking oil and he already knew everyone was going to loathe it, himself included. He passed the barista counter and did a thoughtless visual sweep of the first floor.

And spotted Isla by the window, packing up to leave.

Ewan let out the breath he'd been holding for almost two weeks. She looked paler than usual. The skirt was navy blue today, with a short-sleeved, Peter Pan–collared brown shirt. Her shoes were dark-blue-and-brown oxfords. God, she was cute.

"Hey," he said. Isla jolted like a cat. "How have you been? Why didn't you come upstairs? It's been *ages*."

Her gray eyes held the color of a misty morning, dewy with moisture and wide as an owl's. They suddenly reminded him of the mists at the summit of the Ulsanbawi trail. Her small hands twisted the strap of her laptop bag. "I couldn't. I tried . . . and I couldn't."

"Why? What's going on?"

It looked as if the very thought of answering that question overwhelmed her. Isla looked away to the window, then down at her feet, then opened her mouth to speak, then closed it. She swallowed hard. "I'm sorry," she said on a soft, sad laugh. Her eyes widened, bewildered by her very presence in the coffee shop, as if she had just come back to herself and didn't know how she had gotten here. "I shouldn't have come here today."

"You definitely should have," he countered, his heart stirring at her soft confession. He shouldered his own bag and steered her outside with a hand on her shoulder to get her away from the crowd. He recognized the uneven, rapid rise and fall of her chest. She was probably having another panic attack, but this one felt different than from before. Something about Isla's demeanor triggered some alarm deep inside him. She was currently delicate in a way that made him feel he'd break something if he squeezed too hard.

"Talk to me, Isla," Ewan said.

"I can't. Not like . . ." As soon as the last word passed her lips, she looked horrified. She covered her mouth with her hand, and her eyes filled with tears.

That alarm grew louder. "Isla?" he asked carefully.

"I need to go," she whispered.

He didn't like the thought of her getting in a car and driving that distracted and distraught. When he took her hands, they trembled. Ewan kept his voice soft and firm when he said, "Come with me."

Isla looked too overwhelmed to argue, so she did. When they reached his car, he took care of her one, faint protest of

"My car!" with a "We'll take care of that later." She sat rigidly in the passenger seat and kept her gaze fixed straight ahead during the short ride back to his apartment.

"Take deep, slow breaths for me, Isla, just like in the cave," he said, and watched her out of the corner of his eye to see that she was trying—and also trying not to cry. Sympathy pangs banged around his heart, looking for a way out and finding none, trapped in there as surely as she felt trapped and helpless to the whims of her own mind. Watching this smart, quietly capable and artistically brilliant woman shaken to pieces again was like watching a hurricane tear into a house, shingle by shingle, until the architecture was stripped to its skeleton. He wanted to shield her from those damaging winds.

When they reached his apartment, he had her lie down on the couch, and although it was warm out, she was shaking. He didn't know if some of it was from the air conditioning, so he pulled the throw blanket from the back of the couch and wrapped it around her, forming an Isla-shaped burrito. Their gazes clashed, and her face crumpled.

"I'm sorry I didn't talk to you or stop by," she whispered brokenly. "You didn't deserve that."

Oh, sweetheart. He didn't try to quell the urge to hug her. It surprised and pleased him when she latched on immediately, her grip strengthening until she squeezed him like a well-loved teddy bear. A small, sad sigh escaped her, and he held her tighter. Ewan held the hug for as long as he could, rubbing her back soothingly and making the unconscious shushing noises his mother used to make when he was small. Nothing felt more right and necessary than hugging Isla Abbott in this moment. "There's nothing to be sorry for," he murmured into her ear. "The only thing I want you to do is keep breathing and make yourself comfortable right here. I'm going to make you tea. I'll be right back."

When he came back with a steaming cup of tea—chamomile blended with peppermint, thank you, internet—he found her curled up on her side. She had been crying, judging by the faint sheen to her cheeks, and to help preserve her dignity, he said nothing. She wouldn't look at him as she thanked him for the tea and sat up to drink it. Isla was clearly embarrassed at having had a panic attack in the first place, and that's when it clicked.

She was ashamed of them. She'd had a panic attack in the cave and didn't know how to deal with the aftermath. Tae said Jun-su had been like that when he used to get them more frequently. He'd shut himself up in his studio for days after one and only come out for food and the toilet. He didn't rejoin the rest of the household until he was good and ready.

Isla didn't come back until she was good and ready.

"Listen," he said. "I have to step out for a bit to make some arrangements with work." Her eyes widened as she suddenly remembered that it was a weekday morning and they both had jobs. "Don't worry about it. My schedule can be pretty flexible. I want you to stay here and rest, okay? Promise me you'll be here when I get back?"

A blush colored her cheeks. Isla kept her eyes on the mug of tea as she nodded.

"If you get tired and you want to sleep, you're welcome to use my bed. I don't mean that in a weird or creepy way, I just know it's more comfortable than the couch." He was rewarded with a slight uptick of her mouth before it settled back into a dreadfully serious thin line. "I'm a phone call away, but I shouldn't be long. And if you're hungry, help yourself to anything in the fridge or the cabinets." He squeezed her shoulders and stood to leave.

"Ewan?"

He glanced back. This time, she met his gaze and held it. "Thank you," she said.

Leaving her was harder than he'd thought it would be, but he wouldn't be gone long. She was fine now; she'd get some sleep, eat some food, and he'd find coverage or reschedule his afternoon appointments to keep her company. The possibility that he wouldn't be able to get right back to her was a troubling one, though, a kernel in his teeth he couldn't dislodge, so he picked up his phone and dialed.

"Hey, how's your day looking?"

*　*　*

Rain pattering softly on the roof woke Isla up. The living room was overcast, as if it were much later than it actually was. It took Isla a second to remember where she was. Embarrassment tried to get a foothold, but her mind was quieter, her body still as she remembered once again the simple pleasure of a warm blanket and the sound of rain on the roof. The medicine must have kicked in.

This was the second time she'd had a panic attack in front of Ewan, and he'd handled this one just as well as the first. Back in that cave, for the first time, she'd heard *her* version of Ewan in his calm, kind words.

And realized she couldn't live up to any version of Isla that would deserve him.

Or thought she did. It was a mean thing to think about herself, and it was a backsliding thought, so she'd made an extra appointment with her therapist to talk through it. She was so unbelievably tired of taking a few shaky steps forward before the entire staircase collapsed underneath her feet and forced her to climb on her hands and knees to keep moving up. Tired of her body's signals telling her she would quite literally die at any given minute if she had to endure even a moment's social discomfort.

She couldn't face anyone while she mentally worked through the episode, much less Ewan. Then over a week had gone by, and suddenly too much time had passed—much too much. She didn't know how to explain herself, so she'd ignored his texts, and then the pressure to *do something* had built and built until she was paralyzed and did nothing. She had sabotaged everything. He'd have forgotten her and completely moved on. She'd let him slip between her fingers because she'd fallen into her old habit of ignoring the world away, then wrapped that habit in a *You will only drag him down anyway* bow.

Sheer desperation drove her to the coffee shop, and the forward motion had jerked her panic into gear like rusty train wheels shuddering to life on a track. She couldn't climb those stairs to go see him. Every step in the staircase's direction fed the storm of panic and terror whirling inside her until she couldn't face it anymore. The relief of giving up was instantaneous.

Yet he'd found her anyway, so it was obvious he knew she was avoiding him. Then the storm winds had sucked her in.

But . . . he hadn't forgotten her. He looked relieved, confused, *affected* by her absence.

She had been missed.

When Isla sat up, she winced as a post-cry headache pounded at the base of her skull. She dropped her head onto her knees and slowly rubbed circles into the stiff, aching muscles of the back of her neck.

Which was why she didn't hear anyone in the kitchen until she saw him.

"Oh," she gasped, standing up a little too fast. "Hi. You are not Ewan."

The stranger smiled warmly. "No. I'm a friend of his. He asked me to check on you. My name is Jun-su."

Isla shook his hand. "He's talked about you. It's a pleasure to meet you."

"You too. Are you feeling all right?"

"A little better, thank you." Thank god she'd remembered to call off work today, otherwise the ensuing panic at oversleeping and missing work would have sent her into another tailspin.

"We brought your car here," Jun-su told her as he filled two glasses of water, then handed her one. "Ewan was worried it would get a ticket from the meter."

"That was very thoughtful. Thank you." Isla drank the water gratefully, downing half the glass. "I hope I haven't taken you away from anything important today."

Jun-su waved off her concern. "Work will always be there. Ewan rarely sends out a distress signal."

Isla struggled not to feel self-conscious next to him. He was a few inches shorter than Ewan, and he was beautiful. She was pretty sure his skin had been spun from a cloud, and his hair smelled like the collective hopes and dreams of every human being from Los Angeles to New York City— coconut and seawater and sunshine. He made Isla acutely aware that she had cried a few hours ago and probably looked like it.

"What happened?" he asked her. The genuine concern in his eyes made her sigh miserably.

"I had a panic attack," she mumbled, her heart cringing at even voicing it out loud. "I shouldn't have gone out. Should have known better."

"Shoulda, woulda, coulda." He nudged her shoulder to let her know he was teasing. She envied his ability to be so casually and effortlessly affectionate, especially with a stranger. "I used to get them too. Not so much anymore. It's nothing to be ashamed of."

Her first, instinctual thought was disbelief. This man was gorgeous. The whole world catered to gorgeous people. What could he possibly get that anxious about?

As soon as she thought it, she was horrified and ashamed of herself, as if she'd shouted it in his face. As if attractive people weren't allowed to have anxiety disorders or depression. As if she were the only one with a mental illness. As if other people didn't have a small bully inside them, pushing them around and making them feel less-than. You are a foolish idiot, Isla Abbott, she chastised herself, and if you don't want to be judged for the way you look, then you can't do it to him. You have no idea what his lived experience has been like. She wanted to apologize to Jun-su for a thought she'd never voiced.

He was waiting, giving her space to gather her thoughts to speak. She gripped her glass of water tighter. "Funny how it always feels like it's something to be ashamed of."

Jun-su nodded. "The world is . . . not forgiving of strong emotions that are like a weakness." He squeezed his eyes shut, then shook his head. "Look like weakness. Sorry. Sometimes my English isn't perfect."

"It's just fine," she assured him. "It's certainly better than my Korean." He laughed. "How did you and Tae meet?"

His whole countenance softened. "I met Tae-seok in the military."

Isla blinked. "You served?"

"Korea mandates two years. He conscripted after graduating college." Jun-su cleared his throat, effectively closing that line of conversation, then gestured behind her. When she turned, she saw her painting. "Wonderful impasto technique. It makes you think you can walk right onto the trail."

"Do you paint?"

Jun-su's smile was big enough to hold at least a dozen secrets. "You could say that. I am an artist, like you."

Her eyes drifted to the caged bluebird on the center of the wall. No. It couldn't be. She turned to look at Jun-su, who might as well have had bright-blue feathers poking between his teeth with that grin.

"You're kidding."

His grin widened. He pointedly looked up at the painting.

"You are *not* Woo!"

"Are you not Isla?" he laughed.

"Get out! Seriously?"

She reared back in her seat as if it would help her get a better look at him. She felt as if a rare, beautiful butterfly had landed on her hand and, if she moved, it would fly away. Ewan had not been kidding about knowing him.

"Do you have to kill me now that you've told me your real identity?"

"I've only done that once," he said offhandedly. "If Ewan trusts you, I trust you."

"Why do you keep it separate?"

"Necessity at first." Jun-su scooped his hand through his blond hair. "Graffiti is illegal in, oh, most parts of the world. But the . . ." He wheeled his hand in a circle as if the right word would show up when the ticket stopped spinning. "What is it called, the disguise? The . . ."

"Anonymity?"

He slapped his knee in agreement. "Yes. It made me braver. Brave and stupid. I liked stirring people up, and then pretending to be shocked by it in public." He grinned again, catlike and satisfied. "No one knew, but I knew. All I needed, you know?"

Isla thought of all the paintings in her house that put her emotions on paper, preserved them like a Polaroid. Yes, she did know.

"I bombed Busan, Daegu. Then Kyoto, Tokyo. Beijing. Nearly got caught there. Then word reached me about some businesses wanting legit art from me." Jun-su shrugged. "Paint is expensive, school was expensive. I started doing more contract work to pay the bills, eventually make my way here. I got my green card for my 'artistic merits.'" He air-quoted. "My pieces make money now, so I get to live here with Tae-seok. I'll take it as long as we don't have to hide like that too. I do enough hiding."

"I don't think it's hiding when you're doing it to protect yourself. What you're doing is incredible." Isla felt humbled to even be talking to him. He made her work look like it came from a seventh-grade art class. His work had something to *say*. He'd tackled the Syrian refugee crisis, human trafficking, immigration, and the environment in major cities around the world. "I haven't followed your career closely, but . . . god, you're amazingly talented, and you're using your powers for good. I love your work. I love the piece in Uptown. We were all so jazzed to see your work in our city. If I was half the artist you are, I could die happy. I'm sorry, I'm rambling."

"That's how Ewan sounded when he described you," Jun-su said, sitting down next to her. Isla's cheeks warmed. "It's a pleasure to meet another artist. I've met some in the community, but I keep to myself. For obvious reasons."

"I wasn't very involved in Chicago's art community," Isla admitted, still flushed from Jun-su's offhanded comment about Ewan. "I just observed."

Jun-su nodded slowly. "You could pass a lot of time observing."

Well, ouch. That hit a little too close to home. "What are you working on now?"

They chatted for another hour, Isla's panic attack blown apart by the appearance of a famous street artist giving her tea and talking to her about depression as if they'd known each other for ages. He didn't have the bombastic presence that his artwork did. But then again, neither did she. She didn't tackle current political or social issues, but she did tackle the inside of an ailing, frightened mind and lay it out for the world to see. Not to judge; to recognize. She found herself telling him so, and Jun-su praised the choice as brave.

"You're brave," she countered. "I can barely stand to sell my work. Ewan bought the first one."

"Every piece I do frightens me," Jun-su said bluntly. "I overthink and obsess over every one. I just do it anyway."

I just do it anyway. When Jun-su left, after Isla insisted that he not waste his entire day when she could wait for Ewan by herself, his words rang in her ears. He made it sound so simple, yet they both knew it wasn't. The audacity it took to just do something anyway required a confidence that always slipped out of her reach at the last second, like a dream half remembered.

A wave of exhaustion swamped her. God, losing her shit sucked the very life out of her. Isla wandered around Ewan's living room and then went into his bedroom, feeling only a twinge of guilt at going into his private space because he had told her it was fine to lie down in here.

Wooden floors. A large rug the color of clotted cream underneath a queen-sized bed in the center. The duvet was dove gray, and gray-and-white-striped sheets peeked out from underneath soft, plush pillows. On the wall opposite the bed was a large and stunningly romantic art print of a couple, their faces obscured by an umbrella that was a shock of red in a sea of gray and black. The bedroom's two windows faced the green park of Memorial Plaza.

Isla pulled a soft white blanket off the top of an old wooden chest at the foot of the bed and crawled onto Ewan's bed, tugging the blanket around her as she rested her head on a pillow. And breathed. His scent was all over. She wanted to wear it like a shawl.

She contented herself, instead, with falling asleep.

*　*　*

Ewan returned to a quiet, dimly lit apartment. Jun-su had messaged when he left half an hour ago that all was well, but he didn't see Isla anywhere. Had she left too? He couldn't remember if he'd seen her car out front. He wasn't prepared for an empty apartment. Ewan carefully set the takeout for two on the counter. Well. It was fine. She didn't owe him anything, and if she'd needed to go home because she was embarrassed or didn't want to be here, she had every right to.

It was not fine. He'd just gotten her back, and he wasn't ready to confront another empty space without her filling it.

The afternoon rain shadows deepened the gloom in his apartment, and Ewan kept the lights off to match his mood. His fingers itched to text her, just a check-in and nothing more, but she probably needed space. They weren't really anything to each other but new friends and old coworkers of a sort, and there was no reason at all that her going home was just ruining his day, was there? When did you become so melodramatic, Park? Get a *grip*.

Scowling, Ewan went to his bedroom to change out of his work clothes.

And found Isla in his bed.

He stopped at the threshold, holding his breath lest the whoosh of air prove her form to be a specter that would disperse with the disturbance. Yet she remained, sleeping on top of the covers under a throw blanket. Her bare feet peeked out from underneath, and her dark hair fanned behind her on the pillow. She looked peaceful and disarmingly lovely, her freckles a burst of stardust, one fist tucked loosely under her pointed chin.

Ewan approached slowly, then sat lightly on the edge of the bed. Knowing she had stayed shifted his mood completely; finding her safe and resting in his bed layered his feelings in a way he'd have to examine later, because he didn't know what he would find. He did know that the urge to join her was a thick, drowsy pull he almost caved to. It would be so nice, his brain told him as she breathed deeply, to hold on to this sweet, sad girl and feel her breathe up against your chest. He brushed a few strands of hair away from her face and caught his breath when she sighed and leaned into his touch.

When Ewan left to let her sleep, he was acutely aware of her presence in the bedroom no matter where else he was in the apartment. The whole place felt different with her in it. Different yet . . . familiar.

He rather liked it.

* * *

The rain had stopped when Isla woke again. She could tell it was much later in the day. The setting sun had broken through the clouds, bathing the far wall in orange light. Isla's head still pulsed with a dry throb when she sat up, disoriented, having forgotten where she was again until the smell registered.

Ewan's room. Was he home?

She folded the blanket and put it back where she found it, then slipped quietly into the living room. Ewan sat at a computer desk tucked away in a corner, a single lamp on to let the rest of the living room soak in the dim glow of dusk. Over his broad back, she could see his hands steepled together in front of him, elbows on the desk.

"Hi," she croaked, wincing at the rusty-nail screech of her voice.

He turned around, then stood. She didn't know what to make of the pensiveness on his handsome face; the way his eyes searched her. It raised a very different flush of heat under her skin. "Hello, Isla. How did you sleep?"

"Fine," she said, for lack of a better response. "I, um . . . I pretty much hijacked your entire day, so I should probably go—"

"You can if you want, but . . ." Ewan's gaze swung toward the kitchen, where she spotted a takeout bag. "I have some pretty tasty food with your name on it, if you want to eat first."

He's just being nice, she reminded herself, even as her worn heart that had been through enough today, really, sighed with happiness. "I can stay for food."

They ate side by side on the couch, feasting on bulgogi and japchae. Isla was perfectly willing to let her earlier meltdown die in the past, but Ewan revived it with, "Do you have panic attacks often?"

"Yes." God, it was so heavy to carry it all alone. "Since I was a kid. I'm not . . . I'm not very well." Her voice trembled like a frightened rabbit. "I try to be. But I don't always handle things normally. I have an anxiety disorder that gives me panic attacks. I've also struggled with depression off and on. It can be hard, but I do the best I can. I don't usually tell people unless they find out the hard way." She felt naked in front of him.

Now he studied her thoughtfully, as if she were an art piece in a museum. Her cheeks grew even warmer. "You hide it very well. I just assumed you were shy."

The laughter that burst out of her was the kind of nervous, inappropriate noise that escaped her during funerals. "I am that too. But also quite anxious. Like Piglet from Winnie the Pooh."

The slow smile he gave her was a wrecked ship on the reef of her heart. All her worries washed away like bits of flotsam and jetsam. He didn't look alarmed by her admissions. He wasn't shooing her out of his apartment. He was . . . listening.

"If you're Piglet, I'm Rabbit," he said.

It coaxed a smile out of her. "Won't stand for anyone's nonsense?"

"Everyone needs to get off my lawn." Ewan shifted next to her, and her entire side tingled when his shoulder brushed against hers. "Isla, I'm sorry for taking you to that cave without giving you more details first. I didn't really give you a choice. I know you're too polite to tell me to shove it for doing that, so I'll say it for you."

"No, no, it's not . . ." Isla crossed her legs and stared hard at the rug to gather her thoughts and put this into words. "I mean, yes, information is nice to have up front. But I'm not actually that claustrophobic, or I didn't think I was. I take *comfort* from withdrawing to small spaces. I used to hide in bathrooms at work when I had a bad day. I wanted to be able to do that without having a panic attack, and I disappointed myself when it happened anyway."

"Your expectations of yourself are too high. Isla," he laughed, "it was an underground cave! You had every right to be scared! You may not believe this about you, but I'll believe it for both of us—you were *brave*. You wanted to pet the *bats*. When I took Tae down there, he called me a son of a bitch."

Isla smiled into the fist she propped her chin up with. "I guess."

"You were."

"Okay, okay. I was brave. But I didn't feel brave at the time, and then I worried it would keep happening every time I try to push myself through this fear to do things I want to do. I worried that you'd . . ." Isla dared a glance up at him. ". . . that you'd get tired of it. I like your company. But I know my company is not always fun, or predictable."

"Why would I want predictable?"

Isla didn't have a response to that, but she was sure her face had a lot more to say.

"How do you feel now?"

"Better. And thank you, for today and for the cave. It's not always intuitive to know what to do when someone's having a panic attack, and you did the best you could have in both situations."

Ewan nodded and went quiet for a while. "Some of my patients talk to me, since I see them for a long period of time. I've heard some . . . really depressing tales of dead parents, spouses, children. Disease and depression over their injuries, amputations, what have you." Her skin came alive when he rested his hand on top of hers and squeezed her fingers. "It was cathartic for them to have someone listen. I've never really experienced it myself, so I can't say I know what you're going through, but I know it helps to talk about it, and I'm glad you told me. Please let me know if there's anything I can do to help. As a friend. At least, I hope we qualify as friends now. You slept in my bed."

Even if nothing else worked out, and even if it hurt, Isla wanted nothing more than to be friends with this sweet, kind man. "I think we qualify as friends. Especially with the bed sleeping. That's like the number-one qualification. It's comfy too."

He playfully nudged her shoulder. "I told you."

Isla never wanted to leave. But it grew late, and she had to get home. Ewan walked her out to her car after bagging up her leftovers for her. As they faced each other, she blurted it without thinking. "I felt safe with you today, when I normally don't feel very safe when things get bad like that. I . . ." Why did admitting her affection feel like handing over a mortal weapon? "I'll see you for coffee on Tuesday?"

Why was this so hard?

Ewan smiled slowly. "I look forward to it."

CHAPTER SEVENTEEN

"Got a delivery, Ewan," Barbara said in a sly, suggestive tone. Her cat-eye glasses were perched on the end of her nose, the costume jewelry rhinestones of their chain flashing under the fluorescents. He'd always thought Barb resembled one of those Russian dolls that hid another doll inside it, and then another and another. Round, brightly colored, just a little gaudy.

He slowed, frowned. His lunch, a sandwich from a shop around the corner because he'd forgotten to pack one that morning, was in a bag clutched in his hand. It had been a shit day from the start, because he'd spilled coffee all over his pants, like a winner, then had to go home to grab a fresh pair. And *still* forgotten his lunch. "I can't . . . place that tone, Barb." She made it sound like someone had mailed him porn.

"Came in while you were out. Check your office, sweetie."

Ewan's teeth ground together as he flashed her a smile and walked away. This woman had a way of making him feel like he was twelve instead of a grown ass man.

His annoyance fled, however, at the sight of the flowers on his desk.

A bouquet of delicate, fragrant flowers in a clear vase: purple tulips, lavender roses and hydrangeas, clusters of violets. Among the sea of purple shades were little bright sunbursts of yellow buttercups. He set down his lunch and plucked out the card.

Thank you again, Rabbit.
—Isla

No one had ever sent him flowers before.

He leaned down and pressed his nose against the velvet-soft petals, breathed in the potent hydrangeas, the delicate scent of the roses, the radiant buttercups. He sat at his desk and pulled a lone buttercup from the bunch, slowly twirling it by its slender green stem. Receiving the bouquet from Isla felt like receiving another long, tight hug.

Thank you for the flowers, Buttercup, he texted.

He meant it to lightly tease, to match her silly Hundred Acre Wood nickname for him, but Ewan knew it was spot on as soon as he typed it. It was exactly the right nickname for her. It fit.

I hope you like purple, she replied.

It's my favorite color, he typed. *What are you doing Saturday?*

* * *

Isla had been standing in front of the red brick house for a good five minutes now, and so far the universe was denying her even an ounce of the confidence required to knock on the front door. There was no reason on earth for this. She had already met Jun-su, and she had definitely already met Ewan, but this was different. He was inviting her into his life now, and the weight of that request kept her shoes stuck on the sidewalk.

Until the door opened.

"Hey," Ewan greeted her. "You've got the right house."

Isla eagerly grabbed the save he'd unknowingly handed her. "I wasn't sure. Hi! I brought dessert."

"Oh good, because that was a requirement I forgot to tell you about. The entry fee is a baked good."

"I like to be prepared." Ewan took the plastic-wrapped chocolate chip banana bread loaf from her, then wrapped an arm around her shoulders and pulled her in for a hug. Isla sighed into his shoulder at the feel of his warm, solid body against hers, then tentatively snuck her arms around his waist for a quick squeeze. She kept her head down after so he couldn't see the complicated feelings that hug gave her, which he would not understand and she could not explain.

Because he'd called her buttercup.

Thank you for the flowers, Buttercup.

That string led to future Ewan, the first sign that the two were linked, one and the same, and it made her feel untethered to the ground. As light as dandelion fluff careening through the air at the whim of puckered lips.

It's been a long week without you, Buttercup.

"Isla!" Jun-su appeared from the kitchen with a taller man in tow. "Welcome. This is Tae-seok, my boyfriend."

Tae-seok was tall, his skin a deep bronze, his short, wavy black hair parted down the middle and framing a longer face with high cheekbones and a pointed chin. He was cute in a different way, a little like her. He looked at her speculatively, seriously enough that it made Isla nervous. Then he broke out into a smile so sunny that Isla couldn't help but smile back reflexively.

"Tae is fine," he said. "You are the painter."

"Yes. Ewan told me you work at the Missouri Botanical Garden. What do you do there?"

"I keep the plants alive."

"It's a little more involved than that," Ewan said as he came up behind her. "He's a horticulturist."

"I make the gardens pretty too."

"On behalf of the plants in Ewan's apartment, thank you for keeping them alive," Isla said. Ewan feigned shock at her audacity as Tae laughed.

"Want to come see my worm farm?" he asked.

"Don't do it. He means it," Ewan warned.

"Are you kidding?" Isla turned to Tae. "Show me."

No, he was not kidding: he led her down to the basement and showed her the worm farm hiding in an inconspicuous cooler and gave her a fifteen-minute lecture on why worm composting was excellent for a garden, then took her outside and showed her his beautiful backyard garden. She wandered the rock path past towering sunflowers, blush-pink roses, short stalks of mint, and vibrant green basil. Tae gave her a sprig of lavender, instructing her to crush some of it between her fingers, and the bloom of lavender scent that spritzed the air lay sweet and clean in her nose.

By dinner, Isla had lost count of the number of fruit-flavored soju shots she'd sampled. The number was high enough to equate to a drunk Isla. It made her braver and freed the words she trapped in her head, even when those words wanted to help her make new friends.

"Tae, have you ever gone with Jun-su to tag a city?" she asked. Their couch had hidden recliners, and Isla curled up on one next to Ewan, whose close proximity cranked up the heat in the living room. Tae was sprawled on the other couch, and Jun-su sat on the floor so Tae could play with his hair.

"Germany," Tae replied, closing his eyes and smiling. "We drove to the Alps."

"We went to Austria too," Jun-su added. "It was Tae-seok's first time in Europe. We've been all over East Asia."

"It must be amazing to see so much of the world," Isla sighed.

"You will," Tae said confidently. "Now Jun-su, ask her."

The street artist finished his shot and then climbed to his feet. "Isla, how would you feel about collaborating with me on a project?"

The thought of collaborating with him on anything made her light-headed. "Um, pretty fantastic about it. But I've never created art the way you do."

"Not a problem we can't handle."

So he thought. "What's the project?"

He told her the Korean folktale of Gyeon-wu, a shepherd, and Jik-nyeo, a weaver, a pair of lovers who lived on opposite sides of the Milky Way and were forbidden from seeing each other but once a year because they failed to uphold their duties after they fell in love. The universe's crows and magpies took pity on them and created a bridge so the lovers could meet on the seventh day of the seventh month of the year. It was said, Jun-su told her, that the tears they cried at their parting were the start of the monsoon season.

"It's one of my favorite Korean folktales," Ewan interjected. "My umma used to tell it to me when I was a kid."

Jun-su aimed to recreate the lovers' meeting over the magpie bridge, with the Milky Way scattering stars all around them, and he wanted her impressionist style to build the background his art would lay over.

The more he talked about the logistics of collaborating, the more trepidation Isla felt at painting with him. He was so damn talented, and she didn't know how she would do at painting with an audience. It was a very solitary endeavor for her. Jun-su was a peer who had an artist's perspective when he looked at her work. He's trying to help, she reminded herself. And any feedback he gives you is meant to build you up, not tear you down.

"You would be credited and compensated," Jun-su told her, growing so excited that he paced around the living room. "This could be good for your career. It's how I broke into the community. Can we sketch ideas later?"

"Yes!" Her gaze clashed with Ewan's, and he gave her a wide grin that almost matched her excitement. Well, excitement and utter terror.

One of these days, she'd learned to get comfortable with good things happening to her as well as bad things. One day, her heart and her mind might be able to tell the difference between the two.

*　*　*

Seeing Isla in more spaces outside the coffee shop felt like letting the world in on a secret only Ewan knew. Isla admitted that she rarely showed herself in public spaces other than the coffee shop but was trying to get comfortable with doing more.

The first few times she appeared at Jun-su and Tae's to work on the sketches for the commission piece, she'd ghost around the house like every hour was midnight. After the third visit, she'd grown comfortable enough to help herself to water in the fridge and ask Tae questions about the plants he grew inside the house.

Ewan didn't need to be there when Isla stopped by to work with Jun-su, but he had no reason *not* to. He'd never seen her paint before, so he sat in Jun-su's studio and observed them, bringing a book with him so he wouldn't make it obvious and fluster Isla with an audience.

Something curious happened to her the further she got into a painting. Her face became its own canvas of concentration and wonder and intensity while the scene came to life under her talented fingers. Isla, it seemed, was her most confident while she lived in a painting. Once, when her mind hadn't quite shaken the space it went into while she worked, she aimed those dove-gray eyes at him, direct, single-minded, *alive*, and his breath caught and held, held, as long as their eyes met before hers broke away, still in that other place, and perhaps she hadn't seen him at all.

They were friends. But sometimes he wanted to see what his friend would do if he slipped that sweater off her shoulder and kneaded those tight muscles, then slid his hand up her graceful neck to position her just so, just right for a kiss. And maybe he would make her smile and he'd get to see that pair of charmingly crooked lower teeth, turned into each other like lovers.

He wanted to be alone with her.

The thought stopped him in his tracks, quite literally, as he'd been at the store when the realization popped into his head, and a woman with a cart behind him accidentally rammed her cart's wheel against his bare ankle. *Jesus*, that hurt.

"I'm sorry," she said distractedly, and her child, a towheaded toddler with something dark and sticky on his fingers, twisted around to look at Ewan and laugh.

"It's fine." It was not fine. It hurt like hell, and she'd broken the skin. Her child gave a birdlike shriek, and Ewan wanted to hiss at him and the mother, who was too busy looking at her phone to even deliver a proper apology for ramming her cart into him. He walked away with his shopping basket slung over an arm and a throbbing ankle, and it took him until checkout to pick up the thread of the mental conversation he'd dropped in the cereal aisle.

It occurred to him that he and Isla were rarely alone together, and he craved that possibility the way he craved the solitude and beauty of a mountain trail on a clear morning.

Ewan couldn't find the day or time in his past when his attraction and affection for Isla had appeared . . . but maybe there wasn't any one instance. Maybe it was a culmination of little moments. Her unwavering focus when she painted. Her patience and interest when Tae talked about worm farms for thirty minutes. Her cardigans and skirts and lemon-yellow sunglasses. Her flustered horror when she'd thrown coffee on his shirt and her snappy embarrassment when he called her on it. Her willingness to follow him into a cave and face her own fears.

She doled out details of her life and who she was like someone scattering bread crumbs for the birds. Just a little bit here and there, just enough for him to want to know more. But she couldn't hide when she painted. Her whole self was on display in those pieces of art: her joy, her passion, her heartache and grief. There was a story behind every one, and he wanted to hear them. The contained way she carried herself was such a direct contrast to the art he saw her create. He wanted to merge the two somehow. Find the bridge connecting the painter and the shy graphic designer.

There was only one thing left to do now.

*　*　*

When the day came for work to begin on the commission, Isla felt no more ready than when Jun-su had asked to begin with. She'd practiced with sketches and smaller versions at home over the last two weeks and tested out translating the base impressionist background onto bricks in Jun-su's studio, but nothing prepared her for the face of the blank brick wall on the east side of a building that housed a restaurant and a comic book shop in The Grove.

"It's just another canvas," Jun-su told her frozen expression.

"I can't create a new brick wall if I ruin the base," Isla noted, anxiety beginning its fervent pacing within the confines of her stomach.

"I wouldn't work with someone who did not prove they could do this, and you did," Jun-su reminded her. "Now let's paint the primer. You have everything you need here."

Primer, Isla could do. She shoved her insecurities forcibly to the side and helped with the monotonous task of painting a primer coat of paint over the cleaned brick wall. While the primer dried, they left to grab lunch, and by the time they returned, Isla's anxiety changed to a buzz of adrenaline that she could use. They had a painted mural of the work to reference, split into a grid identical to the larger grid they'd sketched on the brick; painting individual squares was the easiest path to creating the whole. She could replicate that mural on the brick. She was capable.

The work was hard and invigorating. Isla's sense of self scattered to encompass that entire brick wall, painted itself onto every brick her brush stroked. Time was a distant idea—all that really mattered was the daylight to work by, the sweet ache in her hands when the sun set. She took two days off for uninterrupted time with the mural, and when she had to work, she arrived early in the morning and after her shift to add to it. At night, Jun-su spray-painted behind her to overlay his detailed work on top of her dreamy, incandescent bridge of magpies and the star-crossed lovers. When their shifts overlapped and they spoke, they did so in short bursts, like bird chatter across a forest.

By Friday, the mural was nearly finished and needed only a few final last touches. It was warm for October, and Isla was in a T-shirt and yoga pants. Jun-su had pushed back his hair with a red bandanna; she could see sweat glisten on the back of his neck from her vantage point below him. Both of them had learned to ignore the curious gazes of passersby. The addition of Isla's painting style wouldn't mark this piece as Woo on sight, but just in case, Jun-su wore a face mask during the day to keep anyone from snapping pictures.

Every minute that marched by saw the mural more complete, as the galaxy's stars scattered around the lovers, as the magpies with their black, blue, and white feathers spread their lovely wings. A fierce pride surged in Isla's chest. She understood now why Jun-su did this. She could feel the story of the painting flow from her fingertips down into her marrow.

When she was out of daylight and had to stop for the day, Isla climbed down the ladder and set her feet on solid pavement. She stretched, dancing awkwardly on her tiptoes, then turned around to face the street.

"Oh!"

Isla jumped back in horror as a paintbrush smeared a blue streak across her already paint-splattered old T-shirt. Ewan stood in front of her with the paintbrush in his hand, adopting a look of surprise that she didn't believe for a second.

"I am *so sorry*," he said. "I didn't think you were going to turn around."

"Why are you holding a paintbrush?" she asked.

"I was going to help."

"Keep away from my mural," Jun-su called from the ladder.

"Here, let me just . . ." Ewan set down the paintbrush, grabbed an old towel in their rag pile, and dabbed uselessly at the paint stain. "Let's try to get this out."

"It won't work," Isla laughed, batting his hands away. "I can't believe you did that!"

"It was really rude of me." Ewan's grin did not match his words. "Can I make it up to you?"

She heard the echo of her own words to him all those months ago and set her hands on her hips. "I think you've done enough."

"Mmm. I haven't, though." He folded his arms, which only accentuated his toned biceps. "How about this. I haven't been able to put my finger on what it is about you, Buttercup, that keeps you in my thoughts constantly. I'm starting to get an idea, but I need more time. With you. Can I take you on a date?"

Isla smiled.

CHAPTER EIGHTEEN

"You can do this, girl."

"Yes. Yep. Totally."

"I don't hear the conviction in your voice."

Isla worried her lower lip as she eyed the white building and domed glass front of the entrance to the Botanical Garden. Wings of excitement and panic fluttered madly in her chest.

And Willow didn't hear the conviction in her voice because she was meeting Ewan.

For a date.

Isla closed her hand into a fist and settled it in front of her heart, right by the source of a deep and fierce ache that was heady and frightening, like staring down at the water from a diving board seconds before the jump.

"You're real quiet, babe. Did you drop?"

"No, I just second-guessed myself a whole lot."

"Quit that shit," Willow ordered. "This is your life. Meet him and enjoy yourself. And come visit before winter. I miss you."

"I plan to."

"Bring your boy."

"He's not my boy yet."

"You slept in his *bed*."

"Just slept." But Isla couldn't tame her grin. "I could probably ask if he wanted to come, if this goes well, but I really just want to visit with you." She missed Willow fiercely. It had been natural to call her before meeting Ewan, and Willow been thrilled to hear from her.

"Aww, I'm still your favorite?"

"You're always my favorite," Isla said. "Even when you make me try gross dry wine."

"Your palate is still unsophisticated. Now don't be late. Don't loiter. We deserve to be happy, bitch. Now go be happy."

Isla laughed shakily and hung up. She took a deep breath and went in. When she tried to pay for her ticket, she found that it had already been paid for, and she was ushered inside to shift through the throngs of couples, families, and kids. She texted Ewan to let him know she'd arrived and thanked him for the ticket, then gave her attention to the quaint walking paths, the trees wearing their crowns of fiery red and dazzling orange, the bundles of flowers in jewel-toned splashes. She found her way to a still, square pond with three pillars rising from the far end. Stone fairy children sprung from the tops of the pillars, frozen mid takeoff, wings outstretched.

Her phone pinged. *Find me at the Tower Grove House.*

Did you leave me a trail of breadcrumbs? she asked.

You'll find your way, fair maiden. I'm sure of it.

. . . but text me if you really get lost.

Isla consulted her map, then carefully followed the paths that would lead to the white house. To her delight, she passed a hedge maze to her left, then detoured to wind through the tall green hedges until it deposited her next to the charming, old white house. Ewan and Tae stood by its main doors.

Ewan managed to look both sharp and dressed down in a white button-down, rolled up at the sleeves, over tight black pants. He had done something different to his hair too; instead of being styled off to the side, it covered his forehead, making him look less professional and more relaxed. His sunglasses were perched on his head, so when he turned to look at her, she saw his eyes crinkle up as he smiled at her.

"Hi, Buttercup," he said, then surprised her with a tight hug and a chaste kiss to the cheek that sent heat pinwheeling out from the place where his lips touched her skin like an exploding firework. "What do you think so far? Can it compare to Chicago's?"

"The jury's still out on that," she replied. "Tae, are you our tour guide?"

"No, I just wanted to say hi." Tae grinned. "Actually, yes, but only for thirty minutes. I have real work to do, *Ewan Sung-ho.*"

He gave her some background on the history of one of the oldest botanical gardens in the country. Tae had an off-handed, amusing way of playing tour guide that kept you listening and on your toes. When they walked back outside and into the sunlight, he put on a tan, wide-brimmed gardening hat that had been hanging on a cord around his neck.

Neither Isla nor Ewan spoke much, as Tae did most of the talking. She was mainly absorbed in her surroundings and trying not to pay too much attention to Ewan, taking in the flowers, tranquil ponds, stone bridges, and artistic works hidden throughout the gardens. Every so often she apologized to

Tae and asked him to pause so she could take photos, hoping she could sift through them later for inspiration for another art piece.

Each time she did, she found Ewan looking at her.

She found she didn't mind.

* * *

Isla herself could have been a painting. She sat on the grass in front of an eye-shaped gap in a decorative wall as she took a picture. The skirt of her dusky rose dress flared out around her in a circle, her back unusually straight and poised as she sat still to get the right shot. Her hair was up in a ponytail, bangs fluttering in the breeze, her head tilted to the side. Ewan could see delicate shoulder blades and the curve of her neck. A slow, dreamy flush of heat ran a river through him.

He wanted to steal a picture of her just like this, but Tae was watching, and he didn't trust Tae not to say anything out loud. He didn't care if he was embarrassed, but he figured it would embarrass Isla. Subtlety wasn't a strong suit of Tae's. So he had to content himself with committing the picture she made to memory.

"You like her," Tae said, switching to Korean in case she overheard.

"Yes," Ewan replied in kind. He took a second to think through his next response to make sure he had the sentence structure right. "I'm starting to realize how much."

Tae studied her too. "She's a nice girl. Not beautiful. Different."

Ewan resisted the urge to smack Tae in the back of the head, even though Tae said it in an observational way, without malice or judgment. He settled for a dirty look. There was a phrase he wanted to use, but he couldn't think of its

Korean equivalent, so he used the English version. "Beauty is in the eye of the beholder."

"What?"

"We decide who and what is beautiful. People are a spectrum, Tae, not a rigid standard. I kept telling myself she wasn't my type, but I don't think that's true anymore. I think she's adorable."

Tae shrugged, hardly fazed by Ewan's glower. "Have you asked her out? And don't say, 'But Tae, we're out now.' I'm here, it doesn't count. Don't make me the third wheel."

"I did; this is the date."

"Then why am I *here*?"

Ewan looked at him innocently. "I needed a guide."

Tae shook his head and stalked off, his gardening hat bobbing furiously as he walked. He said something to Isla, who had been talking sweetly to a duck waddling by as she took its photo. Isla waved, and Tae was off.

She stood and smoothed out her skirt. "Tae told me to let you know he doesn't work for you."

"He'll tell me himself again half a dozen times." Ewan reached out to take her hand, enjoying the feel of her fingers threading through his of their own volition.

He wished he'd taken her picture. But there would be other opportunities in the future.

* * *

Isla marveled at how loose limbed she was around him, how the fluttering in her belly when he spoke was born from thrilling excitement instead of disproportionate terror and bundles of nerves the size of watermelons. Isla breathed easy in his presence even though her pulse tripped over itself. When their fingers grazed as she passed her cocktail to give him a taste at lunch, the jolt from the contact raced up her arm like lightning. Her mind stayed quiet. It behaved. She was just allowed to be.

Who was this girl who flirted with a handsome man and strolled through gardens and casually talked about her budding career as an artist?

It was her. Really her. She could be, and was, that girl.

No, that wasn't quite right. She *let* herself be. You have more control than you realize, her therapist had told her recently. You are not at the mercy of your shadow self.

They got ice cream after their late lunch in Lafayette Square, which had adorable Victorian townhomes. Isla left her car at Ewan's and he drove, chatting about the neighborhoods and things to do all the while. They walked through the park while she enjoyed a scoop of salted caramel, and Ewan had blackberry and sweet cream. He gave her a taste, and she relished licking the spoon that had been in his mouth. More than ever, she had spent her nights wondering what his lips would taste like.

The day was still young, and the air grew bloated with the possibilities for *how* it would end, and so Isla grabbed the bull by the horns.

"Would you . . . would you like to see some of the other work I've done? That's not on my website?"

Ewan's dark eyes lit up. "Yes, definitely."

"They're at my place," she said, hoping it came out casual. God, her palms were sweaty. "I live about an hour outside the city. It's peaceful. I could make dinner tonight and show you the paintings, if you wanted to come. They're not spectacular or anything, and some are unfinished, but . . ." Stop talking stop talking stop talking! "They're, well, there's certainly a progression on my improvement, since some of them are . . . older . . ." Oh god, she wanted to sink into the ground and die. She had no idea what she was trying to say with that last bit, and now she'd made the whole evening sound like it was All About Her when really she just wanted his company and to maybe sit next to him, on a couch.

She wanted to cringe away from the way he looked at her, and she had to glance off to the pavement rather than meet his eyes. Her cheeks were flames and her hands were clasped tightly together in front of her. A bright burst of laughter from a street over made her flinch.

He stepped close, close enough he could have sheltered under an umbrella with her if it had been raining. His warm hands wrapped around her upper arms, where he merely held on to her. She could feel his forehead inches from her. "Let's go," he said.

Isla smiled down at her shoes.

They drove separately, which gave her enough time to take mental stock of the contents of her fridge and panic over what to make them for dinner. The closer they drew to the cottage, however, with her fervently checking behind her to make sure he was still there, the more unreal it felt to bring Ewan to the place where she'd met him for the first time under impossible circumstances.

He got out of his car when she did, and stood with her in front of the cottage with its white wraparound fence.

"You live in a fairy tale," he said, pleasure turning his beauty into something striking.

You don't know how true that is, Isla thought. "Welcome," she said.

Isla let Ewan Park into the house where it had all started.

*　*　*

"What do you miss about Chicago?" Ewan asked.

"Hmm." Isla stared up at the sky as she thought about it. The night was chilly, so they'd started a small fire in the firepit on the back patio, and now they sat close under some blankets, drinking wine and eating slices of lemon cake they'd made together. "The sounds of my neighbors. Not the loud ones. Not, you know, the apartment that blasted EDM until one in the morning, or my downstairs neighbor who used to stream his calls with his girlfriend through the television, so I could hear *everything*."

Ewan snorted, then let out a small, delayed laugh. His foot bumped against hers.

"The smaller things. Hearing music playing from someone's open window while they cleaned. Walking two blocks to a bookstore or café. On weekend mornings, I could hear someone practicing piano from my kitchen window. I used to lean against the stove with my coffee and just listen to it. I miss those small sounds of lives being lived around me."

"You make it sound romantic."

"It is. Things are romantic when you make them be. When you frame it like that."

Ewan clasped her knee. "That reminds me. Show me the fruits of your labor."

It was not as nerve-racking as expected to have him wander around staring at her paintings, carefully peeling one back from another and pausing to take it in. When he particularly liked a piece, he would hum in the back of his throat, almost unconsciously. Isla was grateful he wasn't looking at her, because she was fairly certain her face looked like a bright-red apple at the height of autumn every time he expressed his pleasure in that low, pleased *hmmm*.

"This is nice," he would say while carefully tracing his finger over a line or a curve, as if the canvas were still wet and he were afraid to smudge the paint and ruin it. "This color gradient. I've never understood how artists like you and Jun-su do it."

"Sometimes we're not even sure."

He looked back and smiled. His gaze drifted toward a painting to his right. "That's one of my favorites."

And there it was. The wall of a backyard garden behind a boutique in a Michigan lake town. Its cotton-candy-pink wall, faded and cracked, meeting worn gray stone and the shock of electric blue framing on the windows. Green ferns fanned out in a cluster along the bottom of the wall and one old rake leaned against the painted stone.

"Where is this?" he asked.

"A backyard," she said, her heart in her throat. "Nothing magical."

"Backyards are magical," he objected, his tone light, teasing. His eyes met hers again. "Don't you remember being five? Backyards were the whole world."

It grew dark, and neither bothered to check the time. They sat on the floor of the living room, cross-legged, giggling drunk and still gorging on dessert. She had confiscated Ewan's phone to scroll through his music. She had known all the metal would be there, but it thrilled her anyway to see with her own eyes that future Ewan had been a real part of her life before this Ewan came into it.

"The Gazette?" Isla asked as she hit play. When the heavy guitar riff snarled to life, she unconsciously nodded her head to the beat.

Ewan grinned so cutely that she wanted to . . . well, do to him what cats do when they show affection. Purr, nip, knead. "They're a visual kei band." Over the music, which had transitioned to fast, rhythmic drumbeats and a lot of screaming, he launched into an explanation of visual kei and Japanese metal. Isla let him go, loving his enthusiasm as much as she loved him. Or loving him more because of it. It added another gradient to his character, deepening the shades of him.

"Sounds like their shows would be wild," Isla said. "I'd see one."

"Really?"

"Of course!"

Ewan gave her a long look. "Isla Abbott, I may just have to keep you."

"Would you?" Oh god! Had she said that? Her eyes went wide, shocked at her own damn self for such a bold, flirtatious statement. Who was she? Who was this woman? "I . . ." Her mouth opened, then shut, and then she had to look away from him because he was staring at her with his head tilted, a smile playing at his lips, his eyes bright as stars.

As if he *liked* her. Really liked being here with her.

She saw him move out of the corner of her eye, but she was frozen in her position, as if he couldn't see her as long as she kept still. The breath left her in a shaky exhale when his fingers touched her chin and he drew her head up.

He was so close that she could feel his warm breath grazing her cheek. "Isla, may I kiss you? I'd like to."

Her chest was a sun going supernova. "Are you sure?" she whispered.

There went that slight smile again, where his lips parted and his white teeth peeked out behind a partially drawn curtain. "You are adorable," he whispered back, then closed the distance and pressed his mouth to hers.

Kissing Ewan seized her heart, like a great hand squeezing and then letting go, leaving its warmth all around her. She was out of practice, but Ewan took his time, their lips meeting slowly and languidly until she had the hang of it. The first hint of his tongue sent a shock wave through her, and a little gasp escaped her throat. Ewan clasped the back of her neck, his palm cradling her head as he subtly deepened the kiss and their tongues met for the first time. It was more than she had ever hoped for; the simple act of kissing Ewan.

She wanted to do this with him forever.

When the kiss finally broke, Isla could barely keep her eyes open. They wanted to slide shut in a dreamy state she could just float in for the rest of the weekend. Their noses brushed. Isla took the opportunity to run her fingers through his hair. "It's as soft as I thought it would be," she said, her voice barely audible. He captured her lips again, and Isla eagerly met his growing intensity, wanting every caress of his tongue, craving every second their bodies were connected.

"Do friends kiss?" she asked breathlessly, breaking it off when she felt herself being directed gradually back onto the couch. God, she wanted nothing more than to feel him against her, but she had to be sure. It had to be clear, what this was, what it could turn into. The future she wanted so badly.

"We are friends," Ewan agreed, pleasing her with his unsteady breath. He brushed her bangs back from her forehead. "You have the softest skin," he said, almost to himself. He ran his thumb across her cheek. "But I want to be something more, if you'll have me."

"Ewan," she said, unable to contain a giggle. "Why do you think I gave up all of my remote days just to sit in that coffee shop?"

Ewan laughed with her, and hugged her to him as if she was some precious thing he didn't want to let go of. She clasped him wholeheartedly, practically climbing into his lap. She did not know how all of her vital organs stayed contained inside her, because she was bursting at the seams with joy and excitement and terror.

The man who had loved her in another world—he was here. She'd found him in this one.

CHAPTER NINETEEN

Isla's house in the woods quenched a thirst Ewan didn't know he had. From that first day onward, he loved coasting up her long drive, hearing the cicadas and katydids sing in the trees as he walked up her porch. They were as loud as ambulance sirens this far out. Her decor was all distressed white wood, gray floors, delicate and lacy things lifted from homes of the past two centuries. The soothing atmosphere Isla had built around herself was as welcoming and refreshing as she was.

Soft music played as Isla painted, and Ewan looked up occasionally from his book to watch her work. She stood on the drop cloth protecting the wood floor and painted a remarkably grim, swampy landscape. Sometimes she would pause, sigh, put down her brush, and walk a small circle on the rug, raise her arms above her head and stretch. It was endlessly fascinating to watch the suggestion of a place come to life on the canvas. Random streaks of oranges and blues became a sunset, then an ocean, and then a boat floating on the rippling waters. Tufts and bushels of purple became lavender fields. She stretched again, her T-shirt rising to expose her stomach and the curve of her lower back. Isla stared at the work and sighed again. "I'm not in the right frame of mind to finish this one today."

Ewan put down his book and walked up behind her. Isla's shoulders slumped when he started to massage her stiff muscles. "You carry the entire world on your shoulders," he murmured. He'd treated men twice her age with blood pressure shooting through the roof that didn't have muscles as tight and unforgiving as she did. No wonder she was prone to headaches. Cervicogenic, most likely.

"Come with me," he said. He led her by the hand to her bedroom, then pulled out the small bottle of almond oil he'd stashed in his bag. "Your knots have knots," he told her as he set the bottle on the bedside dresser. Isla's pale skin pinkened behind her freckles as he stepped up to her and traced his fingers along the edge of her gray shirt. He could get drunk off of her visceral reactions to him.

"I need your back bare to massage it, Buttercup," he said quietly. "May I?"

She let out a long, shaky breath, but nodded eagerly. It was so cute that Ewan captured her mouth in a long, sweet kiss. He slowly lifted her shirt at the same time, dragging his knuckles up her waist. They broke the kiss to lift her shirt over her head, and Isla returned to it instantly, making him smile against her lips.

"We're getting off track," he murmured as he felt around behind her for the bra strap.

"I don't think so," she disagreed, sinking her hand into his thick hair and scratching his scalp with her fingernails. A shiver of delight traveled down his spine. He unhooked her bra, and she reluctantly pulled her hand away to take it off. Before he got sidetracked, Ewan turned her around to face the bed.

He gave her a gentle nudge. "Go lie down."

Isla shot a look behind her that he felt in his gut. She hooked her thumbs under the waistband of her pants and tugged them down, leaving her in underwear decorated with pale-yellow flowers. She lay on her stomach, and Ewan took a moment to admire the gentle curve of her back, the wings of her shoulder blades, the fine, wispy hairs at the nape of her neck underneath her ponytail. The hand toss of small moles along her skin fell like shooting stars from the sky of faint, pale freckles across her upper back.

Ewan was careful as he sat, distributing his weight down into his legs on either side of her hips. He removed his belt so it wouldn't accidentally dig into her when he leaned forward. He knew his pants could not hide how happy he was to be here, and the fact that Isla said nothing, only breathed in deeply and closed her eyes, flushed him with even more heat.

"I do not do this with my patients," he said. Isla breathed out a laugh. "Now relax," he said. He brushed her ponytail away from her back and slathered the oil on his hands. "Tell me if there's too much or too little pressure."

* * *

She didn't know how he made that sound sensual, but he did. She could have purred like a cat at the low, soothing pitch of his voice. Isla stifled a groan when he started to massage her shoulders, slowly and deliberately. He used the heel of his hand and his forearm too, running it along her shoulder blades and targeting stiff and sore muscles.

"Is the pressure okay?" he asked. "You will not hurt my feelings if you tell me to change something—I don't want you to be uncomfortable."

"Maybe a little"—Isla bit her lip—"harder." He obliged, and she fell silent, acutely aware of where he was sitting and the heavy hardness pressing into her low back. As much as she wanted—and needed—the massage, she equally wanted to get up, strip him, and let her hands roam like his did. But this . . . this was divine. Before Ewan, she had never realized how starved she was of the simple act of touching another human being. It was intoxicating.

Ewan worked his way down to the center of her back, then lifted each of her arms. He rubbed circles down to her hands, then slowly and deeply massaged her palms. She looked up to see their hands clasped together, hers limp, his deep veined and strong as his fingers wandered her hand. Isla had officially transitioned from a solid being to a liquid state. She could never get a massage from another person now.

She would have completely missed him pulling down her underwear if she hadn't felt the sudden cool air. He said nothing and continued massaging, kneading into her glutes. She inhaled sharply when he flattened his palm and ran it down to the back of her thigh. All the sensation her body could feel had homed into wherever his hands were—she was aware of nothing save the pounding of her heart, the faint smell of almonds, and his gradually unsteady breathing.

Isla gasped quietly when his hand slid down between her legs, then cupped her. Her hands curled into fists. He dragged a finger against her once, twice, and Isla squirmed as he grew more adventurous. His fingers traced her, then slipped inside in a rhythmic motion. Isla rose to her elbows, gasping into the pillow, her hips following the rhythm. He didn't stop until she was shaking and breathing his name frantically.

When she couldn't feel him anymore, Isla tried to get up to meet him, but Ewan stilled her with a quiet, firm, "No, Buttercup. Stay."

She gladly acquiesced to the soft command in his voice and the promise of what would come next. Isla stayed on her elbows and let him position her hips. It felt delicious, wicked; she had never wanted anyone or anything so badly in all her life. She could feel him hover at the threshold as he stretched out over her, gently pressing his now bare stomach against her back. He kissed her shoulder, and their eyes met—his dark and hungry, hers foggy and mesmerized.

Ewan pressed forward with a shuddering sigh, and Isla took him in with a high gasp. He moved torturously slow, and she gripped the sheets. As the pleasure mounted and her whole body throbbed with need, she flailed a hand behind her until she caught his hair again, sinking her fingers in the strands for purchase. Ewan dropped his head on her shoulder and increased the pace by a fraction, but she felt the change like an earthquake.

Her body rushed toward something that would cause her very cells to fly apart. The intensity of the sensations was borderline frightening and Isla had no choice but to meet them headlong, but Ewan was with her, their gasps intermingling in a staggered chorus. They were still so new together, learning each other, and this time it was a tidal wave that would drown her. He sneaked his hand down between them, pushing against her to put pressure right where she needed it.

Isla buried her head in the pillow as she came apart, and Ewan held her to him as he gasped explosively into her hair and climaxed not long after her.

"I like being your patient," she said breathlessly. He laughed huskily against her shoulder.

It was the middle of the day, but they crawled under the covers anyway, wrapped up in each other, talking in drowsy voices and touching, always touching. Isla couldn't get enough. Feeling the wiry, hard muscles under his lean frame, watching his face relax or spread in a lazy smile because of her caresses. The newness of sleeping next to him, of the little, gargantuan touches like his hand caressing the small of her back, stole her breath. Never in her life, until she let him in, had she thought feelings and sensations like this existed. He made her feel . . . beautiful.

* * *

They started alternating weekends between his place and hers, although Ewan seemed to prefer making the drive to her. Sometimes he even beat her to her place, like today, because she had to drop packages off at the post office first. Isla sent a quick text to Ewan to explain the situation and tried to set aside her guilt at not making it home at the promised time for date night. She was slowly training her brain not to flip tables and have a toddler-level meltdown in aisle four over the smallest transgressions, like being late. She really needed to just make him a key.

It helped that the lateness was brought on by how well her website was doing. Orders had been coming in steadily, and she'd seen a spike in online traffic after she and Jun-su finished the mural and unveiled it to the public. Finding the time to fulfill the orders, keeping the website updated, and continuing to paint, on top of working and having a boy-friend, was running her around like an overexcited golden retriever tugging at the leash, dying to get to the dog park *right now*. Sometimes it was hard to keep up, but she still had a firm grip on the leash. Completing each new task and seeing how her buyers gushed over their paintings, how they sent her pictures of her prints hanging on their living room walls, made her feel wonderfully, vividly alive. It put more sound and color in her day.

She was glad to be here instead of just *here*. She remem-bered now what it felt like to look forward to tomorrow. Sometimes she wished she could tell her first Ewan all about it. Find a way to assure him that life was good and she was happy.

She matched smiles with the man standing on her porch, his hands in his pockets, one hip leaning on the railing as he enjoyed the night air.

"What is this? A gentleman caller?" Isla braced a hand on her chest.

Ewan dutifully bowed at the waist. "I do not come with flowers, my lady, but I do come bearing libations." He lavishly displayed a bottle of red wine.

"This is an acceptable offering," she replied. "You may enter." God, it thrilled her to say the inside parts out loud; the thoughts she always had too late, or was too shy to speak into the air.

They ate chili while they watched a movie, since fall had well and truly settled in and the nights were much colder. Halfway through the film, and breathless while Ewan nipped her earlobe and Isla undid the buttons of his dress shirt, she almost dismissed the sound of gravel popping under car tires until headlights swept across her front windows. They both turned to look.

"The boys?" Isla asked, uncertain.

"Not without a text first."

She let the blanket fall away as she got up to investigate, right as a car door opened and slammed shut. She recognized that silhouette.

Her heart dropped off a skyscraper's ledge.

"Hello, Isla," she heard through the open screen door.

"Hi, Dad," she said through a dry mouth. Isla attempted a smile as she slipped out onto the porch. "I, um, didn't know you were coming."

"I called, left a voice mail." His hug was firm and bony, and Isla's body split into two camps: nostalgic and wary.

His hair had thinned and grayed a little more since the last time she'd seen him, but he was still lean and fit and sharply dressed despite a half-day road trip not requiring dress shirts and slacks whatsoever. Frogs started to jump around in her stomach.

"When?"

"Sometime today. I was in the area, thought I'd drop in to say hello."

"I . . ." Isla swallowed hard, smiled again, and felt her face grow hot. Today? Of course—she hadn't checked her phone because she'd been sketching. Nothing had come through at work. "I wasn't prepared at all. I'm sorry." His response fully registered, and then she added, "You were in the area?"

"A work conference in St. Louis," he said brightly. "And I thought, hell, I might as well come visit my daughter."

What was happening? "How long are you staying?"

"It's just a two-day thing, so I packed light."

Isla finally noted the duffel bag at his feet. She felt like someone had handed her a test and all of the questions were in Latin. "I'm . . . sorry, Dad, you're staying here?"

Arnold Abbott laughed. "Well, you wanted me to come see your new place, and I haven't seen *you* in ages. Why not?"

What if she had been out of town? He would have come all this way to find she wasn't home, and then he would have been mad at her for spoiling his plans. Not to mention that she already had weekend plans. She and Ewan were supposed to go hiking tomorrow at Castlewood State Park and then visit his parents for dinner. They'd planned it weeks ago.

She had never handled last-minute changes or sudden plans well—never, not in her entire life. Isla was a planner down to her core. And he always did this. Day-of cancellations on visitation weekends, then suddenly showing up when he felt like having her over for a random weekend. Showing up late to her mother's funeral. But he'd made it, hadn't he? That was what mattered. And Isla wouldn't mind any of that, right? Such an agreeable kid, so forgiving. She'll get over it.

All of it burned in her throat and stayed there. *Don't make him mad. Don't make him feel unwelcome.* "I only have the couch, Dad. I don't know if it's long enough for you."

"I have an air mattress in the car. Don't worry about it."

Oh, well then. *He* had come prepared. Isla could not catch her thoughts. It was like swinging wildly at butterflies with a net. "Okay, well . . . of course, you can stay. I'm sorry, I'm just surprised. I might not have been home. But come on in."

Her dad patted her shoulder briskly as he walked in. "I figured you'd be home; you know how you are."

Isla's stomach knotted when she saw Ewan standing in the middle of the room, watching the exchange. Her father stopped in his tracks when he spotted him. "Hello, Isla's friend," he said.

"Boyfriend," Isla corrected. She welcomed the hot flush of pleasure at saying the word, which tried its damnedest to counter the mountain of awkward filling her brain. "Dad, this is Ewan Park. Ewan, this is my dad, Arnold Abbott."

"Pleasure to meet you, Mr. Abbott." Ewan shook his hand, and his smile was only a touch genuine. He kept cutting his eyes to Isla.

"Boyfriend," Dad exclaimed, drawing it out a few extra syllables. "When did you get one of those?"

"We've been dating for a little while."

"Oh yeah? When were you going to say something?" Now the faucet for Shame was turning on. Every sentence out of Dad's mouth was a subtle accusation.

Whenever you returned my calls, she wanted to say. "I was going to tell you the next time we talked."

"Well, now we really have to celebrate. I've got some time after the conference concludes Saturday night and Sunday. Maybe you could show your old man around, huh? I'd like to drive up and see Hannibal; I've never been. I can take you and Ewan here out to dinner on Saturday, get to know your boy a little. Plus you had a birthday a while back. We should celebrate."

That sounded like everything she did not want to do. But her weekend now belonged to Dad. "We, uh, already had plans for this weekend, but it can . . . we can reschedule." She hated herself for buckling under the pressure again; for giving in, again. "There's a lot to do in Hannibal, I can show you around. Have you eaten?"

"Just something on the road."

"There's some chili in the kitchen, if you'd like some."

"Thank you, I'd like that. This is a decent place, Isla. Better than that closet you had."

"It was a studio, Dad."

"Your bed was in the living room."

"That's what studios are," she said, her voice crossing a very thin and very unsteady plank of wood. "It was all I could afford."

She left him to wander the house while she all but sprinted into the kitchen. Her chest tightened hideously as her brain sent out a siren wail that this did not feel right. She wanted him to go home even as she was genuinely and pathetically happy to see her father after nine months. She hoped he liked the chili. He was a better cook than she was.

"Hey. Hey." Isla jolted when Ewan's hand wrapped around her waist. "What is it?" he said, low enough to ensure her dad's ears wouldn't prick up. "Do you want me to leave?"

"No," she whispered, turning her horrified face to his. *"Do not leave."*

Ewan's eyes narrowed. "Is it safe?"

Isla closed her eyes. God, she was suddenly so tired. "It's safe," she confirmed. "We just have a complicated relationship. I *really* wasn't expecting him. We had plans, and he just . . . he never checks. It never occurs to him. I'm so sorry, I'll text your mom to let her know and we can reschedule dinner, and—"

"Hey, hey, hey." Ewan pulled her closer and rubbed her arms as if she were cold. "It's okay. I'll take care of it, and the hiking trails aren't going anywhere. Take a deep breath and just stay right here." He refilled her wineglass, poured her father a cup, and took care of giving him the chili and wine while Isla collected herself in the kitchen.

Isla took a hefty gulp of wine and prayed her stomach didn't rebel at this sudden upset. She braced herself when her dad sauntered into the kitchen, holding his chili bowl and eating while he looked around. "How's the job?"

"Good," Isla said carefully. She had no idea where that line of thought could go. "The schedule is a lot more predictable. I was able to pick up some freelance."

"That's how we met," Ewan said. He parked himself by Isla, leaning against the counter so their elbows brushed. "She did some work on my office's website."

"I'm surprised Isla said two words to you," Arnold chuckled. Isla smiled tightly. "Oh, Isla, you know it's true. Shiest kid I've ever met."

"Shy, maybe, but she went after she wanted, and she had the talent and the business sense to convince my boss he needed her expertise," Ewan insisted.

God, now Isla was blushing furiously over the passion in his voice.

"Well. She gets that from me." Dad shot her a smile. "I'm a day trader," he told Ewan, and Isla sighed, this time amused and relieved by the subject change.

Dad loved nothing more than talking about his job.

He bored them senseless for the next hour about tales from the trading floor, deals he'd made for the firm, rooftop parties in downtown Chicago, all the attractive young women in his office, his dating life.

Isla yawned halfway through a story about a marketing manager he'd dated when her father suddenly realized the time. "Well, it's getting late. Ewan, do you mind giving us some father-daughter time? I have to tuck in early. The conference starts at eight AM, and you don't exactly live close to St. Louis."

Arnold Abbott had the balls to kick her boyfriend out of her home on their date night. And she was letting him do it. Her stomach was a giant garlic knot.

Ewan handled it gracefully, expressing pleasure at meeting her father and nipping a slice of banana bread to eat on the road.

"I'll walk you out to your car," Isla hurriedly offered. "Dad, make yourself at home."

"I have never seen you look that uncomfortable," Ewan said when they were finally out of earshot, walking arm in arm out to his car.

Isla closed her eyes. "I didn't tell him about you because Dad is really bad at communication. We haven't spoken in four months. And of course he's only here because of a work thing."

"Four months? My mother would assume I was dead if she hadn't heard from me in three days."

Isla smiled mirthlessly. "Dad was married to his job even before he and Mom got a divorce. And growing up, he just . . ." She hugged herself, hating that she had to talk about this now. "He came home to sleep and argue with Mom, and he remembered I was there when I did something wrong."

Like miss school because of her anxiety disorder or forget to do her chores or try to kill herself.

"Also, wasn't your birthday almost five months ago?"

She sighed and scrubbed her hands over her face. "He forgets every year. Eventually he remembers. We really haven't talked much since Mom died. He barely came around when she was sick, and I . . . I haven't really forgiven him for that yet."

I said too much; oh god, oh god, Isla thought. If you keep piling on the baggage, he is going to run in the other direction. Isla took a deep breath, and then another. Forced herself to meet his eyes and smile gamely. "I really wish we were hiking tomorrow instead, but I'd rather step into a bear trap than bring him along on our first hike."

Ewan hugged her for a long time, and Isla wanted to disappear into him; just disappear altogether.

CHAPTER TWENTY

Dad had arrived late enough in the day to give Isla the excuse to retire to her room and let him watch whatever he wanted on TV until he fell asleep. Saturday morning comprised of robust coffee and a neutral subject to gnaw on along with their eggs—Hannibal's history, in this instance. Isla did enough reading up on it to satisfy her father's curiosity and his own knowledge, cobbled together from his travels, love of American literature, and however else one picked up information when they were a white-collared stock trader from the Midwest. In pubs? During golf? She had no idea. Her father was no doubt an intelligent man, but he had the sort of intelligence that talked down from a high place instead of next to you.

When he left for the last day of his conference, promising to return around six PM for dinner, Isla was still too frazzled to try to salvage some portion of the weekend, and told Ewan to just stay put until dinner. She used the afternoon to read, periodically texting with Janelle and Eleanor just to make sure she wasn't blowing this whole thing out of proportion. The verdict: mixed. While they agreed he should have given advance warning, they wanted her to make the most of the visit and just reschedule the original plans she had.

Status report? Ewan texted her at five.

Nothing yet from Elder Abbott, she replied. *Time will tell.*

Six PM came, then went. Then turned into seven. Then turned into eight.

Isla texted her dad a few times to ask about dinner. No response. Her stomach growled. *No dinner tonight,* she wrote to Ewan. *Radio silence from Elder Abbott.*

Is he okay?

He's fine. He just either forgot or he's too caught up with whatever post-conference festivities his company's having.

It was too typical to get upset over. And they hadn't made concrete dinner plans anyways. Isla ate leftover chili, brought her laptop into her room, and left the front door unlocked for her dad.

By the time the screen door creaked open at eleven, Isla was asleep.

* * *

In fairness, it wasn't the worst Sunday morning father-daughter bonding time.

Apologies abounded for missing dinner, and then Dad bought her coffee and a pastry at her favorite café in downtown Hannibal before they started sightseeing.

They met Ewan at LaBinnah Bistro for brunch, right down the street from Twain's Boyhood Museum, which they'd already toured. The restaurant lived inside an old house and had the spirit of an antique shop, which made Isla feel right at home. Fussy flowered wallpaper, Parisian art and decor, dim lighting, gauzy cloth drooping from the ceilings like big white bows. Isla felt a twinge of regret that she and Ewan weren't coming here on their own.

Dad homed in on Ewan the moment they sat down, pulling the stats out of him he hadn't gotten Friday night: job, family, hobbies. Ewan handled it way more elegantly than Isla would have if she were put on the spot, but she supposed he'd expected this. And as her father talked about his work (again), she spent the time admiring her boyfriend. The dim lighting gave his features an angelic, painting-like quality, as if she were back in the Art Institute, admiring a Caravaggio. Finding new, surreal details to the lifelike strokes of paint. His raven-black hair framed his face, strands curving against his cheek. His eyes were dark pools in the candlelight, and she flushed from far more than the wine when his gaze collided with hers and they shared a smile.

He looked edible in a white dress shirt with tan leather suspenders hooked into blue slacks. Isla texted him when her dad was distracted by the menu. *New favorite outfit. Right there.*

Ewan pulled his phone out of his pocket when it buzzed. He gave her an achingly slow smile and winked. He sent her a text, but she didn't have the chance to look at it right away, since their food decided to arrive then. He kept sneaking meaningful glances at her, so Isla took a quick peek. And then a longer one.

I love you, Buttercup. And I'm so proud of you for handling this like a champ.

Isla could taste the salt of tears at the back of her throat. Those three written words swelled in her heart like the tide, flooding her shores with an emotion her body couldn't contain. He met her gaze steadily.

I love you, he mouthed. Then he made an eating motion with an imaginary fork, pointing to her food, his eyes twinkling.

She did it mechanically, and each bite was an achievement through a throat that wanted to close. How was everyone else eating so calmly? The world had tilted, and she was the only one who knew.

". . . your job?"

"Hmm?" Isla looked at her dad, who looked back expectantly. "I'm sorry, Dad, what?"

"Do you get to travel with your new job," he said slowly.

She let his talking-to-simpletons voice roll right off her back—he couldn't touch how loved she felt in that moment. "No, not like before. But I'm selling prints of my work on the side, now that I have the free time to do it."

"That's a shame. These conferences give me an excuse to get out of the city, see a little more of the country. And staying with you earned me a good hundred bucks."

Isla blinked at him. "Pardon?"

Dad gestured with his fork, taking his sweet time while he chewed. "I get a stipend if I don't use company funds to stay at a hotel for conferences. And we got to visit. Worked out great, didn't it?"

Isla set down her fork. She had no idea why, after all the times he had shown her who he was, she still hoped it would be different. "That's why you stayed with me?"

He was the very picture of indignation. "Well, that's not the only reason. We had fun, didn't we? Anyway." Arnold cleared his throat, and when he spoke again, his tone took on a cajoling note. "I'm glad you like your new job. You worked for a good company, and it's a shame this job doesn't have the same perks is all I was saying."

"It *was* a good company," she admitted. "It just wasn't good for me. Besides." She flashed a shy smile at Ewan. "I got a lot more than a new job from this move."

"I'm happy that's working out," her dad said, pausing to take a few bites of his steak. "I was worried about you. Didn't date boys in school, didn't have much to do with them when you got older. You're the first one I've met, Ewan. Thought I'd have a spinster on my hands."

She didn't know what to say to that, and Ewan saved her with a careful "I'm honored, then."

Dad shook his fork at her and added, "Hold on to this one—at your rate, it'd take you ten more years to find another." He chuckled.

It was almost impressive how quickly her good mood vanished and left behind a sting of self-loathing and anger so sharp it took her breath away. She carefully avoided looking at Ewan, but she could see him out of the corner of her eye—his eyes had widened.

He looked like he wanted to say something. Oh, no—no, she did not need him swooping in. She hated public scenes and confrontations, and she would either cry or lose her shit at her dad. A good thirty years' worth.

"I plan to," she said, giving herself a tiny mental pat on the back for how steady and cool her voice sounded. "Too bad I couldn't date like *you*, Dad. You make it look so easy."

Arnold's brow furrowed, as if he wasn't sure whether she was being sarcastic. "I put myself out there."

"And don't we all know it." Isla smiled brightly at him.

Dad narrowed his eyes at her, and she hated the knee-jerk panic that sprung to life inside her. *Don't make him angry*, it moaned. *He is so scary when he's angry.* "That was a long time ago, Isla."

"I didn't say anything about it," she said.

"I loved your mother."

Oh no. Isla set her napkin down. "You know, Dad, I enjoyed the Mark Twain tours this morning, and brunch has been lovely, but you have a long drive ahead of you. It really would have saved you time had we gone to dinner last night."

"I told you, I had too many after-hour cocktails and had to sober up," her dad protested, although he looked rattled by the direction of the conversation. Of course he did—Isla hated making people uncomfortable. She rarely called him out on his no-shows and had never mentioned the affair that became the final straw in his and Caroline's already strained marriage, of which Isla knew entirely too much, since they hadn't wanted to pay for proper therapists. The suicidal teenager in the house would do. She sent a silent apology up to her mother.

"I know," she said bluntly, although her voice trembled. "The next time you'd like to visit me, Dad, whether you're here for a conference or not, you've got to give me notice. I need time to prepare. If you don't, I can't promise I'll be available."

"Now—"

"It's the polite thing to do," Isla said primly. Her hands were shaking and slick with cold sweat. She had never stood up to her father like this. The waitress passed by, and Isla raised her hand to get her attention. "May we have the check, please?"

"That's quite enough," Arnold said, his voice firming into a warning tone, and she almost flinched. "Isla, I don't know what's gotten into you."

His *be reasonable* tone made her want to scream. "I'm asking for a common courtesy that you rarely give me," she said evenly.

"That's a hell of an accusation." Her father's cheeks bloomed as red as roses. Or the blood that wells up after a prick from their thorns.

"It wasn't an accusation." The older couple at the table next to them were looking over periodically.

"I am your father," he said, in the way he used to address her when he told her to manage her emotions better. "If I want to see my daughter, I'd like to think I can do so at any time."

"You didn't come here for me. You visited because it was convenient for you, and then expected me to be available at a moment's notice when I haven't heard from you in almost six months." Horror writhed in her gut, but she couldn't take back any of it now. "But daughters don't fit well into your busy schedule, so I guess I'll take what I can get."

Real fury shone from Arnold's pale-gray eyes. "Don't ever talk to me in that tone again," he said quietly, each word the promise of what would have been a great, booming, all-night-long scathing lecture, the kind that had just eviscerated her as a child. "You act the way I taught you to act, young lady."

"I don't live in your house anymore." Isla's voice barely reached above a whisper.

He pointed a finger at her, and this time she flinched. "Listen to me—"

"That's enough."

Isla and her dad looked over at Ewan, and she knew they had both forgotten he was even there. His face was a cold mask. "We're done. And you're finished addressing her in that tone. Maybe if you didn't spend all of your time talking over your daughter, you'd actually hear what she needs from you, but it looks like today's not that day."

"With all due respect, this does not concern you," Arnold said.

"With all due respect, you're incorrect, and you're upsetting my girlfriend." Ewan pushed back his chair with a grinding drag from the chair legs and whipped his wallet out of his pocket. Isla hadn't known it was possible to flip bills that angrily. "I'm sure we'll meet again, Mr. Abbott. Have a safe trip home."

Ewan tossed the cash on the table, and Isla took that as her cue to get up. She gave one final look to her father. "I'm not going to talk about this right now," she told him. God, the restaurant was sweltering. She had no control of her body's temperature anymore. "Until we've both cooled down. Drive safe."

Ewan waited for her, and they sped-walked out of the restaurant. She had never seen Ewan angry like this, and in other circumstances she might have appreciated it. As soon as they were in the parking lot, she whirled on him.

"Don't do that again." It pleased Isla that she actually sounded firm and not like she wanted to die, which was her body's current consensus. "Please. Don't speak for me. I'm sorry you had to see that, I'm sorry I made a scene, but he's *my* father and I can handle it."

"I couldn't just let him belittle you," Ewan said hotly.

"It's nothing new." No, no, no. Do not cry. Do not cry. Isla was a butterfly pinned down to a board, her wings fluttering madly to escape, but there was nowhere to go. The pressure built like lava pooling under the crust of the earth, waiting for a crack. Dismay replaced Ewan's anger, and Isla hated herself. She lowered her head and put her trembling hand to her forehead. "I want to go home." She hated how tiny her voice sounded.

She heard him unlock his car. "I'll take you."

"I can drive."

"Not right now you can't."

"I am not helpless!" Isla snapped, her throat raw and aching, unused to yelling at Ewan, but his immediate shutdown, his reasonable tone, and the very idea that he'd snatch her keys from her as if she were a drunk person or worse—*hysterical*—made Isla want to scream. "And I am not weak or fragile."

He shook his head at her, approaching slowly but not touching. "No, you're not. But you're having a panic attack, and you shouldn't drive during one. That's all I meant."

Maybe she was on the verge of one, but her anger kept it at bay. And she had to get this out now, or she never would. "Having a panic attack doesn't mean I lose every working brain cell in my head."

"No, it doesn't, but it does mean you're distracted and you might not watch the road as closely. Where is this coming from?"

"I don't need to be managed like I'm a child."

"I'm trying to help you." His voice gained a new, strained edge. "What else am I supposed to do when you get like this?"

Everything in Isla stilled. "Get like what?"

Ewan's face crumpled. "I didn't mean that. I didn't mean it like that. I just . . . sometimes I don't know how something might make you react, and I know you don't always know that either, and it's not your fault. But that was bad in there, Isla, and you would be well within your rights to have a bad reaction to it."

I don't know how something might make you react. As if he was afraid she would crumble at the slightest provocation. Because he'd seen it happen before. Was he always waiting and worrying for the next time she'd "get like that"? Did he dread it?

Could she promise that she would never have another bad moment in public?

No. No, she couldn't.

This wasn't what she wanted. She didn't want his protection like this. She didn't want to be afraid of her own behavior. Rationally, she knew she'd held it together in tough situations before, and she could do it for Ewan. But she suspected he wouldn't believe that. And so he sought to protect her and himself.

By managing. As if she were a child and didn't know any better.

Isla pulled out her keys with shaking hands.

"Don't do that; I can take you home."

"I really don't want to be told what to do right now, Ewan." Isla couldn't look at him as her vision clouded with tears. "I'm mad at you and I hate it and I can't think straight. I can't be in a car with you for half an hour, and I want to go home."

She jerked away when he reached for her, and she didn't have to look at his face to know how much that hurt him.

"I meant what I said in there," he said, his voice thick and unsteady. "If you believe nothing else, believe that."

Isla nodded, her throat closing as she whispered, "I love you too." Walking away from him withered her heart into a rotten apple core. She hated how deeply important his opinion of her was. How ashamed she was of her own mental illness. How defective it made her.

She made it all the way the home held together with twine and popsicle sticks. As soon as the front door shut her into her empty house, she burst into tears.

* * *

Isla avoided Ewan the entire week. She went remote to stay out of St. Louis and let all of his calls go to voice mail. By Friday, Isla almost couldn't take it anymore, but she didn't know how to fix it. She missed him fiercely and wanted a chance to clear the air and hear him out. He might have misspoken, but he'd defended her against her dad, and God knew she'd said stupid shit when she was upset too.

She texted him halfway through her remote workday. *I meant what I said, too. I love you. I have loved you for so long, and I've loved you every day we haven't talked, even though I'm confused and I can't sort out my feelings. I was too hard on you, and I acted like an asshole.*

She most certainly did not watch her phone for the rest of the afternoon, and her heart did not fly over the moon when he responded back.

Buttercup. What I said was so unfair.

It wasn't. My issues are not a walk in the park. But let's talk about it in person?

He didn't say whether he was coming over, but she assumed it would be tomorrow. She ended her workday early, mentally spent with the entire week, and drew a bath. While the tub filled, she changed out of her clothes and wrapped herself in a robe, letting the soft material comfort her.

The doorbell rang as she shut off the water. Her heart wanted to weep at the sight of his beautiful face on the other side of the screen door, black hair disheveled as if he'd been running his fingers through it, eyes dark as a bruise while the sun set behind him.

"Hi, Rabbit," she said quietly.

"Buttercup," he said just as softly, his voice as deep and intimate as it had been on the phone all those months ago.

"Come in."

* * *

The bathroom was the perfect quiet of a sunrise walk, marred only by the occasional, soothing drip of the faucet. Isla curled up against Ewan's chest in the water, the tendrils of steam fragrant with the lavender bath salts scattered like tiny jewels across the surface.

He could tell by her expression when he'd arrived that she hadn't expected him to show up. She was probably used to people breaking their word—especially if they were men named Arnold Abbott. The week had given him a lot of time to think about her anxiety disorder, the panic attacks, the stomachaches and headaches, and how they were all linked. He was beginning to understand where they stemmed from.

"I'd like to say it out loud too," Ewan said, rousing Isla from her thoughts. She looked back at him, uncomprehending, her gray eyes sparkling like flashes of light on a diamond. Ewan wrapped one arm around her stomach and ran his fingers up her bare arm. "I don't just love you when you're well," he said softly, praying he got this out right and didn't say the wrong thing again. "I love every facet of you. Even the stuff you hate. It's *not* your fault, Isla. It's just how your mind processes things. I hate that you have to deal with it, but I'll try to keep helping any way I can. I may not always be great at it—I can't promise I'll always know what to say or do—but god, please don't think it's ever a reflection of my feelings for you. You're it, Buttercup. I don't want to go anywhere, because you feel like home."

There. That was as close as he could get to what was inside him for this woman. But there was still more. She might think she just emitted anxious vibes all the time and that she stressed people out when she stressed out, but that wasn't the case at all. Ewan hadn't known a contentment or a happiness like what he'd felt when he spent time with her, in the world she'd carefully cultivated.

Okay, he should probably say that too. She needed to hear it. "Listen. You've done things to both help yourself and go after what you want that a lot of people I know lack the courage to do. And even though it stresses you out, you sell your work and run your website because it keeps you creating. Because you love it. You're an entrepreneur, and that's more than your *dad* can say."

Isla let out a watery laugh and wiped her eyes. "I don't deserve you."

"Yeah, you do." Ewan stroked her face, because it was very strokable, and she charmed him by capturing his hand and kissing the center of his palm. "Can I ask you something? What does it feel like when it's happening? I want to understand."

Isla blew out a breath. "It's devastating. It's total helplessness. You're at the mercy of these grand, sweeping, intense emotions—fear that has no direction and no real cause, so you don't know how to make it stop. Despair, because it's happening *again*, and this time it'll go on forever. Hopelessness. It'll happen while you're doing the most mundane things, so you get to feel extra defective because a simple thing like going to school or being in a crowd or going to an appointment can set it off. I was so young when it started. I didn't know what to do with those huge, terrifying feelings. I just wanted it to stop."

She darted a fearful look up at him, and he nodded his encouragement. Yet she kept pausing, her lips parting, then closing, storm clouds building in her gray eyes. He had a feeling he knew where this was going. "You tried to stop it, didn't you?" he asked softly.

Isla rested her head on his shoulder. "When I was fifteen," she said. "It felt endless. Panic attacks every week, constantly anxious, then these sudden dips into worthlessness. I tried to tell my parents, but it upset them to hear how I was feeling. Therapy is expensive and they were in the middle of their divorce, so I just . . . stopped. I went inward. I had to take a year off before going to college, because I just fell apart. I didn't know who I was anymore. I didn't have ambitions, I didn't have a purpose. There was no point to any of it. I wasn't a normal girl; I was a feeling. I *was* despair. It had no beginning and no end. I couldn't live in it anymore. I wanted away from my own mind."

Isla lifted her arm and turned it so the inside of her wrist faced him. She traced a line, and when he looked closely, he could finally see the faint scar he had never noticed before.

"No one knew except my parents. Not even Willow. You're the first person I've told besides my therapist."

A suffocating pressure closed in on Ewan's chest with every quiet, matter-of-fact word she uttered. "How did things change for you?"

"Being able to afford therapy. Medication. I finally went to a counseling center at the college to get help. I lived with Willow and her family for a little while. I worked and learned how to be in public spaces. It was hard. And when I realized I could actually make a career out of my graphic design skills, I just went for it. Moving out on my own was a huge help. I was finally the one in charge of my own life. The only person who could criticize me was myself. I could fill my space with my own things and make it a place that made me happy. So I did."

"And then your mother got sick," Ewan filled in.

"I started to backslide," she confirmed. "My thoughts were scaring me. I had to try something different. So I moved." Isla ran her hand down his bicep, curving her fingers over the muscle. "I don't want to talk about me anymore. Plus, the water's getting cold."

They drained the bathtub, then washed each other's hair underneath a warm shower. He wrapped them in a big towel, and she laughed when he rubbed the soft cloth along her skin as if she were a child. Isla threw her arms around him and hugged him. "Please endure this hug from your wet and cold girlfriend," she mumbled into his chest. "Who loves you very much."

They stood on the bathroom rug for a long time, holding each other. Isla drew his face down for a gentle kiss, and his eyes slid closed.

It could be like this all the time, he thought. Taking care of each other when the outside world grew too harsh. Listening to each other. Shutting out the whole world and making one of their own that they could retreat to.

"Forgive me?" he asked.

Isla snuggled closer to him. "Forgiven. Forgive *me*?"

"Forgiven, Buttercup." Ewan kissed her hair.

She curled up next to him on the couch and dozed while Ewan opened his laptop and planned their first trip together to make up for the ruin of last weekend. Start small, he reminded himself, although he was already planning to take her hiking in Colorado and, maybe next year, on a trip to Korea.

He had a few tabs of possible hotels open when Isla roused, rubbing her head against his side like a cat before pulling herself up and resting her chin on his shoulder. "The Allegro?" she asked sleepily. "That's downtown. In Chicago, I mean. Gorgeous rooms, classy lobby."

"Mm-hmm. We're going there. To Chicago, I mean."

He'd anticipated a few different reactions from Isla, but stiffening up had not been one of them. "We are?"

"I want to make up for last weekend. You've seen where I grew up, and I want to see where you grew up."

"That's . . . that's a great idea, I love it." Each word was carefully chosen. "I haven't been back there since I moved here." She shook her head, swallowed, and gave him a more sincere smile. "The weather's getting cold, though, and it's going to be even colder up there. Do you mind if we go in the spring?"

"That's fine." Her tense shoulders relaxed, and Ewan puzzled at it. "Are you *sure* you want to go? Is it about your dad being up there?"

She gave him a firm kiss. "No, and yes, I want to go. Just . . . in the spring."

When Isla stepped away to use the bathroom, Ewan went back to securing the trip. Hotel Allegro seemed to be the winner, so he reserved four nights in late April. It would give them something to look forward to throughout the winter.

His phone buzzed, startling him, since it was next to his thigh on the couch. Ewan picked it up and laughed at the caller ID. "Something you want to tell me that can't wait, Buttercup?"

Silence greeted him on the other end. She must have accidentally dialed him from the bathroom. Ewan hung up the call and went back to trip planning.

CHAPTER TWENTY-ONE

Isla's first winter in Missouri passed like the snowflakes falling inside a shaken snow globe. Every first shake of the globe, when the snowflakes were a chaotic storm of flurries, was every new and exciting first with Ewan. Ice skating at Forest Park. He was a terrible ice skater, and she secretly relished how tightly he held on to her hands as they slowly drifted around in circles. He was so often the source of comfort for her that she liked when she could be that source for him, even if it was just to keep him upright on the ice. Sunday dinners with his parents. Learning more Korean for Mrs. Ahn and Mr. Park because she wanted so badly for them to like her. Their first Christmas together. Ringing in the new year on the couch, recovering from food poisoning instead of going to Jun-su and Tae's for a party.

All of the firsts shook Isla up into a frenzy of excited, sometimes panicked nerves, but those flurries eventually settled into a steady snowfall. A contentment the likes of which she'd never experienced before. It was becoming easier to endure the swells of anxiety that were a constant in her life when she began to recognize a new pattern: the calm and the peace of Ewan's acceptance and patience. Of her therapist's presence and partnership on helping her find new ways to weather her panic attacks and think about how to coexist with her anxiety. Of how freeing it was to be honest about her struggles with everyone in her life who mattered to her.

By the time winter thawed into spring, Isla's fear of the city she grew up in had dwindled to background noise she could ignore almost as easily as she'd ignored the sound of the L when she lived near the Berwyn Red Line stop. She even let herself look forward to going back to visit Willow and showing Ewan where she'd come from.

* * *

Chicago's skyline never failed to take Isla's breath away. Homesickness pricked her with a needle, weaving through her with its fine gold thread. The sleek, modern skyscrapers that gave way to brick and old brownstone; the lush green parks, flowers budding among new, fresh green leaf sprouts. The lake was a slate gray, the waves choppy from the wind. By morning, it could be turquoise or midnight blue or the color of rain. Isla missed Lake Michigan's mercurial moods and the dozen shades of blue it shifted through on a whim. Her tiny studio had been on the north side in Rogers Park, right by the lake, and she used to love that first step out onto the street, when she could look to see what color the lake had decided to be that day.

She was excited and terrified to share it with Ewan.

But it would be fine. It would be fine. Ewan drove, and Isla suggested they visit Chinatown for dim sum to avoid Lake Shore Drive before checking into their hotel. She didn't breathe properly again until their car was tucked away in the parking garage and they were back on foot.

They arrived on a Thursday, and Isla took him to Fulton Market for dinner at a Mediterranean restaurant filled to bursting with hanging plants, climbing ivy intertwined with fairy lights, and trees nestled up to glowing orbs. They gorged themselves on short rib hummus, whipped feta sprinkled with crushed pistachios, and lamb kebabs.

Isla took Ewan to breakfast on Friday at one of her favorite brunch spots in Lincoln Park, then to the Field Museum and the Museum of Surgical Science, which she knew he'd dig. Willow didn't have work until the next day, so they drove to Logan Square and met her for dinner at a German pub on Milwaukee.

"Who is this dashing stranger that's stolen my girl from me?" Willow said as she walked up to meet them in front of the Radler.

Ewan and Willow hugged, and he congratulated her on completing her sommelier license. Will waved off his praise with all the demureness of a pageant queen on stage. "You guys talk about me! I'm flattered."

"You're Isla's family; you come up in conversation."

"I like this one," Will murmured in Isla's ear. "Ewan, are you ready for the best German food on the West Side?"

He was. They carb-loaded on Bavarian pretzels, brats, spaetzle, and potato croquette poutine, then walked back to Willow's fueled on ales and ciders. The trio lounged in the four-unit brownstone where Will rented. It satisfied a hunger Isla didn't know she had, and she was full and satiated as she stretched out on the soft, cushy couch with her head in Ewan's lap. They blasted Fleetwood Mac from Will's record player, drank wine, and forgot the passage of time.

Ewan graciously offered to head back to the hotel early to give Will and Isla time alone to catch up. "I say I'll go back to the hotel," he said as he put on his jacket, "but what I'll really end up doing is checking if that coffee shop with the mustache on the door is still open."

"It is," Isla and Will chimed together.

As soon as he went out the door, Will whirled on Isla. "Holy shit, girl, he is *hot*." Isla gave a cheesy grin. "And he's so into you. I wish I would have gotten some pictures of you two being disgustingly cute."

An extremely girly laugh escaped Isla. "He's wonderful, isn't he?" She bounced on the balls of her feet. "We've had such a good time. I took him to the Museum of Surgical Science, and he was so adorable. They had this old-timey pharmacy he couldn't get enough of—"

Laughing, Will wrangled Isla into a hug with a swiftness that made Isla squawk in surprise. "I hate that you're far away," she said, "but look at you! I've never seen you like this! I'm so goddamn happy for you."

"I'm sure St. Louis needs sommeliers," Isla said innocently.

"I'm sure they do. I love you, but no, honey. Just promise to keep visiting, and I'll come down again before the weather turns."

"And you're doing all right?" Isla pulled back to stare into Will's happy brown eyes. It occurred to her that she never quite checked in on Will like Will checked in on her. Willow never seemed to need it . . . but then Will never asked for much of anything either. "Really. How are things going for you, outside of becoming a bona fide sommelier?"

Willow hummed and, arm still around Isla's neck, led them to collapse on the couch together. She idly played with Isla's hair as she thought. "Things are honestly good," she finally said. "I'm ready to move out of Logan, try on another neighborhood for size, especially with the raise this fancy title gave me—maybe Lincoln Square, maybe Pilsen. I like having my space, like you do. I'm not looking to find anyone for anything serious. I have my family, I have you, I have my local friends."

"But you'll tell me if that ever changes, right?" Isla asked. "You're always, always looking after me, and I don't always do a good job to see if you're okay. I know the certification was stressful, and I wish I would have been here more to help you through it." She realized now, years after the fact and with some regret, that in her endless search for someone who would make her a priority—who would put her first—Willow had been making her a priority all along. Before Ewan had ever texted that he missed her.

"You did, though," Willow said, surprised. "Babe, you have always been there for me when it's counted. When Lucas's appendix burst—remember that?—you were at the hospital to meet me before my parents even got there."

Isla snuggled her arm. It never felt like enough, because Will had stuck around for all of it—the divorce, the cancer, the breakdown—and never checked out. "That was scary. Poor kid. I don't know, I just wanted to make sure you know the road goes both ways. And that I'm proud of you, and if you're ever struggling, talk to me. Please. Don't make me feel like the only train wreck, like you're so sane all the time."

Willow laughed. "I did worry about you. Not that you weren't seeing anyone—you don't have to see any-damn-body—but because you were lonely. I could tell. I wanted this to work out, and I think it has, don't you?"

"It has," Isla said dreamily.

"That's what I like to hear."

Will suddenly gasped. "Oh, you know what?" She smacked Isla on the arm as if she were thumping a table. "My brother's playing a show tomorrow night. It's at Reggie's. Bring your man."

It was perfect. Isla hadn't necessarily forgotten that Lucas played the drums in a metal band, it just hadn't been relevant until recently. Lucas had always been a vibrant, talented kid who spent most of his waking hours in the garage with a drum set gifted to him from an uncle, which used to drive Will out of the house and over to Isla's during high school.

Isla texted Ewan before going to find him and take him back to the hotel. *Want to go to a concert, Rabbit?*

CHAPTER TWENTY-TWO

The bass thrummed like a heartbeat competing for dominance with Isla's own beating heart, and she was pretty sure it was winning. The speakers were so loud that there was no escape from the noise in any portion of the bar, except maybe the bathroom.

Edge of an Era, Lucas's band, came on half an hour after they arrived. It was past ten, crowded and claustrophobic, the bar food was greasy and fried, and Isla was having the time of her life. She could get drunk off the happiness on Ewan's face. They'd barely spoken since the bands started and just communicated with clashed gazes and grins, peppered with the occasional "Another drink?" and "I saw cheese fries that have my name on them."

When Edge of an Era finished their set, Willow whooped and rushed the stage to greet her brother. Lucas was sweaty, his black hair slicked back from his face and dripping, but his eyes burned with the fire of making music in front of an adoring crowd. He grabbed Isla in a damp, smelly hug, his thin wiry arms like steel bands.

"You're back?" he asked.

"Visiting," she corrected. "You're killin' it up here, Smalls."

Lucas grinned. "We're playing the Subterranean next week. Should have come for that."

After another round of drinks with Will's family, she went with Ewan back to the hotel. Isla still had her old transit card, and they used it to take the northbound Red Line to Monroe. It would have been a shorter walk to Hotel Allegro if she had gotten them off at Lake, but she wanted to walk the distance with him, breathe in the cool spring air and idly gaze at the city lights and dark storefronts. Even at this hour, the sidewalks still had sporadic tourist traffic and locals coming in and out of bars and pubs.

"I've always loved downtown at night," Isla said, her arm threaded through his. "I wish we had more time; there's so much to see."

"We'll come back." Ewan kissed her forehead. "Thank you for taking me to the show."

"Next time you'll have to wear your proper gear. Especially the accessory bits, like, say, the collar." Isla traced her finger across the curve of his neck. "It'd be hot."

His flush was adorable. He didn't seem to know what to say to that. He did, however, pick up the pace to get them to the hotel faster. The hotel lobby, sleekly modern with a touch of art deco—era furniture and lighting, was a blur as they headed for the bank of elevators.

When they were tucked safely inside, Isla slipped into the skin of a more confident version of herself, the one she pretended to be when she was alone with Ewan and he watched her the way he was now, with a single-minded intensity that less-confident Isla could barely stand to look at. His unabashed desire helped her become more than: more than enough, more than the things she told herself she was. Like this, with him, she became what she wanted to be without all of those less-thans—a partner, a lover, a desirable woman.

"Maybe I would tug on it," she whispered, rising to her tiptoes to nuzzle his ear. "Just a little. Lead you home like a puppy. Slide my fingers underneath to make sure it isn't too tight. Hold you there while I touch you." She lovingly stroked his neck while her other hand snuck down to cup the bulge in his pants and squeeze. "Because you're mine."

Their noses brushed, and she could feel his hot, shuddering breath. He leaned in, his hands sliding underneath her jacket, and then the elevator doors opened. Ewan's hand crushed hers as he led them down the hall, then fumbled with the key card twice before it let them in the room. The door hadn't properly shut before he whirled on her, backing her up against the wall and kissing her hungrily. Somehow they got their jackets off without having to drag their lips away from each other for longer than the space of a shaky breath, and then Isla's fingers sank into his soft hair and his hands gripped her waist.

Ewan groaned into her mouth when she undid his belt buckle, unzipped his pants, and freed him. His questing fingers went for the button of her jeans, and she felt the cool wall against her bottom as her pants fell and his hand cupped her, sliding home with ease.

"I've wanted to have you all night," he rasped between her gasps. "I wanted to drag you into the bathroom at the venue, where no one would hear you scream my name but me."

Isla was a feeling. She was desire, and love, and life. She managed to get his shirt off before they went any further because she was dying to feel the muscles move under his bare skin, to scrape her nails over his back while she held on to him. It took them a few moments and breathless laughs to figure out how to make it work until Isla wrapped a leg around his waist and he gripped her hip to keep her steady.

They made love against the wall, their groans and cries intermingling as they moved together. Nothing else mattered but the man in her arms and the fierce sensation of being alive. Ewan filled her again and again as she desperately gripped his shoulder blades, digging her nails into his skin, their faces flushed as they shuddered and gasped. And then Isla went rigid as the wave crested, taking her down with it. She bucked against him and cried his name as he increased the pace and buried his head into her neck, gasping explosively into her skin.

Isla was fairly certain that the sexiest sounds Ewan made came in the aftermath, when the room filled with his harsh, unsteady breaths laid over her own. She brushed his hair back from his beautiful face, delighted with the exhausted happy glaze in his eyes.

"I'm going to find that collar," he told her.

She laughed and kissed him. "Let's go try out the bath-tub," she murmured against his lips.

*　*　*

Ewan woke up to strong morning sunlight cascading into the hotel room. Isla slept among the tangled bedding and pillows, her rest deep and peaceful. He kissed her forehead and carefully left the bed, tidying his hair and throwing on a jacket to step outside for breakfast. He walked north up LaSalle and grabbed two coffees and pastries from Big Shoulders, enjoying the sunshine, the crisp coolness of spring, the traffic and the screech of the L behind him.

His reentry into the room roused her. Isla gave him a sleepy smile as she stretched, and his heart tried to expand to fit all of his love for her inside it.

"Yum, pastry."

"Yum, Isla." She laughed when he nipped her ear as he sat down on the bed and handed her a pastry and coffee. They ate and drank in bed, lazily planning a day that would take them north of the city.

"I've never taken Lake Shore all the way to its end, so that'll be cool," Ewan said.

Isla froze, and her chewing slowed to a stop. "We're not taking Lake Shore."

"Why?"

"We just . . ." Isla closed her eyes. "We can't."

What did she have against the lake? "I'm not following, Buttercup."

"I know it doesn't make any sense."

"I haven't been down Lake Shore since I was a kid." Umma had driven them up and down that road after one of her conferences ended: once during the day to watch how the sun shot diamonds into the water, and once at night to see the city light up the lakefront. It had been magical. Why didn't she want to share that with him?

"We can take the scenic route through the city to get to the gardens and stop for Jeni's Ice Cream," she offered.

"We can do that *and* drive down Lake Shore," he counteroffered. "It's our vacation, we make the rules."

He could not reconcile the worry that pinched between her eyebrows. Did she associate some bad memory with Lake Shore? But she would just tell him if that were the case. For now, he had nothing to explain the shadows gathering in her eyes or the way she hugged herself. The little nibble on her lower lip would have been cute if not for this weird aversion to one of the coolest urban drives in the country.

"Are you nervous about driving it? Because I'll drive." The tense way Isla was holding herself loosened, and he latched on to that. "You can be my navigator."

Her cautious, almost relieved smile puzzled him, but it was better than the worry. "Okay," she agreed. "But I'll drive back down. Through the city. I want you to see it."

"Of course."

As he drove them through downtown and onto Lake Shore, Ewan snatched glances at the still, blue lake, the people jogging along the thin stretch of beach, the dogs catching thrown Frisbees. It was peaceful, picturesque, this steel-and-glass city curving along the edges of a massive freshwater lake, nature colliding with manmade industry. Whatever misgivings Isla had about driving Lake Shore seemed to have dissipated; she smiled absently out at the water, her chin propped in her hand.

"This view is incredible," he said.

"I never get tired of it," Isla replied. Her oversized white sweater engulfed her, contrasting with the camel pencil skirt and black leggings. She wore big Jackie O sunglasses on account of the sunshine. He was the dark foil to her light in black jeans, a red shirt, and a leather jacket. A goth greaser with the preppy, bookish schoolgirl. They were so fucking cute together he couldn't stand it.

"We could move back here," he said casually.

Isla glanced at him, eyebrows raising over her sunglasses. "You've never wanted to move away from your parents."

"We'd visit. I'd still talk to them every week."

She shook her head. "Chicago is more fun to visit now than to live in. I like St. Louis. You have an established client base. I don't need to come back here like you need to stay."

Isla stroked the back of his hand, letting her fingernails lightly drag up his wrist. He turned his hand over and their palms met, fingers lazily dancing. "Besides," she continued, "don't we have some hiking to do next year? Didn't you promise me Colorado?"

Her enthusiasm and willingness to experience the things he loved warmed him like nothing else ever had. "I did. Buttercup, do we need directions to the Botanic Garden?"

"Eventually. I remember most of the way." Isla double-checked the phone in her lap, and as her gaze swung up, her eyes caught the passenger rearview mirror.

Isla inhaled suddenly. "Get in the next lane," she said sharply.

"What?"

"Do it now! Someone's—"

He heard the crunch of metal and the burst of shattering glass before he felt the jolt.

Before he heard Isla scream.

*   *   *

Isla woke with the suddenness of a thunderclap, her eyes snapping open only to get seared by the lightning flash of harsh fluorescents. They left hazy imprints on the backs of her eyelids. Isla reeled from the disorientation as her fingers clutched . . . bedsheets. She was on a bed. In a really fucking cold room. Where the hell was she?

As her eyes adjusted, she heard movement, then jumped when a hand closed over her shoulder.

"Isla? Isla, it's all right. Keep taking deep breaths for me."

It took her eyes forever to focus and lose the afterimages of light until the formless blot became a nurse in blue scrubs, her gaze steady as she hovered over Isla. "You're at Northwestern," the nurse said. "You were in a car accident, sweetie, but you're all right. Let's get you some water."

The woman walked over to a bedside table and poured water into plastic cup. Isla's hands shook as she brought the straw to her lips. She sucked the water down like life.

"I'm going to check your vitals. The doctor will be here soon."

A car accident.

Northwestern.

She was in Chicago. And she had not been the only one in the car.

His name was a whisper at first—barely a puff of air past her lips. "Ewan," she said, stronger this time. "Where is Ewan?" Every word fought to exist out in the open and not just as a scream inside her head.

The nurse didn't answer her.

He's in another room, she told herself, struggling to remember what had happened. She couldn't remember why they'd been in a car, or when, or what day it was. Every time she tried to grab at a memory it danced away from her, back into the dark.

Her attending physician was Dr. Bhavani. She appreciated that he talked to her in a calm, soothing voice, because terror was quickly replacing confusion. No one else had shown up.

And no one was talking about Ewan.

"You've sustained a concussion from the accident," Dr. Bhavani told her. "How is your head feeling?"

"It hurts. And I'm nauseous."

"That's to be expected from a concussion. We'll get you in for a brain scan to be sure nothing more serious is going on, and we'll most likely keep you overnight for observation."

She let them poke and prod until the question couldn't live inside her anymore. "Ewan Park. Ewan was . . . in the car with me. Is he here? Is he okay?"

Dr. Bhavani hesitated, then glanced at the nurse. She knew that glance. It was the *your mother has stage four colon cancer* glance. The *how much do we tell her* glance. The *is this the right time* glance.

"Mr. Park is in the ICU in critical condition," the doctor confessed.

No. Oh no, oh no.

She stared at him as he explained as much as he could: as he used the terms *traumatic brain injury* and *coma*. As he confirmed her absolute worst fears.

The accident had happened anyway, and Ewan had paid the price for her avoidance instead.

Isla could feel the hyperventilating start deep in her lungs: a hitch of the breath, and then another, and then another as her airwaves squeezed themselves down to the size of straws. The nurse—a Latina woman in her forties, her wavy dark hair in a sensible ponytail—dropped her hand on the blankets covering Isla's knee and left it there, her squeeze as gentle as a kneading kitten's paw as she instructed Isla to slow down her breathing, that's it, deep slow breaths.

There was a waiting inside her chest; an emptiness waiting to be filled by something explosive that hadn't yet arrived. The hush before a volatile argument. The peaceful moments before a panic attack gripped her by the throat. The eerie quiet after a mother stopped breathing and the machines flatlined.

The hospital room door opened, and the swift and violent urge to weep choked her when she saw Willow, Jun-su, and Tae in the doorway. Their beloved, familiar faces. Their wrecked faces.

"They said . . ." Isla hated how weak and small her voice sounded. "But he'll wake up."

Dr. Bhavani and the nurse silently stepped out. Willow sat on the bed and shielded her from the room in a hug. She rested her forehead against Isla's and cried silently.

"He'll wake up," Isla insisted.

Will sniffled, sat up, and took Tae's offered tissue with a watery thank-you. "Babe, I'm . . . I'm so happy you're okay.

You were out for hours, and we were so scared. Mom and Dad are on their way now."

That was fine, that was well and good, but that wasn't what Isla cared about. "Ewan," she said, to get Will on track.

A flash flood of anger merged with the sorrow on Tae's face. He looked away, his chin trembling, his hair tousled by quaking fingers. "Some idiot," he said fiercely. "Tried to merge *drunk*, then hit—then . . . aish!" He cut off, as if the words just wouldn't come, as if he couldn't grab at them any more than Isla could grab at her memories. He didn't attempt again and covered his mouth instead, rocking ever so slightly where he stood.

Jun-su hugged him from behind and met Isla's gaze over Tae's head, eyes brutally dry but pools of grief. "People saw, gave statements. The driver was drunk—"

"Three times over the legal limit," Willow interjected furiously.

"—entered the highway too fast. Ewan swerved but hit another car. He came up from behind. You probably didn't see it in time."

Exactly like the first accident. Exactly. No. It *was* the first accident.

Except Ewan had driven this time. Ewan drove, because Isla had been too eager to shove that responsibility on someone else. And look what happened.

"I want to see Ewan."

The trio exchanged glances. She didn't know why. Of course she wanted to see him. She had no memory of this, no memory at all. The last concrete memory she had was leaving the hotel room, heading for the parking garage and the rental car. Holding Ewan's hand. The flash of his smile.

She needed to see him.

"Isla," Jun-su started. She immediately hated his careful tone. "It's . . . upsetting. Are you sure?

"*Yes*, I am sure."

"His parents are with him," Tae said, his voice halting and wavering.

"What day is it?" Isla asked. She didn't know where these questions were coming from. They seemed to spring out of thin air, plucked from a random language generator and spit out of her mouth with an efficiency that had nothing to do with her. Who was really asking them? What on earth did they hope to achieve?

"Sunday night," Willow said, after a brief hesitation. "It's late. Maybe visit him tomorrow. Maybe he'll be awake—"

"His parents are here?"

Tae and Jun-su nodded. Isla's mind couldn't make sense of the two disjointed concepts—the accident happening in Chicago, just now, just minutes ago as far she was concerned, and Ewan's parents being here in Chicago.

"Take me to him," she told them. She could hear the edge of hysteria in her own voice. She didn't give a good goddamn. "Now. I want to see him." Isla tugged at the IV taped to the back of her hand. She ignored the chorus of protests and tried to push Jun-su's and Willow's hands away.

"Isla, let's not do that," the nurse said firmly as she came back into the room.

"I need to see him," she told the woman, pleading, because Jesus, *someone* had to understand how important this was. She needed to know it was real, needed to see his face, even if it was settled in a deep sleep.

"You will," the nurse said. "But we have to arrange it first. Sit tight, and don't pull out your IV. We'll get you a wheelchair."

CHAPTER TWENTY-THREE

Isla could not reconcile the laughing, easygoing Ewan of her memory with the motionless form of the man in the hospital bed. He was still her Ewan in his strong jawline, marred with cuts from windshield glass; in his thick black hair, swept back from his beautiful face; in the closed lashes of his eyelids.

He didn't respond to any of the stimuli around him, even though the ICU was crowded and noisy. They didn't know when he would wake from the coma; his traumatic brain injury was extensive.

Mrs. Ahn and Mr. Park sat side by side in the two hospital chairs by his bedside. Jun-su wheeled her next to them, and Isla wanted to wither away into nothing from the guilt and shame of facing his parents after doing this to him. They couldn't have known this was her fault, but she expected them to somehow pick up on it regardless. She braced herself for their anger and furious grief because it was what she deserved, but they remained ignorant of her role.

Mr. Park squeezed her hands and expressed how relieved he was that she'd woken up. Mrs. Ahn rose and fluttered around the small enclosure, busying herself and her hands by getting Isla water, asking if she and Jun-su and Tae wanted something to eat. She decided Isla was cold and made Jun-su fetch a blanket from somewhere, anywhere, she didn't care.

Isla wanted to ask for more updates on Ewan, but her questions died on her tongue when Mrs. Ahn's fervently bright and wrecked eyes met hers. His mother was barely keeping herself in one piece, and the last thing Isla wanted to do was hammer into Mrs. Ahn's veneer and shatter it in public.

Jun-su settled a warmed blanket on her lap, and she let her fingers graze his arm to get his attention. "Can you bring me closer to him?" she whispered.

He pushed her forward, on the other side of Ewan's parents, until she was relatively level with his head. All of the liveliness and quiet loveliness of Ewan Park had been drained out of him, leaving behind a shell of the man she fiercely loved. She reached out with a trembling hand and swept her fingers through the dark strands of his hair until the world blurred and she couldn't see him anymore.

"I'm so sorry," she whispered brokenly.

"It is not your fault, Isla," Jun-su said, his hands closing over her shoulders and squeezing.

Oh, but it was. She almost told him so, but she knew she'd choke on her words and have a total breakdown in front of all these people.

She stayed. They all stayed. Eventually, Mr. Park left to get everyone food from the cafeteria, and Jun-su and Tae volunteered to go with him. Isla found herself alone with Mrs. Ahn.

For lack of anything better to say, Isla offered a "Do you need anything, Mrs. Ahn?" Besides your son not being in a coma?

A brief, humorless smile quirked Mrs. Ahn's lips. Her eyes never left her son. "Nothing anyone can give me right now."

Isla nodded jerkily, and they fell into a silence a few degrees off from comfortable. She fervently wanted to break it again, but the only things she wanted to say revolved around profuse apology and groveling that would end in an ugly showing of tears. She had no intention of embarrassing Ewan's mother today, so she left them unsaid.

Mrs. Ahn did her the favor instead. "Ewan." She stopped, squeezed her eyes shut, as if uttering his name physically hurt. "Ewan told me your mother passed away recently."

"Almost two years ago," Isla replied. In this very hospital.

"Cancer, he said."

"Yes."

Mrs. Ahn did look at her then, not unkindly. "He said you cared for her."

"She needed me. No one should go through that alone."

"No, they shouldn't," Mrs. Ahn agreed quietly.

The conversation freed up more words, enough for Isla to compile sentences. "Ewan won't be alone, either. During his recovery, I mean. Obviously, he has you and Mr. Park and . . ." Isla closed her eyes and instead of stammering, gave herself another second to restart. Mrs. Ahn graced her with that space, and she appreciated it. "I meant that I will be here when he wakes and after. I know I haven't been dating your son long, but he is so special to me. Ewan has helped me become a better and stronger person."

The words made Isla's chest feel like it would cave in on itself. But she wasn't done. She gathered her courage and continued, even though the tears built a dam in her throat. "And he loves you so much. He talks about you all the time. You're his hero."

Mrs. Ahn stared at her son with unshed tears glistening in her eyes. "He is mine."

Isla held herself together with frayed twine and twigs while they waited by Ewan's bedside, willing him to wake.

Willing him to be all right.

* * *

They wanted to keep her overnight for observation, which was just fine with Isla. She'd stay as long as they'd let her to stay close to Ewan.

The next morning, some of the fog and confusion had cleared, and Isla could arrange her thoughts in an order that made sense. Or as much sense as she could make of how the world had changed. Her head still throbbed like a rotting tooth, but the scans didn't show any signs of a traumatic brain injury. Her hands stopped trembling. She retained all of her fine motor skills and had no problems holding a pen to write or a fork to eat. She was healthy.

It was all wrong.

Every passing minute was another minute progressing into a timeline she did not recognize, had no blueprint for, no way forward that eased the agony down in her marrow, down into the very fabric of her. There was no separation between it and her, fused as they were by a fire that would not go out. One that reminded her every waking minute.

She'd put him in that coma.

The hospital door opened for the thousandth time, and Isla gritted her teeth. There was no true rest in a hospital, ever. People were constantly in and out, and that door opened and shut, opened and shut, all hours of the day.

"Hey," Willow said with way more cheer than Isla wanted to hear. Fake cheer. Isla had used that same tone on her mother when she was in the hospital, and she deeply regretted doing that now. I'm so sorry, Mom, it is the fucking worst.

"Mmm, pudding." Will sat gingerly on the side of the bed after giving Isla a kiss on the forehead. "Are you gonna eat all that?"

"All yours," Isla replied. There was little point in eating, no matter how hollow her stomach felt. No matter how much it gurgled and twisted around itself, seeking the food she wouldn't give it.

She didn't miss the way Willow watched her. She knew her affect had been flat since she'd found out that her lover had been ejected from a car and languished in a coma. In an accident meant for her, and only her.

"When they release you, which I guess might be later today or tomorrow, I'm going to bring you some tamales from the tamale guy."

Willow prattled on about this, that, and the other, and Isla could only follow for so long before it became white noise in the background of the film reel playing on repeat in her head. Trying to fill in the holes of the accident.

Trying to remember the moment she'd asked him to drive, and to take her place.

She'd made him take her place.

Isla's mind wanted to buckle under the weight of it.

". . . your dad come by?"

Isla blinked. Stared at Willow uncomprehendingly. "What?"

"Did your dad come by?"

"No. Well. Yes. He left . . ." She gestured vaguely at the flowers crowded on the windowsill. She wished people would stop sending so many goddamn flowers. They weren't coming home with her. They were all going to die. Nice, empty gestures. Will's parents. Jun-su and Tae. Dad.

"Did you see him?"

Isla snorted. "No. He left a note, said he came while I was sleeping. Told me to call him if I needed anything."

Willow's expression could have shattered glass. "I see. Well, if you need anything, you call me or my parents."

Isla rewarded Willow with a small smile that felt foreign and forced on her face. It didn't belong there, and it knew it. Willow stayed, and Isla was grateful to have her, but also eager to be alone again. She just wanted to sit with her guilt and grief and figure out what to do next.

Because there *was* a next. Eventually she would be discharged and flown home. Eventually they would leave her alone with a bottle of pain medication. If Ewan didn't recover, if his injuries were so severe that it killed him or he never woke again, she knew what to do next.

She could not wait.

Isla startled badly when Willow touched her hair, and Will reared back, raising her arms. One hand held a bottle of hair product. "I'm sorry, I just wanted to spritz some detangler on that mop of hair. We've got some tangles in there we should probably get out."

"No." Isla disagreed.

"Honey, I love you, but those knots are spawning new life and spreading their li'l babies all over your head."

"That's gross."

"I know, and it's not even my hair. I'll be as gentle as I can, I promise."

Isla batted Willow's hands away. "I can do it."

"Let me. Please."

She hated the plea in her best friend's face. *It's the least I can do.* Isla very suddenly despised herself for not even allowing her friend to be her friend while the world was blowing apart. Her shoulders slumped in acceptance.

Will showered Isla's matted hair with the detangler, then carefully (tenderly, Isla noted in the deepest recesses of her angry, grief-stricken mind) worked a comb through the tangles. "I brought some dry shampoo," Willow said absently, just to fill the silence. "We can throw it up in a ponytail until you can get home to have a real shower. Being hospitalized is the worst, even for a little while."

The great dignity robber, Isla thought. That's what her mom used to say—being hospitalized was the quickest way to have your dignity stripped away for the sake of your health and safety. Where you were no longer in control of your body or your decisions. And hell, she wasn't even really injured—this was *healthy* Isla, waiting to be discharged once they deemed her well enough after the concussion. It was amusing to assume she had any control over her life or her choices at all. Fate, it seemed, was determined to march on regardless.

And punish her for even trying to thwart it.

"I did this to him." Isla wasn't aware she'd said it aloud until Willow stopped pulling the comb through her hair.

"No you did not," Willow replied quietly.

"Yes, I did," Isla said slowly. "We thought we could stop it. He thought . . . it would make a difference. And it did, for a while. But none of it mattered. It happened anyway." She looked up at Will, who blurred through a sheen of tears. "And Ewan was driving. I *put* him there. It was supposed to be me, and they gave it to him instead to punish me." Hot tears streaked down her cheeks.

She knew it didn't make sense to Will, but she had to say it—get it out of her like poison. Let someone else know that she'd done this to the only man she'd ever loved, and the only thing he had ever done was try to save her. She didn't even know who *they* were. God? The universe? Whoever had decided to give her and Ewan a second chance that was just as doomed as the first.

"Honey, no, no." Willow gathered her in a hug. "There is no vengeful god out there punishing you for anything, because you have done nothing wrong. It was a senseless, tragic accident, and I can't even begin to tell you how sorry I am that this is happening to both of you. I can't imagine what you're going through. But you are not being punished. And he *will* get better."

Isla let Willow think that, and let all of her other thoughts go unspoken, because if she voiced them, the grief might strike her dead before she had the chance to just do it herself. Ewan was in a coma he might never wake from. Even if he did, he'd sustained a traumatic brain injury. No TBI was the same, and she had no idea how severe it would be for him. And it was her fault. These were the facts in this new nightmare timeline.

After Will left, her nurse Elena lingered, busying herself with Isla's vitals and moving the tray of untouched food off to the side. "Isla, you have to eat," Elena said quietly. "I know you've been through something terrible. But you have to give your body the nutrients it needs."

She didn't wait for a response and left Isla alone with the plate of cold food. The howling in her stomach grew louder.

At her core, Isla was a coward. She gave in and ate the pudding.

* * *

He died in the middle of the night.

While Isla slept, whole and uninjured, Ewan died.

By the time they told her, his body had already been removed. Sent back to St. Louis to prepare for a funeral. Somewhere in that conversation, with Jun-su talking as calmly as possible and Tae in tears, barely able to speak, someone vaguely mentioned that they'd waited to tell her to spare her the pain for as long as they could. Since she had been in the car with him. Since she wasn't fully recovered herself. The words floated around in her brain out of order, half remembered. Maybe the conversation hadn't even happened.

Isla didn't remember anything the doctor had said to her when they discharged her and gave their condolences. Her brain was stuck on one thought, in an endless loop.

Ewan was dead. While she slept, he had died of injuries she had given him.

She had to put on the clothing she'd worn when the accident happened, since a hospital gown was no longer needed for healthy women who'd dodged the injuries meant for them. The skirt and sweater were the only belongings she had with her, except for a purse in surprisingly good condition. She still had to go back to the hotel to retrieve the luggage. Possibly. She'd called to let them know what happened and authorized Willow to get her and Ewan's things from the room, because there was no way she could set foot in that hotel room. She couldn't enter the last place they had been happy and whole together. But now she couldn't remember if Willow had the luggage or if the hotel was holding it.

Ewan was dead.

Discharge meant being handed pain medication for the lingering headaches, signing papers to okay billing her insurance for whatever exorbitant amount her two-day hospital stay would be. The equivalent of her college debt, most likely. Isla stared around the room, at the flowers making a garden on the windowsill, the lake glittering a hard blue beyond. She couldn't look at it. Chicago felt like a foreign city to her now. She didn't know where to place her feet if it wasn't by his side.

One by one, Isla picked up each vase of flowers and dumped them into the trash can until the windowsill was empty.

A knock on the door sent her flying out of her skin, a glass upset off the table and shattered.

"Sorry," Tae said, his hands raised in a calming gesture. He hid his hair beneath a beanie, appropriate for the cool spring weather, and the baggy jacket he wore swallowed his thin frame. His foot tapped relentlessly against the tile, a nervous tic that spoke of his discomfort with the hospital, with the entire trip, with every aspect of this reality. His red-rimmed eyes could not settle on any one thing for longer than a hummingbird's flight pattern. He looked like he hadn't slept all night. Like he'd just lost his brother.

"We didn't mean to scare you." Jun-su gave her a small, sad smile. He looked, as always, adorably handsome: perfect ash-blond hair swooping into his eyes, dangling earrings, ringed fingers sweeping back the hair, only to have it fall in his face again. He also looked tired, his normally bright brown eyes dull and careworn. "Ready to go?"

Isla blinked stupidly. "Go?"

Tae jangled a set of keys. "Home. They let you out, yes?"

She nodded. She'd heard every word they said, and not a single one made sense.

"Let's get you home." Jun-su said it like it was the most natural, obvious thing in the world. Isla wanted to reject it, to not believe it, but she couldn't hold on to the lie because Jun-su had never, ever been anything but honest with her. He deserved to be believed.

She managed to speak over the tightness in her throat. "You didn't have to stay. To take me back. I would have found a way." Eventually. Isla didn't actually have a plan to get home yet, because they'd driven Ewan's car to the city, and Ewan's car was totaled.

"You're our friend, Isla," he said patiently. "You haven't stopped being our friend. And we have your luggage; Willow gave it to me this morning."

Her eyes slid away from his, at the same time Tae's gaze dropped to the floor at the reminder. She swallowed once, twice. "Thank you," she whispered.

It was strange and uncomfortable to be back in a car. Isla didn't care for it one bit. She avoided looking at oncoming traffic and braced her hands against the seat as Jun-su drove. Tae tried to fool them into thinking he was as cheerful as his old self, but she could feel his pain in the pockets of silence, when he couldn't hold on to the smile any longer and stared out the window into nothing.

Isla didn't remember anything about the four-and-a-half-hour drive afterward. Nothing anyone said, nothing she saw along the way. They rarely spoke after Springfield, preferring instead the silence of shared grief. It weighed as much as wet summer air in New Orleans.

Seeing her cottage come into view gave Isla her second jolt of the day. It looked as it had when she'd first seen it: not yet hers, an empty vessel. Even the gravel popping under the car's tires sounded unnaturally loud and unfamiliar.

Jun-su got out first and went to the trunk. Isla saw them as she stepped out of the car and joined him—the suitcases. Hers and Ewan's. Jun-su carried them in, and Isla stared at Ewan's tidy little black suitcase as it bobbed along under his grip.

Isla expected the living room to be cold and choked with stale air, even though she had been gone only a week, but it was the same. Jun-su went into the kitchen and tinkered around in there doing . . . something. She was worn out from the travel, so she huddled under a blanket in the living room with Tae to keep her company.

She must have dozed off, because when she woke up, it was dark outside. The house smelled like apples and cinnamon, and her head only hurt a little. A bearable nagging along the crown of her head.

"She wakes," Tae commented. He was sprawled on the living room rug, watching something on television. Jun-su had taken the armchair. He put down his sketch pad and went into the kitchen, then came back with a mug full of something steaming.

"It's a night for cider," he said. She took the cup with a thank-you and sipped the hot cider, feeling the warmth of it trail through her.

Isla didn't feel deserving of how they had taken care of her since the accident. Perhaps it was a distraction for them, but it was far more kindness than she'd expected nonetheless. "Thank you. For everything. I don't know how to repay you."

"By taking care of yourself," Jun-su answered. "I didn't intend for our collaboration to be the only one."

Isla stared down at the amber liquid in her cup. She didn't deserve to create anything with him after killing his best friend. "I'd like that," she said, her voice small and pathetic. Every word tasted like ash.

Jun-su joined Tae on the floor, sitting cross-legged next to his lover and idly stroking his back as he watched the movie playing and sipped cider. The pang of longing that lanced through Isla hit the very center of her, like a stomach cramp. Watching Tae and Jun-su together fragmented her until there were too many broken pieces to put back together. She would never have this with Ewan again, or anyone else. No one would ever compare to what he was to her—what he did for her.

You know you have a way out, her brain reminded her.

She did. And she felt it as strongly as the longing now, as if giving it space in her brain to grow and develop made it real. If this was it, she didn't have to bear it for long. And for once, Isla let herself feel the full weight of it. Mentally acted it out. Sending the boys home. Drawing a bath and bringing her pain medication with her. One long, endless sleep. It was so tempting she could taste it, the want so huge that it frightened her and calmed her at the same time.

But you made a promise. Not in so many words. Ewan isn't here to lose you again, but other people are.

Like the talented street artist who came up to hug her from behind while she put her cup away in the dishwasher. She twisted to embrace him properly, and felt love and a sweet ache swell in her chest. She stroked his hair and held him tighter when a soundless sob rocked him. Isla beckoned the lanky, loitering figure in the doorway to come forward, and Tae joined them, his long arms wrapping around them both, his eyes bright with unshed tears.

Could she disappoint Ewan again? Leave her new family and the new life she'd built? Just because it was hard?

No.

No, she couldn't.

So she tucked the action away in her back pocket. It was oddly comforting to have it there, even if she never pulled it out to use it. She would, instead, schedule an appointment with her therapist to find a release valve for some of this pressure. To find a way to live in her skin without wanting to tear it off.

She sent Tae and Jun-su home with the promise of getting together for dinner the following weekend. They wanted to stay the night; she could tell they didn't feel comfortable leaving her home alone and wanted to stay over, but she needed the space and solitude. The funeral would happen soon.

Isla needed to prepare for that alone.

* * *

Hell was a cold funeral home heaped with flowers.

Someone must have drained all the oxygen out of the room, because Isla could not breathe in any way that satisfied her lungs' desperation for air. The contents of Ewan's life were strewn all about her: childhood friends she'd never had the chance to meet, college friends, coworkers she knew, a few other familiar faces. Family. Mr. Park and Mrs. Ahn spent the majority of the evening in a corner near the casket with an elderly Korean couple, greeting guests. She could barely look into the eyes of Ewan's grandparents, which were haunted by the grief-stricken shock and jet lag of flying halfway around the world to bury their grandson.

Everyone in the room looked as if they had stumbled out of that car on Lake Shore, asking strangers if they knew what had happened. When Isla approached his parents to express condolences, her voice abandoned her. Mrs. Ahn gave her one slow nod that Isla returned, and Mr. Park's greeting and questions fell on ears that could not make sense of what he said.

Isla did not hear a word of the service. She spent it parked in a chair, clasping Tae's hand tightly next to the rungs. He shivered in a way that had nothing to do with cold, hunching into himself as he stared at the casket housing his best friend, eyes bright with anger and shedding tears he didn't bother wiping away. He was unmoved by Jun-su's hand on his back, where it stayed motionless, ready to pluck him back from the ledge if needed.

She had avoided the casket all night.

It wasn't until the crowd began to disperse that Isla approached on feet weighed with lead to greet the not-Ewan resting inside gleaming mahogany. A poised, still shell of the man whose smiling photo she'd passed on the way in—the one she had taken for his company's website.

We have both been here now, Rabbit, she thought, holding tightly to the memories of the first Ewan to keep herself from floating away on cut balloon strings. She'd float until the wind burst her wide open, scattering what was left of her to the four corners of the earth. Had he, too, felt this sense of being unmoored, unmade, unreal? Had either of them ever thought they would both be in the same place quite like this?

She stayed at Jun-su and Tae's to ride with them to the graveside service in the morning. They dragged all the bedding into the living room to cocoon like children, and Isla lay awake into the night. Perhaps his parents were now putting together or had already created the shrine at home to remember their son by. Perhaps they were giving his grandfather the painting Ewan had bought for him to tether a loving memory between the two of them across all that distance. That thread only went one way now.

By the morning of the burial, Isla had descended into a beautiful numbness that carried her like a boat over the still waters of death, all the way through the service. It enabled her to look Mrs. Ahn and Mr. Park in the eye as she apologized, which they took as a condolence for their loss when she actually meant it as an apology for robbing them of their son.

Isla went home. Whole and healthy and alive.

And a murderer.

They were going to cremate him, she remembered as she sank onto her couch in the quiet living room with its lake walls. There'd be no place to visit him like there was for her mother. Ewan was gone. The idea of both present Ewan and future Ewan gone permanently, forever and always, was unbearable. She had walked away from that accident with her future unhindered by injury, and it had cost him his life.

*　　*　　*

Isla drifted for days. The hours were meaningless, empty pockets of time passing that she barely felt. She ate only when the hunger pangs grew unbearable. Every phone call went unanswered. She locked herself inside the cottage that was no longer a haven, no longer a comfort. It was a constant reminder of her failure.

Ghosts of Ewan's voice traveled the air in all the rooms. He teased her in the bedroom, whispered sweet nothings in her ear. Laughed in the kitchen at something she said. He mourned her from another timeline, asking her to say his name again because he wanted to hear it from her lips.

He had been taken from her, twice. And so she asked the universe again: how much pain could be inflicted on a single person before they broke completely?

"Why?" she asked the empty room. Her vision blurred. This couldn't have been what future Ewan intended. He couldn't have known. He was just trying to help her, and look what it had done to him.

Her chest heaved. She rocked herself into a ball and wept until the evening light slanted into nothing between the drapes.

There was no point to any of this. Future Isla had been such a weak idiot. Taking her life when she *had* a Ewan. As if the brain injury were the worst thing. As if it could compare to killing her lover while trying to avoid what was evidently inevitable.

She lost time inside her own head, her thoughts replaying the last nine months over and over. At some point, she must have slept. The sun dared to show its face again, reminding her that time was still a real construct and another day had arrived.

There was something important forming, some thought, just out of reach. A normal sensation at this point, but this time it really bothered her. She was on the cusp of a realization that felt vital.

It dogged her as she stared blankly at her laptop screen. She attempted to log into her work desktop to check her emails and ended up merely staring at a slog of unread emails that she would have rather printed out and set on fire in a ceremonious burning than read.

It didn't hit her until she remembered that she needed to pay the mortgage.

Mortgage at her house. The house she still lived in. The house past Isla lived in too.

If Ewan had been able to reach her here . . . could she reach herself?

Oh god, oh god, could she undo it? The whole fucking thing? Isla nearly threw her laptop to the ground as she stood to pace. Could that actually work? And if she managed to reach herself *after* she knew about Ewan, then she wouldn't have to go through the rigmarole Ewan had to. The message was simple.

Stay the hell off Lake Shore Drive.

But as soon as the flare of hope lit up her chest like a beacon, it died before she could use it to signal for help. Because the accident had happened twice now, in the exact same spot. So maybe she avoided Lake Shore and thwarted it a third time and saved Ewan, but what about the fourth time? And the fifth? What if he kept dying? What if someone else died too? Could she keep doing this, just to save herself from her injuries? Just put the accident on repeat—have it, undo it, worry about the next time, have it, undo it, and worry some more about when and who it would involve?

She wanted to. Oh, god, a part of her wanted to throw the blankets over her head and avoid it until she left this mortal coil. She didn't want her life to change like this. She wanted to keep trying until the ball landed on the number she'd bet on and the roulette wheel could stop spinning. Until it gave her the health she had now and the man she loved at the same time. She wanted to be able to paint without pain and not kill her lover, and that did not seem like much to ask of the universe.

But she couldn't guarantee it. And she wanted a life with Ewan more. She wanted him to *not be dead*. So what's worse, Isla? she asked herself in the dead silence of her living room. What's worse? An accident you can recover from, or running the risk of killing Ewan over and over just to stay physically healthy?

Accept it. Accept it the way your mother had to accept a cancer diagnosis, the way people have to accept limb loss, the way people have to accept all of the shitty, unfair things that happen to them along the way. Sure, she could keep preventing it and live for the next time and the next time and drive herself crazy.

Or she could save Ewan right now, and move on with her life.

If the accident was determined to happen, then the consequences didn't have to touch anyone else she loved. There were worse things.

Oh, there were worse things.

CHAPTER TWENTY-FOUR

Isla reached for her phone and went into her messages. She could not stop the jolt of pain and grief at seeing Ewan's thread. She started a new one, and typed in her own number.

She had no idea if this would work. At all. Before she could let her brain go down that rabbit hole, she messaged herself.

Isla? It's future you. I need you to listen to me, but I need to know you're there and that you got this message.

She hit send.

It sent.

And the phone spat it back out at her. Delivered to herself.

She frowned. Did that mean it didn't take? How would she know?

Ten minutes went by, then fifteen. Then an hour. Nothing. Isla wanted to break her phone into a thousand electronic shards.

Did it need to come from a different number? What were the rules? Who decided whether this worked or not? Had she and Ewan been given only one chance, one pathway through time from Ewan's future into Isla's past, from his phone to hers? That was a problem she couldn't solve, because his phone had been lost in the accident.

"Would someone like to explain?" she demanded to the empty room. "There is something *clearly different* about this cottage, and someone is responsible for it. Help? Please?" Her voice cracked.

Silence.

No. No, this wasn't acceptable. There had to be a way to undo this. If Ewan had been able to connect with her, damn it, she should be able to as well. His death *wasn't supposed to happen.*

Technically, neither was yours, the devil's advocate inside her reminded her. You chose to do that, not anyone else.

"And I'm choosing not to do it," she said aloud sharply. And it had nothing to do with the accident—it did and it didn't. If fate chose to right itself by causing the accident, fine, whatever. But it should never have taken him. She didn't care if she was messing with forces she didn't understand by tampering with the timeline again. Ewan had done it for her. Now she could save him too. Something about this cottage had let that line of communication open up between them. Or maybe it was a glitch in the system, or an anomaly that a few people just stumbled upon, but either way: if it had worked once, it stood to reason that it would work again.

The universe could not be that cruel and unfeeling.

Are you sure about that?

Isla wanted to growl at her own negative self. She wished she had another phone to try it out on, but if that phone was texting her current number, it wouldn't matter anyway—it'd just go to her phone.

Helplessly confused, Isla glared at Digby, her sweet little northern white-faced owl tucked away in her painting, and wanted to shriek until he flew away in a flurry of feathers. How did this work? How could she *do* this?

Ewan had texted Isla after she'd died. From the future, he'd texted a dead woman's number.

So she had to do the same.

Isla's shoulders slumped. Oh, Christ, she was not ready to contact him. Wasn't ready to put herself in his shoes. But it was the only tactic she hadn't tried. She went back to Ewan's thread on her phone.

Ewan. It's Isla. Are you getting this?

The finger hovering over the send button trembled. Isla stared at the thread. This didn't feel right. She didn't know where in the past her text would go. What happened if she messaged him while her past self was around? Did she want to advertise her existence this way? Would it jeopardize what she was trying to do?

Just see if it works. All of this worry is for nothing if it doesn't work. Isla deleted the text. She took deep, measured breaths to calm her fretful heart.

And hit call.

Isla's eyes slid closed as the phone rang. And rang.

Click.

"Something you want to tell me that can't wait, Buttercup?"

Ewan's voice, rich and warm in her ear, amused and reverberant like so many church bells pealing, filled Isla's ear with a hope so razor-sharp it cut her. She didn't dare breathe, because he could not know how soon he was going to die.

Her shoulders shook with the effort to hold in her elation and terror and grief as he let out a faint chuckle. Was this how her first Ewan had felt when she told him who she was? Like the world had cracked open and he was falling endlessly through it, desperate to grab on to anything that made sense?

Ewan hung up. She dropped her phone on the rug and clasped her hands over her mouth, gasping for air as if she'd broken the surface after a particularly vicious wave. Ewan and Isla could only reach each other through time after death. But she'd reached a Ewan who already knew her. Ewan had reached an Isla who didn't know him.

Why?

When Ewan texted her, she'd been about three years away from dying by suicide. The Ewan she just called could only be, at most, seven or eight months away from the accident that killed him.

Every cell within her rattled the cage of ordinary physics that kept her from understanding whatever magic allowed them to connect in this way. What were the rules? *What were the rules?* It felt like playing a memory game using pictures she had never seen to begin with. The calming blue of her traitorous cottage had turned into the tumultuous waves of a storm, soaking her to the bone and filling her mouth with salt.

There had to be some logic or reason behind the change in time. If she could crack that, she'd stand a better chance at knowing what to do with the Ewan she could reach, because right now it felt hopeless. She couldn't convince him to let her go through with a car accident, and she worried that if she tried, it would somehow damage their relationship in the past.

Isla's thoughts tripped over themselves. What had been so special about the day Ewan's first text reached her? She had worked remotely. Finished a brochure. Picked up laundry. Talked to Will about Will's visit.

Talked to Will about *Isla's* visit.

Will had wanted to make birthday dinner reservations for the trip Ewan told her not to go on—the trip that would cause the first accident. Isla had agreed and scheduled that Friday off in June. Somewhere in their conversation, his text had come through.

So what was special about the day Ewan had picked up the phone? "Something you want to tell me that can't wait," Isla repeated out loud. She wanted to flinch at the sound of her own waterlogged, hollow voice. He'd sounded amused. Her past self must have been nearby, close enough that a phone call was unnecessary. Maybe they were both at the cottage?

Yes. They had to have been. The connection hadn't worked for Isla last spring when she'd left the property. He hadn't started coming over to her place until the fall, but that still left a good six- or seven-month window to comb through for a likely suspect. A glimmer of insight shimmered on the horizon of her memory, but it was too far away for her to make sense of it yet.

She kept it in her sight line as she wandered the cottage, mindlessly picking up clutter, coasting on autopilot until her toe slammed into an object that ordinarily was not in her living room. Cursing and limping, Isla sank to the floor to glare at the suitcase.

Ewan's suitcase.

She hadn't been able to bring herself to sift through the contents yet.

Isla approached the suitcase as if it held a bomb. Or the personal belongings of her dead lover. She tugged the suitcase toward her and laid it on its side. The zipper was unnaturally loud, as if a cicada had snuck in through the window to drone in her ear. She breathed in once, twice, bracing herself before opening the flap and letting it fall back to the floor.

Slacks and light sweaters in neat, orderly piles, meticulously folded. Toiletries to the side. Nice black shoes tucked underneath. *Pachinko* by Min Jin Lee.

Isla lifted the top sweater, a light cream-colored knit, and brought it to her nose. She breathed in his lingering cologne and a *Ewan*-ness that transported her onto a mountain trail. Slowly, as if she were slipping under water, Isla took off her shirt and pulled Ewan's sweater over her head. It enveloped her in a hug she sorely needed, but without the grip and strength of the real thing. It tried, and she thanked Ewan's clothes for giving her a tiny part of him back. Isla spent long minutes taking in deep, shuddering breaths, tears scorching down her cheeks, then lay down on the couch, curling her fingers into his sleeves and putting the material up to her nose again.

Focus. When had they decided to return to Chicago?

"His idea," she whispered. It had been in the fall, after her dad's terrible visit. She'd fallen asleep, right where she was now, and woken up to Ewan looking at hotels. He'd suggested the trip then and booked the rooms later that night.

What did you want to tell me?

Isla jerked upright. He'd said that to her when she came back from the bathroom. The question hadn't made sense at the time, but he'd teased her about it instead of explaining. "What did you want to tell me," she said again, testing every syllable against her tongue.

Oh god. She'd reached him the day they'd talked about going back to Chicago, where the accident would happen a second time. She had gone to use the bathroom, and her future self had called Ewan in that five-minute window.

What did that mean? Had another version of her already tried this and failed? If she remembered that interaction and the accident happened anyway, that meant another attempt failed, right? Was she doomed to repeat this loop over and over, just because she'd prevented that one first accident? "I don't understand," she said in a trembling, pleading voice to the cottage, to the connection, to dead air. A thousand moths beat their wings inside her rib cage, the onslaught robbing her of air.

Had there been other moments? Other weird things Ewan had said or missed phone calls or texts? She had to think, think hard, but her mind was an open book flipping furiously through a thousand pages. She couldn't get her thoughts to sit still long enough for her to examine each page.

"Shh, shh," she told herself, now on her feet, pacing and pacing. Vines of panic and despair crept through her, blossoming poisonous flowers as they went, and she had to cut the growth before it consumed her. Now was not the time to fall apart. Now was the time for action. Put your thinking cap on, as her mother used to say, and figure out what the hell to do now. Isla abruptly sat back down on the rug and bowed her head. Listened to the wind chimes gently collide with one another, creating a haphazard melody of tinkling bells. Slowed down her breathing until the roaring blood in her veins settled into a steady stream.

When had Ewan booked that hotel? She needed a date to know what her specific time difference to him was. "Sometime in November" wouldn't cut it. Isla grabbed her phone and searched her emails to see if he'd forwarded her a confirmation email for their booking.

And there it was: a reservation confirmation from the Allegro Royal Sonesta Hotel. *Thank you, darling, for being so thorough.*

The email had been sent on November 15. It was May 10. They were almost six months apart. The second accident had been one week ago.

She was beginning to understand.

The difference in time between the two timelines wasn't fixed. It was dependent on choices. Isla's choice to take the trip that would cause the accident future Ewan was trying to prevent. Ewan's choice to take the trip that caused a replay of the accident she was trying to undo.

Isla couldn't approach this the way Ewan had. They had different goals, even though they'd fixated on the same event. She needed to save Ewan's life. Ewan couldn't save his own life because it wasn't a decision he could make.

She had to convince herself to let the accident happen as it would have originally. It was the only way. The difference now was the difference future Ewan had tried to make from the very beginning. Not preventing the accident, but showing her a different path. Showing her what she was capable of.

How was she going to do this if her phone connected to Ewan's? How could she reach herself with Ewan in the middle? And *when* should she talk to her past self?

She worried that if she told her past self to go through with the accident too early, it would give the other Isla too much time to panic and avoid it altogether. But then again, if she waited too *long* and didn't tell herself until right before the accident, past Isla might also panic and not go through with it. She knew herself: Isla spiraled when plans changed at the last minute. If she was given such a monumental task with no time to mentally prepare for it, she would avoid it. And if past Isla avoided the accident, it would just happen again, and again, and again. It would hurt Ewan and god knew who else over and over, and Isla couldn't live with that.

If another Isla had already tried this, that might have been the fail point. So she had to contact her earlier.

But when?

* * *

The key was in her camera roll.

Isla had a habit of taking pictures of Ewan when he was sleeping, because he was an outrageously adorable sleeper. Mouth slightly open, hair falling across his forehead, handsome features nearly angelic when completely relaxed in slumber. She opened the album dedicated to him and scrolled through to find any sleeping photos of him from the past six months, when he was visiting at the cottage. The dates and times attached to these photos would give her solid openings to reach her past self while Ewan was sleeping, because she would see her own name on the caller ID and pick it up before he woke up.

There were three candidates. The week before Christmas, the dreaded food poisoning of New Year's Eve, and the weekend of his birthday in March. Isla hated all of these options. Hated that she had to pick the time to ruin her past self's day and make her carry the burden of what she'd have to do in April. She had the choice of giving herself four months or one month to prepare.

She already knew the correct answer. The more preparation she gave herself, the better. But that also meant she couldn't fix this right away. She had to wait for the past timeline to catch up to that New Year's Eve weekend.

The clearer the solution became, the shallower her breathing grew. All the other doors had shut, edges sealed tight, latches secured, handles barred with an immeasurably heavy thing she would never be able to budge. But there was still a way through.

The only thing she could do now was wait.

CHAPTER TWENTY-FIVE

"Isla?"

Jun-su's stare was stocked with careful kindness; a look she had grown used to. Neither man had wanted her to spend Memorial Day weekend alone, so here she was, huddled in a corner of Jun-su's studio above the garage, losing herself in the worlds she sketched for future paintings while Jun-su also sketched out a new mural. Warm, late-spring air swirled in from the open windows. Tae was outside in the garden, where he spent most of his time now when he wasn't working. A month ago, she would have been overjoyed to sit here with Jun-su and sketch out their next projects and chat idly with him about any old thing. Today she felt nothing. Worse than nothing. The paintings were a way to pass the time and give her a buffer from her own thoughts.

"I'm sorry, did you say something?" she asked. It was a chore to inject any sort of life into her voice.

"We should break for lunch soon," he said.

"I'm not hungry," she said. "But thank you."

She ignored the thinly veiled concern that creased his face and went back to the sketch. Three weeks had passed. Nearly the halfway point until she reached back in time again. Isla honestly didn't know what day it was anymore, because her mind paid closer attention to a different timeline now. She just had to get through the days.

So she painted.

* * *

Isla abandoned the idea of having a spare bedroom and turned it into an art storage room. The burst of desperate creativity to distract herself from her grief proved fruitful and she had nowhere else to put the murals unless she rented a storage unit in the city.

She stood among the murals, brooding at them. She resented them for springing forth after he'd died, as if that was the only way they could exist. As if she could have this only in a timeline that took him away.

That was bullshit, and she would prove it.

Because it was almost her birthday, and it was time to reopen the path to the past.

It was New Year's Eve in that timeline, and Ewan was asleep. Past Isla would be on the couch next to him, reading. This was Isla's perfect window to reach herself.

And yet Isla's anxiety soared all the way to the top of the Gateway Arch. She'd taken her medication to keep relatively calm, but the weight of her actions today busted through the chemical barrier aimed at steadying her body's fight-or-flight response. Sitting and staring at the phone did nothing but turn the dial up on the low level of buzzing adrenaline that invaded every inch of her.

She had been framing the argument for weeks now. Playing out the pending conversation, anticipating the protests, building counterarguments, playing devil's advocate with herself to come up with an ironclad defense to convince her past self to go through with the accident.

Because she was painfully aware of what she was asking herself to do. Her past self was going to learn that the accident was a fated, unavoidable tragedy, guaranteed to either permanently injure her or permanently kill someone else. The grief at that realization would be devastating. She could very well say no, and Isla had no fallback plan for that.

She could defy it completely. Tell her past self to cancel the Chicago trip altogether. Keep testing it out to see if one timeline got it right. Avoid Lake Shore forever and be done with it. The accident was fixed in one spot, wasn't it? So she would never, ever drive north on Lake Shore.

Isla's shoulders slumped, and she sank to the floor. As if that hadn't already occurred to her a thousand times. Because what if she forgot one day, and maybe Willow was in the car with her, or she took an Uber or a taxi and they used that route? She could kill someone else too. Lake Shore was avoidable, but not *that* avoidable, unless she vowed to never go back to Chicago. What if it followed her elsewhere, years down the road? Was she going to spend the rest of her life looking over her shoulder?

She either bore the brunt of the accident, or someone else did. And if she continually shoved it on someone else, just to preserve her health, she would have to wait out the timelines again and again and live with the guilt and the grief every time. She could put herself through that hell, or she could learn to live with a TBI.

Isla read up on them, and based on what future Ewan had told her, her alternate self had suffered a moderate TBI. She read that some of those issues could improve with time, even years down the road. Even if that wasn't the case for her, her past self hadn't waited long enough to find out. She also knew that version of Isla hadn't started an art career at all before the accident. Once it happened, she probably hadn't even seen the point in painting again. That uphill battle must have looked like the sheer rock face of El Capitan, which would have worsened the depression *already* worsened by the TBI. And she'd done what Isla always did: suffer in silence instead of reaching out for help. Instead of being honest.

Isla knew better now.

But would her past self agree?

She didn't know. Asking herself to knowingly get into an accident and not try to avoid it was a hell of a demand. But she didn't want to rob her past self of the chance to choose.

The original Isla had never had a choice. Most people were never given a choice when these things happened to them. Isla's unique position gave her the ability to choose the hard thing in order to avoid its harder alternative.

Isla opened Ewan's contact page on her phone and, before she could overthink it, hit call. It rang. And rang. And rang. And went to voice mail.

"Come on, Isla, put down the book," she muttered. It was just past midnight; she knew her other self wasn't asleep yet. She had text messages between her and Willow to prove it.

She called again.

No answer.

The vines started creeping through her mind again, and she got out her shears and started cutting as she took deep, measured breaths and willed her hands to stop shaking. Be patient. You *know* your past self is right next to him, she's just not paying attention to why his phone is buzzing. Do not catastrophize. She will pick up.

The phone buzzed in her hand.

Isla looked down at the caller ID.

Ewan Park.

All the air escaped her lungs. She answered and put the phone to her ear, holding herself very still for who she would hear on the other end of the line.

"Who is this?"

Isla's throat went dry at the sound of her own voice. God, was it really that *high*? She cleared her throat while she tried to find the words. "Isla," she said, as calmly as she could muster.

The silence stretched. Her own voice sounded high and breathless. "Excuse me?"

"Isla, it's me. *You*. From the future."

More silence. She imagined herself checking the phone to see if the number was right. "I knew," she finally replied, her tone trembling on the edge of fear. "I knew when I saw my name on his missed call list. But I didn't want to believe it."

"We need to talk."

"Hold on." She was probably going to the bedroom so he'd sleep undisturbed in the living room. Isla turned her head to stare at the empty couch behind her, heart aching. "What happened? Why are you calling?" Past Isla's voice was hushed and taut as a bowstring.

Isla closed her eyes and took two deep, measured breaths. "The accident happens anyway, and this time it's going to kill Ewan."

The gasp on the other end of the line hurt worse than stepping on broken glass. "No. No."

"He's in the car with us this time. And it happens at the exact same location as the first accident we avoided."

"Lake Shore?"

"Yes."

"When?"

"On your trip. This April."

Past Isla's "Jesus Christ" was muffled, as if she'd put her hand over her mouth. "You're kidding. It can't be." Her voice wavered unsteadily. "He's not supposed to die."

Isla pressed her face into her hand, and the effort it took to keep from crying made holding back the Red Sea look easy. "I know. I thought so too. But he's gone."

"So we'll cancel the trip."

"No." The firmness in her own voice surprised her. "Isla, it will keep happening, I'm sure of it. We can't avoid this. When Ewan got through that first time, I don't think the point was to avoid the accident. It was to help us cope better with the TBI. To actually believe in ourselves for once."

"Are you . . . did you get injured in the accident?"

Isla closed her eyes. "No. We walk away perfectly healthy. No TBI. And the price is his life."

Nothing but fast, unsteady breathing on the other end.

Isla faltered under the weight of that quiet, then picked up frenetic speed to fill it. "It's looking like this will happen no matter what, but it doesn't have to kill him or anyone else. Don't let him drive. Or go on the trip without him. That'll cause the TBI and erase this timeline."

"That's a hell of an ultimatum," past Isla snapped.

"He died, Isla," she cried. "We don't do this to other people. We don't deliberately hurt them. After everything he's done for you—" No, no. Use honey, not vinegar. She closed her eyes and pressed the heel of her hand against her forehead. Hard. What did she want? How could she make it okay for her past self to walk right into a terrible car accident that would catapult her into an unknown future?

"What do you want, Isla?" she asked herself.

Past Isla's breath hitched on a sob. "I don't want any of this."

"We're here anyway. There's nothing we can do about that. What are you afraid of?"

"That my life will be over if the accident hurts me. That I'll get depressed and try to end my life again."

Isla felt the pain in that voice down in her own marrow. "We don't know that. You don't know what you're capable of yet, even with a TBI. Stop underestimating yourself! We've overcome so much. We can get through this too. Don't let someone else pay this price. If you try to avoid it, it's just going to happen further down the road, and we'll be stuck in this loop forever. We have to believe that we're strong enough to handle what comes next. You've worked so hard to build a support network and reach out for help when you need it; you'll have that to lean on. And we need to love him right now. He loved us *with* the accident, not despite it. Maybe we could love ourselves that way too."

"How am I supposed to act normal for the next four months?"

"Isla, you're constantly afraid of things that don't even pan out. You have to stop being afraid of what you don't know. You have to stop being afraid *all the time*. This is the right choice. For him. For us. Can you do it?"

No answer.

"Isla?"

Her only answer was the wind chimes tinkling, both on the back porch and on the other end of time.

"Isla?" she called. "What are you going to do?"

*   *   *

"I'm glad you came in today, my dear." Dr. Nowicki's face settled into a kindness that split Isla's heart open like a melon. "How have these last few weeks been?"

"Hard." Her voice wavered with the unsteadiness that had kept her off-balance since . . . well. Since. "Awful. I feel fine sometimes, and then sometimes I feel like I got punched in the face." Because the waiting, the not knowing, was so hard. It was so goddamned hard.

"What do you do when it punches you in the face, Isla?" her therapist asked.

"Withdraw. Hate my life." Hate this timeline and the dead, responseless air on the other end of the only lifeline she had.

The doctor nodded and hummed. "What do you think Ewan would have to say about that?"

Isla wanted to hiss at the pain of hearing his name evoked. The woman might as well have tossed a boiling pot of water at her. "He wouldn't . . . he wouldn't like hearing me say that about myself," she relented, her voice small and beaten down. "He would want me to be kind to myself."

"And what could that kindness look like?"

She shrugged. She had no idea. All she could do was endure until the current and past timelines matched up where she needed them to. It was a marathon she hadn't signed up for. She had no choice but to compete anyway.

"Let's start with the basics. Let's make sure Isla is fed and has clean clothes and does some small thing for herself every day. It could be eating a snack. It could be meditating or taking a walk. It could be contacting someone you love. Just a small thing that would take five minutes of your time. Could we start there?"

Isla nodded at the floor.

"Good. I know things are very hard right now. But I want you to remember that you're not alone. You can lean on people. And you can strive to be a version of yourself that would honor Ewan's wish for you to have self-compassion."

"It's hard," she whispered.

"I know, my dear. But I'll guide you through it."

*   *   *

"Are we ready to go?" Willow stepped out of the bathroom, throwing on a light jacket as she walked.

Isla pocketed her keys and did a final mental check of everything in her bag. "Yes. Got your overnight bag for Tae's?"

"Yes, ma'am."

"Then let's go to the zoo."

"And then the Art Museum."

Isla forced a smile. "Yes, ma'am."

"And then the 33 Wine Shop."

"I wouldn't dream of depriving you."

Willow slung an arm around her shoulder and squeezed. "I'm proud of you for leaving your hobbit hole and rejoining the world this weekend."

Isla shrugged. It had to happen sometime. They were retracing steps back through the places she and Ewan used to go to, but the sting of those memories was lessened by Willow's visit.

The last two months had been a study in blind faith that her past self would do the right thing, because there was nothing else Isla could do to make sure the course correction occurred. Time had worn her obsession over the lack of a real answer from her past self down to a pencil nub.

Will took a sudden, longer look around the living room. "Isla, where did the TV go?"

She gestured vaguely to another part of the cottage. "I needed the room for painting, so I moved it into my bedroom."

"You've been on a roll lately. That art fair is coming up too, isn't it?"

Isla allowed herself a small, real smile. "In three weeks. Eleanor's going to help me watch over the booth." But she didn't want to talk about it anymore. She painted to fill the time; to keep her brain occupied long enough so it didn't remind her of all that she'd lost. "Let's hit the road, lady, we have a lot to see today."

When they got in the car to spend the weekend in St. Louis, Isla squeezed Will's hand before starting the engine. "I'm glad you're here," she said.

"I wouldn't be anywhere else."

* * *

"Why are you awake?" Tae demanded. His dark hair stuck up every which way in truly impressive bedhead fashion. He shuffled into the living room and flopped onto the couch next to her, dragging his hand through his hair with a loud sigh. "Too early," he whined.

"Does your head hurt, Tae?" she asked innocently. He glared at her sleepily. She could *see* the headache behind his eyes.

"Too much partying," he said, as she rose from the couch. Isla drew a glass of water from the sink, located the Advil, and returned with her offering. He extended his hand gratefully and took the glass and the pills.

"Too much soju," Isla corrected. There had been no partying; just a night in with too much to drink, to celebrate the second collaboration she and Jun-su had done in San Francisco. Jun-su was still upstairs, sleeping off the jet lag. She tucked the blanket around them both, and they sat quietly, admiring Tae's veritable forest of plants in the living room. Delicate ferns clustered in the corners like shy wallflowers; aloe vera stretched up to the sun on the windowsill; succulents nestled on the end tables like baby birds in nests; strings of pearls let their hair down from hanging vases.

"I miss him," Tae said quietly.

Isla leaned her head on his shoulder. "Me too," she whispered. "Every day."

None of her friends knew how she kept time these days. How she wrote old dates inside the current dates on the calendar to mark the passage of time in another world.

The dates stopped next Friday.

The waiting was almost over, and it both soothed the edges of the ache in her life and ramped up old anxious feelings that had been dulled by grief.

She still didn't know what would happen when the dates stopped.

"You should move closer," Tae suddenly said, pulling her out of her thoughts. "Why do you stay out so far?"

"I need it."

He made a noise of disapproval. "For what? You're making that artist money now. You can afford a nice place in St. Louis."

Isla lifted her knees up to her chest and hugged them. "I do, but this cottage is important to me. I'm keeping it for a little while yet."

She wished she could say that one day he'd know why, but that was between her and the cottage.

* * *

Bright sunlight drenched the living room, announcing the heat of an unseasonably warm October day just outside the door. Isla sat in the center of the room, phone in front of her. All her paintings were safely stored away, ready for transportation to an art gallery showing.

It would be her first solo art show in downtown St. Louis. Something she had never even dared imagine for herself.

It was surreal to recount the sheer amount of progress she'd made in the past year, especially these last few months. Showcasing her work at a booth during an art festival. Increasing her print sales through the website; selling originals and taking commissions. Applying to a dozen juried exhibitions and finally getting the one yes she craved. Every act had terrified her, and she regretted none of it. Especially since her art had become her refuge ever since . . . well.

Isla was grateful for every opportunity this timeline had given her in such a short span, despite what it had taken away. All of it was a dream she'd never thought she'd realize.

And all of it meant nothing if it came at the cost of Ewan's life. Of grieving parents. Jun-su's long, pensive silences. Tae's silent tears as he gardened. She was sure now, more than ever, that this success was not contingent on complete physical health.

It was contingent on mind-set.

In the past year, Isla had done two collaborations with Jun-su, and each had been lavished with praise over the mixture of techniques and the dreamlike, transportive nature of the murals. She had a literal art showing in four days.

Isla even six months ago would have doubted she could have this if she added another disability to the disabilities she already had. She would have thought having perfect health was the only way to achieve this, even though she'd never had perfect health to begin with.

It was a lie. The kind of lie her anxiety fed her all the time. She would have this again.

If her past self did the right thing.

It was the morning of the accident in that timeline. They were in Chicago, getting ready to leave the hotel. The accident was going to happen at 10:01, and Isla only knew this because she remembered looking at the clock right before she saw the car swerving at them and thinking it reminded her of binary.

Past Isla had never called or messaged again after their conversation. Never confirmed if she would do it.

Isla had tried calling one more time, right around Ewan's birthday in March. Her past self had never responded.

If 10:01 passed and nothing changed, Isla would know she'd failed. She would be stuck in this timeline without Ewan, and there would be no undoing what had been done. No second chances.

She had to have faith in herself. In all of the care and love she'd tried to direct at herself over the past year. All the work and support future Ewan had showered her with. It couldn't be for nothing.

9:59 a.m.

"Please," she whispered.

10:00 a.m.

Isla closed her eyes.

10:01 a.m.

EPILOGUE

Art covered the bare white walls of the gallery.

A wild, green-black forest path at twilight.

Gray-and-blue woods, fresh white snow collected at the bottom of the painting, with an owl in the center perched on a snow-covered branch.

A series of sparse, rural winter landscapes, with a crow on one fence post, frostbitten grass; a road meeting the dark, naked trees.

Isla stood alone by a table of snacks—there was a word for the fancy, bite-sized morsels on tiered platters, but she couldn't remember what it was—and tried to will herself not to sweat through the sleeves of her floor-length dress. She wished she could sneak off her shoes. She'd chosen poorly, and they were already setting her off-balance.

The entire gallery housed nothing but her own work. Pieces she had painstakingly sketched and painted, now pitched in dramatic lighting for people to take in and critique and perhaps bring home. Each mural held its own origin story that she could lay out like a map.

Or a timeline.

Doors opened in five minutes.

"Are you ready, Isla?"

Jun-su rounded the corner from wherever the restrooms were hiding, looking surprisingly subdued in an unbuttoned black blazer and fitted slacks. Tae strolled next to him, absolutely refusing to trade his beloved plaid for anything, although this time it appeared on his pants and he wore a dress shirt he looked vaguely uncomfortable in.

Isla grinned. "Looking . . ." She couldn't think of the word she was looking for, so she gestured vaguely at Tae's person and nodded approvingly.

"Annoyed?" Jun-su supplied helpfully. "Like a pouty child dressed up for picture day? Like—" He laughed when Tae pinched his side, spinning away gracefully. When the front door to the gallery opened, Jun-su cleared his throat and fixed his hair, putting on a winning smile for whoever walked in.

"I have never been in an art gallery before," Eleanor said, her eyes drawing up to the walls. "This is a first. Holy shit, girl, these are amazing!"

"I am going to spend all night analyzing these paintings, but first?" Janelle breezed by with a squeeze of Isla's elbow. "Ah, there we are." She selected a glass of white wine from the table. "It has been a long day."

"Thank you both for coming," Isla said. Her nerves warred with genuine excitement and pleasure that her friends had shown up to her first solo art exhibit.

Though truthfully, they weren't the ones she wanted to show all this to.

While Eleanor, Janelle, Tae, and Jun-su caught up, Isla discreetly tucked her shoes underneath the food table and wandered barefoot farther into the gallery, past the pink-walled boutique backyard in Michigan and the streets of

Chicago in full bloom. She could smell the fresh grass and flowers as she passed.

She stopped at a painting of a mountain path in Colorado. Her first fourteener. The beauty of that curve in the trailhead, overlooking a valley of pines below, had struck her to the heart and stayed there, like capturing lightning in a bottle. What a victory it had been to climb.

"You lost your shoes, Buttercup."

Isla turned around to face the gorgeous man standing behind her, hands tucked casually in the pockets of his black dress pants. His presence brought the mountain back to her; she could smell it on him still.

"I don't need them," she said.

Ewan's hair fell boyishly across his forehead, his dark eyes sparkling as he smiled down at her. She didn't know why or where it was coming from, but that smile made her want to weep. Seeing him standing there felt like a second chance.

He wrapped his arms around her waist, pulling her close. She buried her nose in his hair and breathed. She wanted to cloak herself in his scent, wear it like protection. "I love you," she said, her breath hitching in her throat.

He smiled against her shoulder, then kissed it. "I love you too," he said in his deep, quiet voice. He drew her back and smoothed her hair away from her face, letting his fingers twine around the falling strands like threading silk. "Ready for your admirers?"

Isla looked away bashfully. "I suppose. I'm worried I'll get . . . overwhelmed." Ever since the accident, she'd had a hard time concentrating. It had been worse in the beginning, when reading was difficult and she couldn't concentrate long enough to carry the sentences through to a cohesive narrative. She kept forgetting what came before—couldn't hold the story in her head long enough. Her neurologist assured her that it was normal for a TBI and that it would get better. Slowly, it had. She still didn't have the focus to read an entire book, but she could feel the improvements in small increments. It was always worse in a loud environment. When too many people talked at once, it all became white noise that she couldn't distinguish. She couldn't pick out the individual threads of conversations, because it all registered as one gnarled ball of yarn. Ewan called it sensory overload.

"You can take breaks if you start to get overwhelmed," he reminded her. "You don't have to push through it just because it feels like it's something you should be able to do because you *used* to be able to do it. When you start to panic, politely excuse yourself—I know you won't want to be rude, but they'll understand—and come to me, or Jun-su, or Tae. We'll help you. Or you can take a walk outside to clear your head. Does it hurt?"

"A little." It hurt most days, but she also had good days where it barely hurt at all and the depressive episodes saw themselves out the door. Dr. Nowicki was great about taking last-minute appointments, and Isla had gotten better at telling Ewan when she needed help and when the bad days were coming. But today had been good. She'd slept in, as usual, because lord knew her body required far more sleep than it used to, and Ewan walked her through her ongoing therapy exercises. They'd hung a chalkboard in the living room of their house by the entryway with Ewan's work schedule, Isla's exercises and therapy appointments, and other basic logistics written down to help Isla keep a routine and remember the things she needed to do. She still couldn't remember *anything* leading up to the accident itself, but she doubted she'd ever get that back.

"Is Gertie okay?"

Ewan snorted. "Babe." He pulled out his phone, scrolled, and then turned it to face her. Isla laughed at the picture of Gertie sitting on her haunches, staring up expectantly at Mrs. Ahn as she held out a treat. Isla could practically see the long-haired collie quivering with excitement. "She's more than okay. She loves visiting her grandparents." He tilted up her chin to kiss her softly. "Don't worry about her," he said. "This is your night. You've worked hard for this. I want you to enjoy every minute."

She *had* worked hard. Starting up her art career again had been like building a car engine blindfolded. It had taken well over a year for the weakness and trembling in her hands to become manageable for short periods of time, for everything from cutting meat to washing her hair to holding paintbrushes.

But.

She hadn't been alone through any of it. Ewan had taken a sabbatical from work to stay with her while she went through rehabilitation. Jun-su and Tae had helped Isla work on her fine motor skills. That first Christmas, they'd made crafts on the living room carpet together, building Popsicle stick snowmen ornaments, cutting out glittery snowflakes, and painting pinecones. She, too, had taken a sabbatical from work, because her vision issues and light sensitivity made extensive computer work difficult and the laptop screen had to be on the dimmest light setting. Most of her work took twice as long as it used to, but completing a mural was twice as satisfying for it.

More people filtered into the studio space, including old coworkers and people she'd met at the art fairs she'd participated in. It was easier to talk to people who already knew about her memory lapses; easier to laugh it off with them while she hunted for the right word. She could stare at a thing she absolutely knew how to name and not be able to name it. Or she'd *almost* get it, but not quite. Like the times she'd forgotten what to call instant coffee, or the kind of paint she used, and just now, when she hadn't been able to name what kind of owl Digby was. She used to feel so stupid whenever she couldn't think of the right word, but once, when she'd voiced that to Jun-su, he'd smiled and said, "Don't be hard on yourself. Look at it this way—sometimes Tae and I don't have the words either." He'd flashed her a sweet smile and added, "We can find our words together."

The conversations grew fatiguing, and Isla soothed herself by playing with the slim, narrow engagement ring nestled next to her wedding ring, an aquamarine jewel set in its center, pale and lovely like cool, fresh water. Like her old cottage. She had sold it the previous spring. It had been easier to move in with Ewan, especially since she couldn't drive that first year after the accident, and rarely did so now. It also made perfect sense. There was no need to stay in the house anymore. It had been good to her, but she knew in her bones that her time with the house was over. She was never meant to stay there permanently—maybe no one was.

Just when her insides began to coil up too tightly for comfort, Ewan came up next to her and placed a reassuring hand at the small of her back. Isla remembered to slow down her breathing.

"Want to get some air?" Ewan asked.

"Yes," she said on an exhale. "Would you excuse me for one moment?" The couple in front of her nodded, and she and Ewan headed for the door after he swiped her shoes from underneath the hors d'oeuvres—*that* was the name!—table. She tugged on a jacket before the chill of the autumn evening hit them.

"You're doing great," he said. "I'm proud of you. When this is done, let's go get ice cream."

Isla slid her hand in his, then kissed him. "Thank you for believing in me, Rabbit."

"Always," he murmured.

"I love you. And I love . . . I love me too." The words slid into place like a key turning a lock. She knew it like she knew she loved him. All this time, everybody had been telling her to be kinder to herself, but she'd had a hard time complying until she held up a mirror to her accomplishments and her courage and her passion and decided that she could love this person too. Maybe not all the time. Maybe loving herself more often than not would be a hard, long journey. But she wanted to keep trying to love her regardless. Like her. Root for her.

Just as much as Ewan did.

"Hey, break it up." Willow grinned at them as she got out of her car. "This is a professional establishment for serious artists only, not a couple of kids making out in the street."

"I don't see any serious artists here," Isla quipped back, curling her fingers tighter into Ewan's shirt. He winked at her. The crisp night air cooled her skin, warmed from his embrace. Her love was here, her friends close by, her past adorning the walls of the building behind her, her future unmapped.

With Ewan's hand in hers, everything was in its place.

Help is available if you need it. You are not alone.

National Suicide Prevention Lifeline
988
suicidepreventionlifeline.org

Crisis Text Line
Text HOME to 741-741
crisistextline.org

The Trevor Project
1-866-488-7396
Text START to 678-678
thetrevorproject.org

ACKNOWLEDGMENTS

I always said that if I never published another book in my life, I would be happy if this one book made it out into the world. This is the book of my heart. I put a lot of myself into it, because a younger version of me needed to read about a woman who had panic attacks and chronic conditions who was also joyful and in love. This book would not be in the hands of readers without the help of so many wonderful human beings who believed in it as much as I did. My heart is full to bursting with gratitude and thanks for the following people:

To my former agent, Devon Halliday, thank you for taking a chance on me and Isla. Your steadfast belief and your passion for this story bolstered me when I wavered. You worked tirelessly with me to make this manuscript shine. You stuck through countless rounds of emails and edits while we hammered that ending and those timeline logistics into a recognizable shape. You took such expert care of this story that I knew without a doubt you would help find it a home. Although it saddened me that this would be the only book we partnered on together, I feel all the more fortunate to have worked with you, and I wish you nothing but the best in your future endeavors. To my current agent, Laura Cameron, thank you for taking me on and jumping in with both feet. I can't wait to see what the future brings!

To my editor, Melissa Rechter, thank you for championing me into a book deal. You understood Isla and Ewan and Isla's journey so well that I knew it would be a joy to work with you. I loved reading through your comments and reactions as we worked together to make sure the book was ready for readers. You helped the ending stick the landing with your insightful questions and suggestions. A big thank-you to my copy editor, Rachel Keith, as well!

To Alcove Press, thank you for giving *Twice in a Lifetime* a home and making my wildest dream come true. Thank you to Rebecca Nelson, Madeline Rathle, Dulce Botello, and Kate McManus for your marketing guidance and efforts, your tireless work to promote my book and all the other amazing authors at Alcove and Crooked Lane. Your passion and dedication is noticed and appreciated.

To my beta and sensitivity readers, thank you for providing amazingly detailed, thoughtful feedback. Bridgit Davis from Quiethouse Editing, for your meticulous and much-needed feedback that was a joy to read through, because it was my first taste of how readers would react as the story unfolded. Dr. Linh Anh Cat, for your balanced feedback and words of encouragement. Dani Moran of Tessera Editorial, for your outstanding attention to detail and thoroughness. You are incredible. Your insight into Ewan, his parents, Tae-seok, and Jun-su was a tremendous help, and I am so grateful to you. Lisa Konst-Evans, for untangling my timeline woes and being my second pair of eyes on those dates and times.

To my readers and cheerleaders, I owe you everything. Candice Velasco, you were there when *Twice in a Lifetime* was a series of spoken word ideas and a half-written outline. Thank you for being game to discuss that plot into the ground, even while you made us dinner and I paced in the background, spitballing ideas and writing none of them down. Tara O'Shea, thank you for your support and your willingness to drop everything for a friend in need. Dr. Matthew Sutherland, thank you for being the very first person to read the finished draft of the manuscript, and for answering all of my TBI-related questions.

My thanks to you, dearest reader, for choosing to go on this journey with Isla and Ewan.

And finally, to Art Sangurai. Thank you for carrying enough belief for both of us. For brainstorming edits and timeline logistics, well into the night. For reading everything I write, no questions asked. For walking this road with me from querying to publication. For being my biggest advocate. I love you.